FIND

"We knew from s⸺ ⸺ ⸺ letters that Nakasen kept a lifelog from very early on—"

Jak all but gasped. A lifelog was a record, maintained by an AI complex running in background on one's purse, downloaded into a more permanent location at every opportunity. The AI complex watched from your purse through all the years and events of your life, snapping copies of everything that might be of interest to a biographer—rough drafts, messages to friends, shopping orders, school work, anything—keeping a running organization and catalog as it went. Nakasen was humanity's greatest single religious teacher. Finding Mohammed's home movies, Jesus' agent's appointment calendar (with the rough draft of the Sermon on the Mount folded between the pages), and Buddha's complete sent-email file would not have been as important.

ALSO BY
JOHN BARNES

Orbital Resonance
A Million Open Doors
Mother of Storms
Kaleidescope Century
Encounter with Tiber (with Buzz Aldrin)*
Earth Made of Glass
Finity
Candle
The Return (with Buzz Aldrin)
The Merchants of Souls
The Sky So Big and Black

JAK JINNAKA NOVELS
*The Duke of Uranium**
*A Princess of the Aerie**

*available from Warner Aspect

IN THE HALL OF
THE MARTIAN KING

JOHN BARNES

WARNER BOOKS

An AOL Time Warner Company

WARNER BOOKS EDITION

Copyright © 2003 by John Barnes
All rights reserved. No part of this book may be reproduced in any form or by any electronic or mechanical means, including information storage and retrieval systems, without permission in writing from the publisher, except by a reviewer who may quote brief passages in a review.

Aspect® is a registered trademark of Warner Books, Inc.

Cover design by Don Puckey/Shasti O'Leary Soudant
Cover illustration by Matt Stawicki

Warner Books, Inc.
1271 Avenue of the Americas
New York, NY 10020

Visit our Web site at www.twbookmark.com

 An AOL Time Warner Company

Printed in the United States of America

First Paperback Printing: June 2003

10 9 8 7 6 5 4 3 2 1

For Sean Walbeck. Lose the hat.

"Since people will say everything in the world about Jak Jinnaka, now, as long as it's bad—maybe I should say something true and simple. We met just casually, before either of us was anybody, and then we were friends, and then we stayed friends while we worked together as colleagues, then I took on that assignment you keep harping about (which I was <u>ever</u> so glad to have failed at), and then there was our long period of a close relationship. In all that time, he never brought up any of our past. We were what we were to each other, right then. From that first mission to the Harmless Zone when **<NOT INCLUDED IN THIS MESSAGE DUE TO REASONS OF NATIONAL SECURITY>** right up until the moment those **<NOT INCLUDED IN THIS MESSAGE DUE TO REASONS OF NATIONAL SECURITY>** and I lost my best and oldest friend, Jak Jinnaka always just accepted that your relationship was what it was right then, whether he was your tove, your pizo, your target—or your lover.

"Of course I know which of those relationships you want me to talk about, masen? There's only two really interesting subjects, sex and violence . . . which should I start with? And do you mind if I ask you something? Are you aware that for a media heet, you're an exceptionally attractive young man? Would

you mind sitting here, a little closer, so I don't have
to raise my voice?"

**From "Looking Back on a Long, Eventful Life: Jin-
naka's Onetime Mistress, Would-Be Assassin Says
She'd Do It All Again,"** Reasonably True news, **vol.
1344, Story 336, page 9, see catalog for over one
million Jinnaka stillpix.**

CHAPTER 1

Everyone Knows Your Uncle

Jak Jinnaka swam through the air carefully, watching where he was going, because even the widest tunnels swarmed with Deimons. His face was less than half a meter from the feet of the girl in front of him, and the small child behind him occasionally tugged Jak's ankle. The tunnel seemed dim even with the bright central light, for almost nothing reflected from the glass-coated gray-brown natural rock of Deimos.

Tunnels on Deimos were crowded even at midshift, because there were as few tunnels as possible. According to a report Jak was supposed to annotate, drilling new tunnels on Deimos cost more than on any other airless, low-gravity world in the solar system, because the waste you bored out was mostly chon. Deimos circled Mars, which was literally covered with chon, so it was like having a sand quarry near the Sahara.

Jak was glad he could link *Hive Army Report 737FEB08F26: Current economics of construction at Hive Possession Deimos,* with the fact that he was perpetually about to bounce his face off the girl's sneakers.

Most of the airswimmers were in uniform—bureaucrats, maintenance workers, Army, and crewies (many in the black-with-red uniform of the Spatial; most of the young women were depilated, another depressing feature of Greasy Rock, as every non-Deimon called the place whenever there were no Deimons apt to hear (or whenever they wanted to fight a Deimon).

As it was for billions of workers around the solar system, midshift break was, too often, the highlight of Jak's day. And it always began with a very stale joke.

Jinnaka could not help that he spoke Standard with the fast, flat, nasal accent of the Hive, stubbing his consonants and barely opening his jaw; he had grown up on the Hive, he had only been away from it for brief periods, and it was the way everyone else he'd grown up with talked. Thus when Jak airswam into the Sweet and Flaky, every day at fifteen-thirty, Avor Brindoneshta, the owner, would say, "Udlakka lardubba cuffy untuh binyezzplizz."

"Ahem," Jak said, trying to sound like an unusually stuffy actor showing off his diction, "I would very much like to purchase a large, double-strength coffee, and two beignets, if you please, and I would like that with some *new* humor, now that we have established that I talk funny."

Avor smiled and shook his head. "Old pizo, I don't think you're ever going to pull off an air of wounded dignity. Are you going to sit in the centrifuge, or hang out here at the counter so I can make fun of you?"

"Serve it for micrograv," Jak said, hooking his feet into the stirrups of the stool. "If your life isn't too busy."

"Only if I get a rush, and who can predict that? *Eros's Torch* is due but the quarkjet liner crowd goes to lighter places than mine. You didn't bring work with you today? Shouldn't you be working out complicated rules to mess up citizens' lives?"

"Probably I should, but my brain aches and I'm falling

asleep at my desk." Jak sighed. Besides the food, the Sweet and Flaky's other attraction was that Avor was always willing to listen to him complain.

The year before, to the surprise of everyone who had known him when he was younger, Jak had graduated with honors from the Hive's Public Service Academy, and been chosen late in the first round of the Agency Draft. It was good to be in the first round, but better to be early in it; Hive Intel, the Spatial, the Army, and the other glamorous fast-track agencies picked first. Jak had been drafted by the Protectorates Administrative Services Corps.

PASC administered the strategic real estate that the Hive had acquired via the not-unrelated factors of being the largest single nation in the solar system, unbeaten in war for more than four hundred years, and the possessor of the largest Spatial in history.

Deimos, Mars's outer moon, was vital to the Hive as a military and intelligence base against the Martian nations, a trading post, and a political base of operations for preventing Martian reunification. It was invaluable as a counterbalance to the Jovian League base on Phobos. For a flying mountain of tar with less volume than any of the major volcanoes on Mars below it, Deimos was an important place.

"Tell you what your problem is, pizo," Avor said. "You're spoiled three different ways, and it's hard to get over all three of them at once."

Jak took a sugary bite of fresh, hot beignet. "So, nothing short of the sun blowing up would stop you from telling me, masen?"

Avor grinned at him. "Toktru, pizo. One, you're spoiled because you grew up on the Hive, and you're not used to living on a big military base. Two, you're spoiled because you grew up rich, and you could always buy more amusements, and we don't have nearly as many for sale here. And three, you're *really* spoiled because you've had two big adventures in your life, running and scrambling and getting shot at and barely getting away. Compared to that, sitting at a desk and deciding whether or not to permit a mercantile company to open a department store in Malecandra Pleasure City is pretty dull. Oh, and four: you also got to stick it in a princess."

Only his Uncle Sib, or perhaps Dujuv or Myxenna (his oldest toves), would have been able to tell that Avor's casual teasing had wracked Jak like a backhand to the balls. Jak's eyelids tensed slightly, his breathing hitched, and for a fraction of a second, his jaw muscles pulsed. Jak's two great adventures had both been directly caused by his having had, as his high school demmy, the sweet but vague Sesh Kiroping—later revealed as secretly Shyf Karrinynya, Crown Princess of Greenworld and utter bitch on wheels. In his first great adventure, Jak had rescued Sesh/Shyf, and made many friends; in his second, she had nearly enslaved him with the psychological conditioning techniques that the aristos used to create perfectly loyal servants and to destroy captive enemies. She had then set him to tasks that had cost him most of those friends.

Even now, Shyf's name, spoken aloud, sent a tremor through Jak's guts and made him feel heart-ripping insanely sixteen-years-old-and-fresh-in-love again. A casual reference to sex with her could send Jak to the brink of a killing rage; unfavorable stories about her on news accesscasts sent him into depression; and each message from her made his heart scream upward in pure joy.

"On the other hand," Jak said, marveling that Avor had

no awareness of how close he had come to a broken neck, "objectively, my life *is* very dull, which is scientifically proven to cause boredom. *And* it's about to be duller, because Waxajovna removed anything that requires judgment or initiative from the in-box."

Avor shook his head, smiling sympathetically. "You aren't going to be here for long," he said. "Whether you realize it or not, you aren't. Reeb Waxajovna is." Waxajovna, Jak's boss, had been Procurator of Deimos for ninety-five years. "He's been here forever and he'll stay here till they fire him out the casket launcher. But all vice-ps leave within a couple of years. Either they aren't good at things, and Reeb gets rid of them for the good of Deimos, or they *are* good at things, and Reeb gets rid of them for the good of Reeb. He'll find some perfect position for you somewhere else, as soon as he can."

Till Jak unbelted from his seat to leave, the rest of the conversation was about the chances of Deimos's minor-league slamball team. Then, as Jak gripped his stool to push off, Avor added, "Don't worry about getting stuck here. That's not going to happen. You'll get out of here like everyone else. Nakasen's pink hairy bottom, old pizo, that's what I envy you most. Every few days I think about selling the Sweet and Flaky and moving back to the Hive. I'm past two hundred years old now and I still like to talk to people, but it would be nice to talk about something new."

"What are you tired of talking about?"

"You know, sex, war, sports, taxes—"

"In the Hive, nobody talks about taxes. Otherwise it's the same."

"You have a gift for keeping Deimons on Deimos," Avor

observed. "Of course, you are a Hive bureaucrat and that is Hive policy."

"That also means I've accomplished one thing that I was supposed to, today, so I guess I should go back and write a bunch of memos claiming the credit. I'll see you."

Jak airswam into the tunnel, merging between an older kobold (diligently paddling along with an expression of utter boredom) and a group of teenaged boys (airswimming in cylinder formation, discussing how dull life was).

The visit with Avor had been nice, but Jak was still discouraged. His first independent command, beginning in less than two hours, ought to feel more significant, more like a moment when all of history changed, or more like the heavy hand of doom, or just more *something*.

Reeb Waxajovna was going on vacation. Like any PASC administrator, he had little choice: he went on vacation whenever his accumulated leave time, desired days at destination, and possible shipping schedules specified a solution to a scheduling equation at PASC headquarters. He wanted to go back to the Hive, which sat at the Earth-Sun L5 Lagrange libration point, sixty degrees behind Earth in orbit. A scheduling algorithm somewhere back in the main office had spotted a chance: *Eros's Torch*, a downbound quarkjet liner (twenty-two days from Mars to the Hive), and *The Song of Copernicus*, an upbound sunclipper (two and a half months from the Hive to Mars via a Venus assist), would provide Waxajovna with three more days at the Hive than the sixty minimum he had requested. While he did that, Jak Jinnaka would be administering Deimos, for a total of five months.

Waxajovna was waiting for him. "Mister Jinnaka. Let's go over everything one more time, so that your obsessive, neurotic supervisor will not worry himself ill while on vacation."

"I never said anything like that about you, sir."

"Of course not, you're not crazy, Jinnaka, but you are not stupid either, and considering what I've been putting you through for the last few weeks, you *have* to have been thinking it, now and then. Now, humor me on this. Then I have a few last notes."

The Procurator for Deimos was an unmodified human, a medium-brown-skinned endomorph with slight epicanthic folds, flat cheekbones, and a snub nose. In messages to his more closely trusted toves, Jak sometimes called Reeb Waxajovna "The Modal Man" because he seemed to have the most common type of everything. He even looked the average age; only the tired crackle in his voice revealed that he was older. "Now, then, let's run over each area budget first."

After area budgets, there were culture grants, infrastructure financing, projects advice to the local government, revenue enhancement relations with Deimos's tax bureau, and some issues about Wager orthodoxy. Only the last of these really mattered; though individual nations were continually at war, the essential unity of humanity (against the Rubahy if another war were to break out and against the Galactic State if it ever issued its long-expected Extermination Order,) was absolutely a matter of survival. The Wager, the religious-philosophic system followed by nineteen out of twenty humans, was the basis of human unity, and though there were local variations and minor differences in its practice, so far, in seven hundred years, there had been no major schism. The Hive itself had been founded, in part, to be the center and sustainer of the Wager.

But even on the Wager-related matters, the real creative

thinking was done; Jak would merely follow orders and fill out paperwork.

Almost all arriving and departing ships would be Deimos-based Hive Spatial patrols by orbicruisers and armed sunclippers. Patrol in-and-outs required no real effort; their crews already had quarters, and for every ship that left its berth to go out on patrol, another came in.

All the real headaches during Jak's five-month watch would derive from the eleven ships from extramartian space: two downbound quarkjet liners, four upbound sunclippers, a down-bound sunclipper, and four warships—a downbound armed sunclipper from New Hamburg making an allied-port call, and a task force of three Spatial ships, the battlesphere *Like So Not*, warshuttle carrier *Actium*, and orbicruiser *Tree Bowing to the Storm*, upbound to the Neptune system to relieve the Hive's task force guarding Triton (whether the Spatial guarded Triton from the Jovians, the Rubahy, or the Tritonians themselves was always an interesting question).

"That armed sunclipper will be no problem at all," Waxajovna observed, "because nobody's going to be allowed off it. New Hamburg has a major defection problem, so *Bunne* will co-orbit rather than dock, and send over officer parties by longshore capsule.

"But any trouble that the Hamburgers save you, our own task force will make up for. Battlesphere crewies always drink and fuck themselves silly, and *Actium* will be worse—two hundred fifty warshuttle crews. *And then* add in that they're all going up to Triton on a direct ride from here—so after this one port call they're in for thirty-seven more weeks of training on simulators, then two years at Triton, where Forces personnel are confined to base due to terrorist threats. And then at least forty weeks in all getting back down to the Hive.

"Which means their lives are looking to absolutely stink for the next three and a half years, and their last ten days to blow off steam will happen here.

"So the pilots, navigators, weaponeers, and beanies will all be roaming bar to bar and whorehouse to whorehouse, looking for chances to beat each other up, and the officers will all be publicly telling them to cut it out and privately betting on whose crewies can stomp whose, and the warshuttle crewies will clash with the battlesphere crewies . . ."

"And you haven't even factored in the orbicruiser," Jak pointed out.

"*They* won't be the problem," Waxajovna explained. "Orbicruiser captains and crews are usually tight little families that don't like anyone else. They'll come onto Deimos for about ten minutes, spend all of it buying liquor and hiring prostitutes to go back on board with them—"

"Isn't that contrary—"

"If you even think of enforcing those regulations, I'll see that your next post is administering sanitation at a methane mine in the Kuiper Belt. Half the art of administering, Jinnaka, is leaving well enough alone. Now, everything is in good shape and you have worked hard to make sure that it is. I would imagine that you are specking that, headaches of the port call excepted, the next five months will be spectacularly boring."

"As a matter of fact, sir, yes."

"Well, don't bet on it. Let me emphasize that, again. *Don't* bet on it. The world can always become lively. The *kind* of surprises that can happen is a surprise all by itself."

Reeb Waxajovna stretched and yawned. "I always hated old farts who told war stories, but there *is* some purpose in it at the moment, so let me just tell you about a few things that can break up the routine, in a 'routine' temporary command. I promise I won't go into detail, slap me if I do, all right?"

"Looking forward to it, sir."

Waxajovna grinned. "I would, too. Anyway, in my first ten years of occasional commands, I had to deal with a sudden outbreak of mutated chicken pox. And I was temp acting station chief at Tycho during the week the police stumbled across a serial killer with thirty bodies in a rented cold locker.

"Then there was arriving at a miserable little asteroid out at Saturn L5, as the vice procurator—same job you have now. My ferry docked six hours after the procurator had been shot dead by a jealous husband. The previous vice-p was already on the ferry out to the sunclipper, past the point of no return. And the Hive was in inferior conjunction with the sun, so I had to send the message around relays.

"Five hours later PASC's reply arrived. Four instructions. One, bury him. Two, assume command as acting chief for at least the next three years. Three, in eighty-four hours the battlesphere *Up Yours*—never a better named ship in history as far as I was concerned!—would be bringing me a secret weapons project with a staff of twelve hundred people, all of whom would have to be housed, fed, and cared for, and which would also require a couple of cubic kilometers of new space to be constructed for the project. That was more people and more space than the colony had at the time."

"What was four?"

Waxajovna winced. "They told me to buck up and quit whining. Now, as I said there would be, there's a point to my old war stories. And the point is: my experiences are why I insisted on making sure you were so overprepared before I left. I've been preparing you to be a juggler with a baby in the air."

"Um?"

"It's a metaphor I learned from a mentor a long time ago. A juggler is supposed to keep lots of balls in the air, that's what makes him a juggler. Nobody's very interested unless he juggles something very dangerous or very precious—a rare glass goblet, or a jar of nitroglycerin, or a baby. And if you're juggling a baby, no one cares about any tennis balls or oranges you've also got in the air—just get that baby down unhurt, and the audience thinks you're the greatest juggler they've ever seen. Have I stretched this metaphor far enough to tear it yet?"

"We're getting there. So the point is that if some emergency does come up—"

"Solve one big problem, brilliantly, once, and you will look brilliant. And if it's easier because everything else is all wrapped up and running on automatic, you can look more brilliant than you really are. Which means you'd be promoted away from here, which obviously benefits you, and also benefits me politically—since you have talent, it's better to have you as a protégé than a rival, masen?

"So if all the accelerated drudgery of the last few weeks pays off, you'll have a tremendously better chance at the sort of brilliant success you need to be promoted away from Greasy Rock."

"Um, I thought—"

"I forbid the term officially because it offends Deimons. For that matter it offends me. But I know perfectly well that to you, this place is Greasy Rock."

"I dak. How likely do you really think it is that something like that will come up?"

"Based on all past experience, maybe fifty percent. After all, you and I have had two things that could have become real emergencies—that almost-war between Yellow Magenta Green Blue and Yellow Amber Cyan Red, and that sewage strike that the Jovian agitator—what was her name?"

"Vala Brnibov."

"Yes, right, I remember the software wouldn't accept her death warrant at first because it wanted there to be one more vowel in her name. Held her up in the airlock for half an hour—must have been terrible for her, not knowing what was going on and having to wait for the door to open for that long. Well, anyway, as a very junior vice procurator in charge, if you had coped with either situation solo, it would have worked wonders for your career.

"By the way, don't suffer an attack of cleverness and *make* something come up. I say that because, though I know that *you* are smarter and more circumspect than that, your uncle—"

"I'd already thought of that, sir, and messaged him on the subject, very bluntly, and you can depend upon it that I'll watch him toktru close while he's here."

Jak's Uncle Sibroillo was coming down from Ceres to Deimos on *Eros's Torch*, the same ship on which Waxajovna would be departing. He was a leader in Circle Four, a notorious zybot that was tolerated (barely) in the Hive and hunted zealously everywhere else. All zybots were theoretically illegal everywhere (no one wanted to let any social engineering conspiracy have a free hand) but most of the great powers tolerated a few zybots as clandestine auxiliaries to their own covert operations. Even then they had to be watched, for a zybot was a weapon that could turn in the hand.

Thanks to Uncle Sib, Jak had had his wild adventures on Earth, the Aerie, and Mercury; Sib's Circle Four involvement had gotten Jak nearly killed more times than he could easily count; and Sib had implanted, deep in Jak's liver, a microscopic memory sliver containing enough information to convict and execute one of the solar system's most dangerous criminals, Bex Riveroma. Riveroma wanted that sliver at any cost, and did not regard damage to Jak's liver as a cost—given his choice, he'd rather just have the liver without Jak.

But Sibroillo was also the man who had raised Jak, all the family he had. Jak was fond of the old gwont. Besides, Sib was supposedly not coming here on zybot business; he was celebrating his two hundredth birthday by going out on the Big Circuit, the trip around the solar system that took a few years to complete if you stopped and visited all the major inhabited places—the four lower planets, Earth's moon, the Aerie, Ceres, the moons of the upper planets, and at least a flyby of dark, cold Pluto/Charon where the Rubahy civilization squatted in its last haven.

"Luckily, sir, Uncle Sibroillo is traveling with Gweshira, his demmy, and she's pretty good at slowing him down and keeping a leash on him."

"But isn't she—"

"She's Circle Four herself, sir, yes, but she doesn't have his compulsion to rush in where angels fear to tread. (Nobody has a compulsion like his, believe me, sir.) Gweshira and I will sit on him, one way or another. Since he lived on Mars when he was young, and has toves to visit, I'm hoping he'll stay down there till I stuff him onto a departing ship; he's got departures for Venus, Vesta, or the Uranus system possible within a few months."

The Big Circuit never went in up-from-the-sun-and-back-down order. Planets move, sunclippers travel in arcs rather than straight lines, and quarkjets very nearly ignore solar gravity. Weaving among the complex tangle of possible trajectories, tourists on the Big Circuit bounced up and down the sun's gravity well on sunclippers, or leapt across it on quarkjets, picking up a few worlds on each bounce.

"I'll keep a tight rein on Uncle Sib," Jak reiterated, mentally crossing his fingers.

"You really do have considerable administrative talent." Waxajovna smiled. "That was exactly what I wanted to hear, and as Principle 106 reminds us, 'Telling your boss what he wants to hear is the very essence of administrative talent.' Now, you are no doubt aware that I have a great-great-granddaughter, who lives with me, and who is named Pikia."

"It would be difficult for me to be unaware of it, sir."

Waxajovna tried not to smile. "Let me just guess at your private opinions."

"Um."

"I see your diplomatic technique is coming along, Jinnaka.

"Now, life is very dull for Pikia. If I were to take her to the Hive with me, she would have ample chances to make life exciting, and do ten or so things that would keep her out of the PSA and therefore out of any decent career, forever. It's a family phase that I have now seen through five generations, masen? I need to keep her out here in the dull until she's ready for the world, and boost her record so that she's admitted to the PSA.

"Now, I've arranged the sort of internship here, in our office, that one arranges for a relative. So she will be calling on you, here, first thing tomorrow. Her job is to help you. Your job is to cause whatever she does to constitute help, so that later you can write a glowing report about how helpful she was. And this way, everyone gets some help, and after all, we all need help, don't we?"

"I was just thinking that, sir."

"Good thinking, pizo. Now, I really must go back to my quarters one last time, and make sure that my bags really were picked up and are on their way to *Eros's Torch*. Unofficially, hello to your uncle, tell him to behave, and tell him to stay away from the ones that look like opossums—uh, better tell him that when his demmy's not around."

"You knew each other?"

"Much too well. *Everyone* knows your uncle. It's a miracle that anyone named Jinnaka can get a job anywhere." With a happy wave, Reeb Waxajovna airswam out of Jak's office, leaving Jak, for the first time, in charge of forty thousand people living in and on a tiny world.

CHAPTER 2

Your Special Little Princess

In interplanetary travel, momentum is money, changes in momentum have to be paid for in scarce and expensive energy, and therefore ships rarely descend into orbit, preferring to pass the planets, moons, and big stations at distances of anywhere from one hundred thousand to one million kilometers, exchanging passengers and cargo via ferries, launches, or longshore capsules.

Reeb Waxajovna was now on a ferry headed out to *Eros's Torch,* but had many hours to fly until his ferry would catch it; Sib and Gweshira were coming in on a different ferry, had only just left the ship, and would not arrive until early the next morning. At least, Jak reflected, orbital mechanics usually gave you enough time to clean the bathroom and hide the sex toys before off-planet visitors arrived.

Jak's official quarters were one of his few real perks—850 square meters on three levels, which gave him space enough for exercise and full-viv rooms, a centrifuged lap-swimming pool, and a ballroom perfect for a party if he'd had any friends.

He stripped into the laundry freshener, raised his left hand to his mouth, and told his purse to "have the butron clean, press, and hang all this. Order my standard Lunar

Greek meal from Kosta's, and have it delivered. I'll want it after I practice the Disciplines."

The fingerless blue glove asked, "Shall I start preparations for an early bedtime?"

"Yes, thank you." Jak stroked the reward spot as he walked into his dressing area. He opened the charging locker and pulled on the fighting suit and viv helmet for the Disciplines.

Uncle Sib always said that the Disciplines was a martial art in about the same way that sex was a biological activity or chocolate was a food—technically true but it missed most of what mattered. Most afternoons, when Jak began Disciplines katas, he was instantly calm, focused, and alive. But his mind was not on it today. As he fought the endlessly attacking black figure, flickers of color and flashes of light all over Jak's own body indicated when his hands and feet were not on the right trajectory at the right time, and to his disgust, he actually missed twice with the short blade and once with the slug thrower in the weapons katas.

He had his purse delay his bath, and sat and meditated for a short while, but he found that even meditating was difficult, and whatever was bothering him, it remained elusive. After a time, he sighed and gave up, asking his purse, "Bath ready?"

"Yes, at temperature."

Jak pulled off his fighting suit and dropped it into the freshener; the butron would move it to the charging locker once it was clean.

In the bathroom, Jak set his purse down within easy reach (purses were waterproof but disliked immersion in dark, sudsy water). He had barely settled into the suds when his purse said, "Two messages from top priority people."

Jak leaned out of the tub and pushed the reward spot again. He might be spoiling this purse slightly, but it was essential that it be loyal. The purse did so many routine tasks for its wearer that the right to wear one was part of the Hive Charter. But to have the necessary judgment and sensitivity to be the constant companion of a human being, a purse had to be far too smart to be programmed; it could only be trained. And like any personality, much of its nature was determined by the subtle accidents of its physical nature.

Thus, when Bex Riveroma had forced Jak's old purse to suicide—murdered it, really, as far as Jak was concerned—his new purse had had to be trained all over again to be able to access the restored memories, in much the way that a new arm grafted onto a tennis player had to re-learn, before it could play as well as its predecessor—and it would never play the *same*.

This was a good purse, but Jak missed the old one. One more score to be settled with Riveroma. (If Riveroma didn't settle first.)

"All right, then," Jak said, "you can put the first message up on the wall across from me."

Jak looked into the utterly expressionless face of his old toktru tove and oath-friend Shadow on the Frost. Shadow lived among humankind, instead of in the Rubahy colonies in the Pluto/Charon system, for reasons that probably made sense to a Rubahy. Human and Rubahy politics and institutions intertranslated badly, but as far as Jak could make out, his Rubahy tove was thought to be so promising that too much was expected of him for any Rubahy to fulfill, thus offending both his allies and his enemies whenever he succeeded (because it damaged their own relative standing) and whenever he failed (because it showed him unworthy of either their love or their hatred). Or it could be something else entirely. Perhaps in another thousand years human and Rubahy would dak each other better, if they didn't annihilate each other and if the Galactic Court didn't order both species exterminated. Meanwhile, Shadow on the Frost was a pizo to have with you when it all went into the soup, and a toktru tove, and that was all Jak really needed to know.

Shadow was slightly short for a Rubahy, which meant he was tall for a man. His large jaws and long front teeth, with extra slicers, marked him as hereditary warrior caste, and as on most warriors the pinfeathers that densely covered his body were white with one black patch on the back of his right shoulder. His scent organs, on top of his head, were two big loose flaps of flesh covered with special feathers, and looked much like ears. His were unusually long and elliptical, causing other Rubahy to call him "Bunny," a nickname that he hated passionately.

Because of the scent organs, square jaw, and black button eyes, speciesist humans sometimes called Rubahy by the insulting term "terrier," but there was really nothing doglike about them. Rubahy looked something like tall thin feathered apes with baboon-jaws, and something like thin tyrannosaurs with gorilla arms, but to anyone who had ever seen them, they looked like Rubahy; once you knew a few, they tended to look like warriors, truth-tellers, makers, teachers, or any of the about ninety other castes; and to Jak, Shadow just looked like Shadow.

"Jak, my toktru tove, it is my obligation to message you now and then, since we are oath-bound. I have no real news; being bound to both you and your tove, Dujuv Gonzawara, I have chosen to be where the danger and excitement are greater, thus giving myself a somewhat better chance to win

real honor, but to tell you the truth, Jak, old tove" —
Shadow's soft, whistling voice, which was as much like a
flute as the human voice was like a trumpet, dropped into a
warmer, more informal style—"it is so dull down here that I
cannot imagine how it can be duller up there. We travel from
capital to capital within the Harmless Zone, we see five or
eight or eleven nations a day, and the greater part of my time
is spent sitting watchfully as Dujuv signs his name and puts
his thumbprints on various documents. I have concluded
that the nations of the Harmless Zone are a very elaborate
prank which you humans are playing on we poor Rubahy."
He told some stories of how they had flattered this petty
king or that one, observing that "Your nations are like dogs,
and whereas the large ones will merely emit a disgruntled
woof when small children tug their ears, the small ones go
into yapping frenzies for every fancied insult. And the
Harmless Zone is filled with toy poodles and chihuahuas."

The Harmless Zone was called that, not for its harmless
people, but because it was an area for nations that were engineered to be harmless to other nations. Nakasen's Principle 23 was that "A functioning metasociety meets the
demand for as many different kinds of society as possible."
The Harmless Zone was where Principle 23 was most ag-
gressively applied. The Chryse Basin had been an industrial
center almost from the days of early settlement, and afterward the economic heart of the Second Martian Empire, but
at the end of the Seventh Rubahy War, the Second Empire
was dead, and the all but depopulated, ruined Chryse was
demilitarized and divided among hundreds of refugee
bands. Today, of the six thousand human nations, more than
one thousand were in the Harmless Zone, and not one of
them had the significance of a fruit fly fart.

Since Shadow would not care that Jak was in the bath, Jak fought down his Hive-bred impulse to get fully dressed before messaging, and recorded a short reply immediately, confirming that it really *was* that dull on Deimos, and passing on what little gossip there was.

The butron brought in dinner, the Lunar Greek meal that Jak had loved since he was a small boy (baked hamster with bechamel on glutles, mango pastry for dessert), and set it up on a lap table over the tub. Jak finished the main course and another glass of wine; it was so pleasant to eat his favorite meal, and to have something to hold off loneliness this evening. He had saved the second message from a friend to enjoy over dessert. Maybe Dujuv would have an interesting story to tell, or perhaps Phrysaba would want to talk about the concept of solidarity and why it was necessary, something she had been arguing with Jak about for years—"All right, let's see the second message."

"It's from Princess Shyf."

Jak swallowed hard. "Mark for reverse semiosis, then."

"Marking . . ." for about two minutes the purse analyzed the message, identifying hypnotic effects and enhanced images. It restored Shyf's original message, putting in a small green "emphasis bar" in the upper right-hand corner to indicate where effects had been added.

"Ready." Jak would have sworn his purse sounded as if it were bracing itself.

"All right, let's see it."

Shyf was nude, her back turned. Gracile genes in the Karrinynya Dynasty's official genome (some ancestors had liked models and courtesans) gave her long limbs and small globular buttocks; her red hair brushed them as she stretched up on her toes, arched her back, and turned her hip. She revealed one beautifully formed breast, and peeked at Jak with one twilight blue eye beside the beautiful red curtain of her hair. "Hello, Jak. I know it's been a while, but you'll forgive me, because after all" —her smile deepened—"I know that I'm your special little princess. I know what I mean to you, my darling." The tip of her tongue delicately rested on her upper lip.

His usual surge of desire proceeded directly into his usual overwhelming feeling of guilt.

"A long walk together sometime, Jak, just you and me, holding hands," Shyf said, in the message, turning to show herself full on. "You know how I hate the silly ceremony and restrictions in the Royal Palace. How I wish I could be plain old Sesh Kiroping, your demmy, once again . . ."

"That's a lie," Jak said, to her unhearing message.

The green bar flickered. "And you've lost all those people that you thought were your toktru toves—they deserted you as soon as times got tough—"

"You did your best to make me lose them," Jak said, staring at the steady, bright green bar. Whatever she wanted was coming next.

"It kind of makes me feel extra bad that while you're so lonely and stuck in such a dull job and feeling so deserted by your friends, I have a wonderful new correspondence with Duke Psim. I so need to know that you love me and I'm still your princess, and I want you to look into my eyes and pledge yourself to me, and then . . . if you do that . . . maybe sometime soon . . ." She smiled and struck a more overt pose.

Jak tensed, grunted, and sighed. "Frankly," he said to her image, "fucking you isn't half the fun of taking a good dump." His bowels coiled at having said that to her.

The message clicked off, and Jak said, "Report that call to Hive Intel, please."

The purse said, "Accessing Hive Intel AIs. This might take several minutes."

"Thank you," Jak said.

He gulped his cold, tasteless mango pastry, and thought about having the tub rewarmed—no, too much trouble. He set the tray aside, swished in the not-quite-right slightly-too-soap-gray water, and stood up to towel off. All around him, blobs of gray bathwater, drifting in the microgravity, swirled away into the exhaust system.

"Call in high-private scramble. It's from Doctor Mejitarian, Hive Intel, Deimos office," his purse said as he slipped his hand back into the fingerless blue glove.

"On screen."

Mejitarian was a kobold, with that breed's characteristic large scoop ears and big intelligent kind-looking eyes like an orangutan's, about 175 years old, gray hair just starting to come into his curly beard. "I've been through your latest message from Princess Shyf. We'd better apply some de-conditioning. Can we download software for that to your purse?"

"Please do."

"The message was reinforcement for your existing conditioning; otherwise, there was no hidden content we see. Do you have any unusual sensations or feelings?"

"Just sick and disgusted. Nothing unusual about that."

While he was at Greenworld, Princess Shyf had drafted Jak into the Royal Palace Guards and had him conditioned to her; conditioning was one of the favored tools of the aristos because it produced a state of psychological slavery that was far more reliable than mere loyalty, self-interest, or terror. Jak had returned to the Hive from his second great adventure completely conditioned into doggy devotion to the Princess's whims.

Seeing an opportunity, Dean Caccitepe, both the Dean of Students at the PSA and a senior Hive Intel operative, had recruited Jak to serve as a double agent. Hive Intel doctors had deconditioned him enough to be able to resist commands, but left as much conditioning in place as possible, so that Greenworld Intel continued to think Jak was conditioned, and that they had a valuable asset inside PASC. Hive Intel obtained copious information, and Jak's career in the colonial bureaucracy was supposedly being pushed along. Caccitepe and Mejitarian often assured him that if he performed this assignment well, he would eventually cross over to Hive Intel with high rank and a dossier full of strong recommendations.

When Jak had first arrived on Deimos and been assigned to Mejitarian, he had thought him kind. He knew now that the kobold was merely a thorough professional, good at expressing empathy and warmth for the same reason that Caccitepe was good at putting together clusters of stray facts, or that his uncle was good with a gun. Mejitarian's job was to be Hive Intel's doctor, not Jak's, and he was indifferent to everything except his job.

As he usually did, Jak gazed steadily at Mejitarian's right eye, to avoid looking at the notched left ear and the faded outline of a brand in the fur of Mejitarian's left cheek. On Mercury, where banking and other archaic horrors were still practiced, several banks marked children born into peonage in that way. How Mejitarian had gotten away from that life, and into his present one, was doubtless an interesting story, and one Jak was almost certain never to hear.

The kobold seemed to be seeing something in Jak's face. "Something else? I've told you to report unusual feelings and thoughts. Something you're not sure you should report, perhaps? Or something you feel curiously reluctant to report?"

"Oh, I know what it is, and it didn't come in the message," Jak said, shivering because he was still wet and naked. He set the dial on the towel to "extra absorbent" and gently pressed himself all over with it. "It's frustration. How long will I have to live like this and do this? I know you don't have an answer, like a fixed date or anything, but I want to get really deconditioned, go into Hive Intel on a regular mission, draw a Hive Intel paycheck, and stop infiltrating PASC. Sometimes it's hard to wait."

"Perhaps Dean Caccitepe has not been clear. If you rise to be the head of PASC while giving us a marvelous backchannel into the Karrinynya palace, and you do that across fifty years, you will have been a very successful agent. There's no particular virtue in drawing one of our paychecks, after all—rather the contrary, since the whole idea is to accomplish as much as we can within our budget, so having our agents paid out of other offices is good. You are in your most valuable possible assignment. You are a fast-rising star within PASC, which is *noticed*. And you are invaluable as a double agent. You are extraordinarily useful where you are, doing what you are doing. Now, when you sleep tonight, be sure to run the deconditioning program that we've downloaded to your purse. Any other questions?"

"No, sir."

The screen blinked off.

"Do you want to record your script now?" the purse asked. "Hive Intel has already sent it over."

"Sure," Jak said. "I'll put on a shirt and let's do it in the recording room. Prompt it from right below the camera."

After each message from Shyf, the Hive Intel AIs wrote a short script, which Jak then read from a prompter with as much sincerity as he could manage; its purpose was to convince Greenworld Intelligence that Shyf still had functional control of Jak, plant some disinformation, aid the Hive, and keep Greenworld from gaining too many advantages. *It's nice that we're allies,* Jak thought. *Because if we were enemies, this whole business might be toktru nasty.*

The room camera recorded him reading the script as it rolled across the end wall of his sitting room, and his purse uploaded it to Hive Intelligence for editing and enhancements. Nowadays he tried not to think about any of the words he was reading.

"Time for bed," he told the purse. He slipped into his prewarmed bed. "Play the deconditioning program that they just sent you. If it doesn't specify how often, repeat it all night. Wake me at four. Bright lights, lively music, lots of coffee, and something I like to eat."

"Tomorrow's going to be a good day," the purse said, cheerfully, trying to catch his mood—something at which it was still less than perfect.

"Tomorrow's going to be a day," Jak corrected.

CHAPTER 3

I Have the Most Complete Confidence in You

The next morning, the bright lights came on almost with a pop, some gutty old blues singer belted out a lively version of "Saint James Infirmary," and the waitron flew into the room towing a container with a big flask of hot strong black coffee and a mountain of delicate pastries.

Jak untethered and pushed off the warming pad, feeling as if he had a hangover, and slowly, slowly dispensed coffee into a bulb. Usually when he was sleep-deconditioned, he had threatening dreams, frightening dreams, dreams that made him weep, none of them coherent, all of Shyf; this time had been no exception. Jak had a sour taste in his mouth, a raw feeling in his throat, and an oozy gray mess in his brain.

He drew a breath, told himself to be a grown-up, and stripped off the old "PSA Maniples First Chair" shirt he usually slept in.

The music changed over to a medley of medieval American musical theatre songs, bright bouncy happy things about cockeyed optimists, four-leaf clovers, and figuring that whenever you're down and out the only way is up. (Conservation of momentum was apparently unknown to medieval Americans.)

He ate only two small puff pastries, despite all the temptations the waitron offered. It would be close to dinnertime for Sib and Gweshira, and Sib always sprang for a great meal.

Not that he would ever admit it to Sib, but Jak was looking forward to seeing him. Sibroillo Jinnaka had raised Jak, taught him the Disciplines, pushed him to excel at everything, and usually been everything you would want your uncle to be. Of course, there was a downside. Jak had gotten caught, more than once, in Circle Four's deadly feud with Triangle One. Jak's life could have been much easier had his family name been something other than Jinnaka. But still, Uncle Sib had been right there whenever Jak needed him, and if his advice had sometimes proved dead wrong, he was still Jak's model of brains, skill, and courage.

Besides, I haven't seen the horrible old gwont, or had a chance to tease him in person, for a whole year, Jak thought as he airswam swiftly through the tunnels. *Hope I haven't lost my touch.*

Most passengers off *Eros's Torch* had taken the launch directly down to Mars. Sib and Gweshira were the only passengers on the ferry. As Hive citizens entering a Hive possession, they cleared security swiftly, and were out in the receiving area, pounding Jak's back, hugging him and laughing, within a minute of the green pressure light.

They went to the Parakeet, a pleasant-enough all-shifts restaurant. On the way, Sib commented, "Except for some minor changes in the uniforms, this could be a hundred eighty years ago, when I used to come up here to go drinking and whoring."

"Since I'm in charge of the place, I'm supposed to go somewhere else for that."

"The burden of command," Gweshira said, her eyes twinkling. She was a tiny woman, all muscle and gristle, and the deep brown skin stretched over her square jaw was still firm and tight, though she must be close to two hundred years old herself. Her silver hair had escaped from its clip, bobbing around her face as they airswam.

The Parakeet was centrifuged to one-tenth g, the grav that made "light" synonymous with "rich" or "high class," in which soup stayed in a bowl and one could walk, but lying on a hard floor was comfortable and motion easy. On the partitions in the dining room, which blocked the view of people dining upside down over one's head and doors whirling by every few seconds, screens showed views from outside cameras; the restaurant appeared to be freeflying in Mars orbit.

One side of the dining room showed the red-green-blue-white landscape of Mars, spattered with small lakes, interrupted by tight white cyclones and smeared with the black smoke of prairie fires. On the opposite side the screens were lit with the wild rainbow flame of *Eros's Torch,* a stream of exotic matter tortured to the borders of existence, cooling into a thin smear of plasma, fifty thousand kilometers long and a million kilometers away, against the black star-showered velvet of space. "Well, the ferry with my boss on it should be reaching *Eros's Torch,* right about now," Jak said. "And since they don't turn them around for anything, I guess I'm in charge. How long do you think I should wait before staging a coup and declaring a provisional government?"

Sib laughed, coping with difficulty with his mouthful of salad. "You should call and ask him. It might be a welcome stimulus. The poor man is about to be bored to death."

Gweshira nodded vigorously as she picked bones out of her fish. "Neither of us had traveled in decades, you know, we'd spent all our time on the Hive, and before when we traveled, it was always 'business.'" The way she said it meant "Circle Four business." "We hadn't quite realized what a month on a quarkjet liner would be like—nothing much to do but the Disciplines, gambling, reading, and catching viv entertainment . . . they're mainly set up for younger people to stand around watching each other try to be beautiful. I'm afraid we're turning into a couple of old gwonts who think life was better in their youth."

"Well, maybe it was," Jak said.

Sibroillo half smiled. "At least our youth was better for us, eh, old pizo? Just remember that someday you're going to be describing this as the golden age."

"I don't think Deimos has ever had a golden age, Uncle Sib. At best it's had a tar age. But I appreciate your not being too discouraging. I'm looking forward to some very dull months, and my orders are to keep them that way if at all possible."

Sib beamed. "Now, that was nicely put, pizo. Very nicely put. You'd rather not offend me, but you'd rather not be left holding the bag for whatever I might do."

"Um, very blunt, but toktru."

"Well, Gweshira and I, having had one good meal and a night's sleep here, are going to head down to Mars. Deimos is only interesting because you're here. Is that good news?"

Jak made a face. "I never thought I'd be saying this, Uncle Sib, but I want to stay out of trouble."

Sib and Gweshira roared with laughter so merry that Jak joined in. "What's the joke?"

Gweshira shrugged. "Back when we were both at school

on Mars—this was in different decades, by the way—each of us had the experience of a certain teacher—also the teacher of Bex Riveroma—"

Jak shuddered. "That data sliver still in my liver—"

Sib shrugged. "In a few years the information will be out-dated and he won't care. Till then just be careful. He's crazy, evil, and dangerous, but rational enough—in fact that's why he's so dangerous. This teacher whose name we won't men-tion always said he thought of Bex as one of the two most dangerous people he'd ever trained."

"Were you the other one, Gweshira?" Jak asked.

Jak and Gweshira waited to laugh until Sib's face was a mask of fury. A moment later Sib was laughing too. "I don't know why I always fall for that."

"Because it gives us such pleasure," Jak suggested.

"Possibly." Sib held up a finger, recalling his point. "Well, anyway, when you said you wanted to stay out of trouble, it reminded us of something. During our training, believe me, *we* said that often. 'Out of trouble' was all we wanted. And every time we even thought that phrase, this teacher-we-won't-name would say (I can't intone like he could), 'You are invoking the Great God Murphy Whose Will Is Law, and he will be moved to act.' And because we're planning to visit him as soon as we fly down to Mars, he was on our mind, and you triggered the memory."

When Sib and Gweshira had finished eating, they were tired, so Jak called a sprite to guide them to their hotel, and they airswam after the little twinkling glow.

At the office, the tasks accumulated overnight consumed ten minutes, and it still wasn't officially start time; Jak had nothing to do for the rest of the day except interview Pikia.

While he waited for her, he set up a flask of coffee and two bulbs.

"Pikia Periochung is here for her interview," Jak's purse said.

"Send her in."

The door dilated and Pikia, dressed in a nicer-than-required coverall, airswam in. Jak had met her at many receptions; he was usually the only person present within fifty years of her age, so they often chatted, but only about his brief periods of media fame (which he would rather have forgotten), and the usual "do you like school" things that adults use for awkward small talk with teenagers.

"Pikia, my good news is your bad news. Your great-great-grandfather left things in really good shape. There isn't much for us to do right now, so you will be doing what everyone else does—filling out forms, rechecking administrative decisions made by the AIs, doing human-contact follow-throughs—all terribly dull."

Her big-eyed vigorous nodding indicated that Jak was now old enough to constitute Authority to a teenager. Therefore she had not listened to a word he'd said. (Nakasen, how he envied her that!) "Any questions?" he asked.

"Well, I did look at the list of optional projects for this office, and the one about the descendants of all the pretenders to the Old Martian Imperial throne—"

Jak shook his head. "Sorry. Whenever anything new comes up about open projects, we authorize some AI searches to make sure there's still nothing to do—but that's all we do. I looked into all of them when I got here and your great-great-grandfather had to tell me the same thing."

Pikia made a wry face. "Well, I tried. Great-great-grandpa Reeb's job really is as dull as it looks, isn't it?"

"Probably even duller, now." Jak explained about all the preparations they had made for Waxajovna's trip. "Furthermore, rank hath a privilege, so if anything interesting turns up, *I'll* grab it. In the unlikely event of a brief flurry of excitement, it probably won't fall on your desk."

Jak's purse chimed. He looked down at the palm display. URGENT MESSAGE YOUR EYES ONLY. "Hunh."

"What?"

"Eyes-only message. Usually these turn out to be some overzealous clerk pushing security as high as it will go to make his job look more important, or something that would embarrass some administrator if her underlings read it. But rules are rules, so shoo, scat, get out of here—grab a terminal outside and ask the clerks to show you how to handle tax exemption evaluations. We're always backlogged on those and nobody gets to avoid them for long. If it gets too exciting, lie down and breathe deeply, per the employee stress management manual."

She smiled; at least she was a good sport. "If it's about saving the universe from evil or anything other than office work, consider me volunteered."

"Weehu, Pikia, I wouldn't leave a fellow human being to do tax exemptions if I had somewhere else to put her. Now, scoot."

She scooted.

Jak floated up from his chair and spoke to his purse. "All right, lock the door, opaque the windows, vibration-suppress external surfaces, turn on security verification, adjust the central rear wall to a white surface, and use that as the screen. Let me know when you have all that done and the message cued up."

"Check on procedure, please?"

"Yes?"

"Since you have done the same things for the last five eyes-only messages, I would like to name all the sequence of all those procedures 'prepare to receive eyes-only message,' okay?"

"Approved. Suggest it anytime I receive an eyes only message." Jak touched the reward spot and listened for the cheeble; then he said, "Now, message up on screen, please."

It was Hel Faczel, the head of PASC, Jak's boss-of-bosses. He was a large man, some kind of kobold-simi hybrid, with big pointed ears, heavy brows, and a completely hair-covered snouted face. "Hello, Acting Procurator Jinnaka. We have an extraordinarily urgent situation which calls for your full and immediate attention." His expression became very serious. "The following message was received via the General Secure Common Routing Office at the Hive, a bit over nine hours ago. The person you will see in the message copy that follows has been authenticated as Teacher Xlini Copermisr, who has been doing Nakasen-related archaeology in Chrysepolis."

The great ruin of Chrysepolis, half-submerged in Bleak Lake, was where anyone went to do Nakasen-related archaeology. Paj Nakasen, founder of the Wager, had lived most of his life there. His bones were somewhere in the ruins, for the city had been destroyed in the opening minutes of the Seventh Rubahy War. When that last desperate struggle with the Rubahy was over, nothing was left of the Second Martian Empire. The League of Polities had no money. Nothing and no one would rebuild the wrecked city that had once been home to six million people.

But though Nakasen was dead, the Wager must go on—time enough to find relics later. It had been centuries before archaeology even started on the ruins. By then, forgeries, propaganda, archive viruses, and disinformation from thousands of nations, corporations, and zybots had hopelessly tangled the trail.

Xlini Copermisr looked to be between forty and a hundred years old. She had very dark skin and thick curly pale hair, like Gweshira and many people from the old Hive families. She had broad shoulders like a panth, but a delicate, fine-boned face like a gracile's, so perhaps she was unmodified but athletic and pretty. Her dark eyes seemed to reach through the screen to scratch along the back of Jak's skull.

"I am Teacher Xlini Copermisr, currently on detached service from Old Imperial University. I'm a Hive citizen working for the Nakasen Archaeology Project, whose purpose is to shed light on the early development of the Wager and to recover relics of the life of Paj Nakasen. We had already had a remarkable breakthrough earlier this year, identifying a complex of buildings as the Stanford Grand Chrysepolis Hotel, where Paj Nakasen was staying on the night of the initial Rubahy attack. Three days ago, the recovered black box of their business records revealed that Paj Nakasen had indeed been a guest there on the night of the attack, and gave us a floor plan and his room number."

Jak shuddered; though a secret unbeliever, he felt the same awe an ancient Skeptic might have had at the true site of Omphalos, or a medieval atheist might at the discovery of the True Cross or Marx's grave.

Xlini Copermisr went on, her eyes looking steadily into the camera, her voice level, and yet the excitement seemed to leap out of the screen to grab him by the neck and shake him. "Though we did not locate Nakasen's body, we did find the crushed remains of the room in which he had stayed. We knew from some of his notes and letters that Nakasen kept a lifelog from very early on—"

Jak all but gasped. A lifelog was a record, maintained by an AI complex running in background on one's purse, downloaded into a more permanent location at every opportunity. The AI complex watched from your purse through all the years and events of your life, snapping copies of everything that might be of interest to a biographer—rough drafts, messages to friends, shopping orders, schoolwork, anything—keeping a running organization and catalog as it went. Nakasen was humanity's greatest single religious teacher. Finding Mohammed's home movies, Jesus's agent's appointment calendar (with the rough draft of the Sermon on the Mount folded between the pages), and Buddha's complete sent-email file would not have been as important.

Copermisr was still talking—"under the bed, protected by several structures from falling objects, and the room was not burned. It seems to be absolutely undamaged.

"Physically it is a small dark blue memory block, a square about eighteen centimeters on a side by four centimeters thick, with Nakasen's signature embossed in white on its upper surface, designed for playback in a Harris Fastbox, a format so common that we keep a Harris Fastbox simulator in the field laboratory. We have established that it is not encrypted; it appears to contain multiple early drafts of *The Principles of the Wager, Teachings Concerning the Principles,* and *Suggestions Regarding the Teachings,* extensive notes, a large volume of message traffic in and out, and a daily diary covering the last eighty-nine years of Nakasen's life.

"Aside from a hundred random samples of pages, images, and words, by which I determined that there seems to be no encryption, I haven't looked at anything other than the index. A real examination of Nakasen's lifelog would be a job for a big, carefully chosen, international team of specialists, once the lifelog has been safely secured for the Hive and is firmly in our physical possession.

"That brings me to our problem. At the moment, Nakasen's lifelog is not secured and not in our physical possession. Chrysepolis, as you probably know, is in the Harmless Zone, and the discovery fell within the territory of Red Amber Magenta Green." She made a face. "Of course we could just seize it . . ."

Jak could hear her clear implication; no Harmless Zone nation would be able to withstand a determined grab by the Hive. Officially nations in the Harmless Zone were limited to 2500 square kilometers of territory, fifty thousand permanent residents, three thousand trained soldiers, and only weapons light enough for three unmodified humans to lift, which released no more than a thousand joules per pull of a trigger.

Xlini Copermisr had been talking on, and Jak had not heard a word of it. He told his purse "go back to where she first mentioned Red Amber Magenta Green."

". . . discovery fell within the territory of Red Amber Magenta Green. Of course we could just seize it . . . but King Witerio has generally been friendly to the Hive. I think we can buy it from him if we're polite and careful.

"Officially, King Witerio of Red Amber Magenta Green is His Splendor King Witerio Smith Guntrasen, first and sole recognized scion of the Gunemabuv Branch of the Kaesenedi Dynasty, the Probably-Rightful Leaders (that's a title) of the Splendor of the Splendiferous Chrysetic People. Like every nation down here, though they use their color designation to communicate, they strongly prefer to be called by what they call themselves—the Splendor. Every member of the royal house may properly be addressed as 'Your Splendor.' Except at formal occasions, the King prefers 'King Witerio.' The Prince stands on his dignity and prefers to be 'Your Splendor,' all the time, though he will answer to 'Prince Cyx.' (A few of his older guards still call him 'Sonny,' but I strongly advise not doing that.)

"Now, I am reasonably sure, because the King is a reasonable heet, that he will probably be reasonable if we pay him some gigantic ransom, labeled as rent or a licensing fee.

"Also, Prince Cyx intends to be a thoroughly modern monarch. He attended the PSA and he wants bureaucracy and diplomacy and a constitution and all the other modern toys. If he thinks giving us the lifelog is the 'modern' thing to do, he will.

"It is my opinion that the local Roving Consul, Dujuv Gonzawara, *could* handle the whole thing on his own, and toktru it would go better if he did. He knows the territory and he's good."

"Of *course* he's good," Jak muttered. Jak didn't know anyone kinder, more generous, fiercer in a fight, or more loyal to a tove.

"Remember that although this is the Harmless Zone, they're not savages, and they're *not* fools, and they know it. You can expect to pay plenty for the lifelog, in both cash and ceremonial honor—but it's a bargain at any price, at least in the opinion of *this* scientist. I therefore request a diplomatic team to negotiate for the lifelog of Paj Nakasen, immediately. Voiceprint signature: I am Teacher Xlini Copermisr, permanent assignment Old Empire University, temporary assignment Nakasen Archaeology Project." The screen blurred into a swirl of colors.

Hel Faczel reappeared. "We have confirmed everything she said. This is clearly a job for PASC and the Roving Consuls, but there's a major turf war on behind the scenes and Hive Intel will jump in with both feet and try to grab the whole show and all the credit. You will indeed be working closely with Dujuv Gonzawara—the two of you are toves and that's a lucky break for us. Reeb Waxajovna speaks well of you, also. We expect great things of you, and when you do them, they will be noticed and remembered.

"One point on which I must be blunt: we are getting into a turf war. Hive Intel is going to move in fast and hard. Therefore, since we can't hit as hard, we have to move faster. You're the only administrator with command rank who can get there within one day—so *get going*.

"The secret services invariably decide that if a thing is important, it is theirs. But if Hive Intel controls access to that lifelog, they will have taken control of humanity's religious and philosophical future. The spiritual life of the human race must not be dictated by the spymasters of one nation. The Hive may be the center of the Wager, but if the Wager is ever perceived as *belonging* to the Hive, the Wager is dead. There would be worse things than the loss or accidental destruction of that lifelog—its capture by Hive Intel would be one.

"Now, give orders to your staff to keep Deimos running, and go get that lifelog. Succeed, and you'll be remembered for a very long time. Fail, and you'll be remembered even longer. Good luck."

Jak clicked off, and drew a deep breath. His purse said, "Vital message, highest priority, eyes only, for you."

"Put it up," Jak said.

It was Reeb Waxajovna, messaging from *Eros's Torch*. "Well, I do suppose you're seeing the wisdom of a clear desk at the moment, Jak, so I wanted you to remember what a clever heet *I* was for having gotten the decks cleared for your success." Waxajovna seemed to parody his own smug smile.

It was so unexpected that Jak laughed out loud.

"And I also did want to tell you that I have the most complete confidence in you that I have ever had in any junior officer in PASC, ever, and if all this had to happen with me not there, thank Nakasen and all the Principles that you were. And I do believe my word carried some weight with Hel Faczel. Now those are reminders"—he paused and his smile deepened—"of how you got into this potentially tremendously advantageous situation, and they remind *me* of why I feel a *little* badly about imposing an additional difficulty on you. But this favor would do me and my family so much good that it would be wrong *not* to ask it. Since my greatgreat-granddaughter needs to distinguish herself, please take Pikia along on this mission, as your aide or whatever you want to designate her. *(Don't let her do anything and keep her completely out of trouble!)*" His eyes twinkled, and he smiled pleasantly. The screen clicked off.

"You know," Jak said to the blank space in front of him, "I liked you better when I thought you were a pigheaded old bureaucratic fossil."

He realized he didn't have much time. He needed to grab that lifelog for Hive Intel and simultaneously make it look like he had tried his heart out to get it for PASC, and he needed to be down on the surface with Dujuv, working the angles, right away.

There was bound to be a military try, too, to grab that lifelog. Within a few hours every officer in the Spatial would be told to delay Jak as much as possible. If he was going to commandeer transport to the surface, he should get it commandeered now and make sure it stayed commandeered.

He lifted his left hand and spoke to his purse. "Identify every officer and techny who has any power to prevent *John Carter* from making a flight down to Red Amber Magenta Green's landing field. Assuming they have one. Nearest landing field if they don't—"

"They have one—all weather, long enough runway. Check for all inspection certificates to make sure they can't block it with missing paperwork?"

"Do it." Jak pushed the reward spot hard, and the cheeble was joyous. "All right, line those heets up by rank, and start blinking them onto the screen, lowest first. As soon as I'm done talking to one, move me to the next. Try to structure it so that anyone who calls his boss about it will find his boss is busy talking to me."

A very junior mechanic's face appeared on the screen, hand on his chest in the salute position. "Sir!"

"I need immediate confirmation that to the best of your knowledge warshuttle *John Carter* is ready to be commandeered for an emergency mission to the surface." The *Carter* was the flagship of the Deimos fleet, suitable for calling on a king.

The techny nodded vehemently. "Sir, it is completely ready to go; get your party aboard and you can launch in ten minutes."

"Thank you, techny. Very unofficially, it's highly likely you'll need to make good on that."

"Thank *you*, sir."

Jak gave the civilian administrator's salute, and his purse blinked off the techny and blinked up a junior officer on the screen. Jak had essentially the same one-minute conversation over and over as he worked his way up the organizational chart in a blinding fury of bureaucratic ticket-punching.

With his purse helping, Jak commed thirty-one technies and officers in less than twenty-five minutes, all on ultra high priority. Because the priority was so high, no one hesitated an instant before answering.

Being a true wasp, and thus among the most modest humans in the solar system, Jak was both pleased and appalled by what he encountered—he thought the first lieutenant who had to step out of her shower was really cute, but it would have been all right with Jak if the senior techny, a simi covered with full body hair, had waited a moment to get off the toilet.

The only conversation that was different was the last one, when he finally spoke to the base commander.

"Acting Procurator Jinnaka, what can I do for you?"

"I am commandeering warshuttle *John Carter* for a descent to the Red Amber Magenta Green landing field, party of two—myself and an assistant—for arrival at fourteen hundred ground solar time. Please have it ready for boarding two hours and forty minutes from now."

"Sir, we can't guarantee its availability, and I don't know if we have any other warshuttle—"

"I've already verified with all of the involved personnel that it is ready for immediate departure." Jak spoke to his purse. "Transmit the relevant records to the base commander's purse, please."

The base commander glanced down at his own purse, his lips pressed tight together. "Very well," he said, "it will be ready. In the future, you need not disturb so many of our personnel here—we are busy and we do have things to do— you can call me—"

"I am aware that I can," Jak said, pleasantly, "and also that I can call anyone I like. Or even people I don't like, if I may be permitted a small joke. The mission is urgent, sir, and I want to commend all of your personnel for their immediate willingness to help and for the pride and confidence with which they were able to tell me that what I needed would be available. Splendidly well done, sir."

"You are too kind."

"You may tell the skipper of *John Carter* that my assistant and I may be somewhat early, but I won't request that his departure time be stepped up. Thank you again, sir."

Jak clicked off and let himself smile broadly. He spoke into his purse. "Draft a short favorable memo—

"From: me.

"To: every officer I talked to, and to his CO.

"Subject: commendation for efficiency and cooperation.

"Content: summarize what I just said to the commander.

"Style: formal."

He airswam toward the door. "Back to regular security level," he told his purse, and all the windows instantly became transparent again. The door dilated in front of him, and he airswam to Pikia's desk.

"Ahem," Jak said.

All four of the human staff looked up, and at least one camera on each of the dozens of robots swiveled toward him.

"I have an emergency mission to the Martian surface; I

may be gone for a period of weeks, and I am leaving immediately. Process all routine cases, defer anything that requires my approval. If it's urgent or an emergency, call me on my purse. I'm taking the only other line officer with me—that's you, Pikia—so all of you should pretend that you miss us."

The ragged cheer was slightly disconcerting, but not as much as Pikia's impulsive hug, which nearly tumbled him backward. "Get packed," Jak said, disentangling himself. "Departure in two hours and forty minutes. Make sure you have enough formal wear, we're going to have to be polite to diplomats. Cancel all your social calendar for the next two weeks."

She was still grinning like a moron. "Jak, boss, chief, whatever," she said, "I didn't *have* a social calendar until you said we're leaving. I'll be back with a bag in ten minutes."

"That should be Mister Jinnaka or sir—" he said, to her rapidly flipping feet, as she airswam out the door.

CHAPTER 4

Not the Most Useless Person on the Team

As Pikia and Jak floated in the cageway, waiting to go aboard *John Carter,* she said, "Can I ask a very immature question?"

"As long as I don't have to give a toktru mature answer."

"Where will we be sitting? I like to get a good view of the cameras and viewports."

Jak glanced sideways at her; he could tell she was excited and trying to hide it. "Don't worry," he said, "so do I. We're on spare acceleration couches in the cockpit. It's my first flight down to Mars; I wouldn't miss being able to see it."

She smiled and her eyes twinkled. "That's what I wanted to know." Then, as if the thought would burst her if she didn't voice it, she explained, "I've been down and up a hundred times at least, probably more, and I still love it. But so many adults pull down the shade."

"Toktru. They don't do it because they're adults. They do it because they're boring. I still love the window, too."

Well, she might be the boss's bratty relative, but she had a nice smile. And the job was simple—watch Duj and Teacher Copermisr talk, say some polite things himself, collect the package, put it on the next warship bound for the Hive.

A crewie came out, gave the Spatial salute, and asked them to follow her inside. They entered through the main doors over the boarding-side wing, where the beanies would storm out in an opposed landing.

Aside from its war room within the worryball, *John Carter* was exactly like every other warshuttle in the Hive's fleet at Deimos, purpose-built to land on Mars, with wings designed to reconfigure to cope with the drastically varying reentry stress profile, the widest range of forces for any world with an atmosphere. The accidental terraformation of Mars by the Rubahy Bombardment had produced as strange a set of conditions as could be found anywhere in the solar system: breathable atmosphere farthest up, but lowest pressure at surface; very viscous low-density air that exerted high shearing but low heat on a reentering spacecraft; a thermosphere with easy aerobraking, and a troposphere with a steep glide ratio. An orbit-to-ground shuttle for Earth could be fixed geometry (though it would heat up like a furnace while high and fly like a brick while low), but the Martian atmosphere required continuously varying the exposed surface. Warshuttles and launches entered shaped like dolphins and landed shaped like condors, morphing constantly.

Inside the boarding airlock, *John Carter* was folded down to almost a bare fuselage, a long ellipsoid with small curved fins on all sides, nose bulbous, tail conical, resting on the track.

Atmosphere-flight craft always looked wrong to Jak; he had grown up in space. Spaceships should be spheres joined by struts, with platforms, discs, or squares stuck on at any convenient angle, and the working guts out and visible. Craft made for air were weirdly seamless, squashed-and-squeezed alien phalloi, with big, awkward-looking wings stuck on like some equally alien birth-control device.

"Welcome aboard," Tror Adlongongu, the captain, said, and traded forearm grips with them both. He was short but not small; his heavily muscled frame suggested many years in garrison without much to do but resistance lifting, and perhaps kobold or panth genes. He was depilated like all Spatial crewies. His skin was a coppery shade of brown, and the faceplate-shaped patch of deeper tan around his face indicated frequent EVs. His habit of having a hand on something solid at all times confirmed him as a long-term crewie. "Well," he said, "though they told me that what we're making this flight for is none of my business, they did confirm that this is important, by telling me that if I messed things up it would be bad for the Hive, the Spatial, Deimos Base, and me personally—in rising order of badness."

"They weren't exaggerating," Jak said. "They told me much the same thing. Sorry we're making you land in a backwater."

"Oh, yeah. At least Red Amber Magenta Green has a landing field," the captain said. "Some of the Harmless Zone nations would have had to build one for us first, or we'd have landed on a beach or a lake and brought along a disassembled cradle and some engineers to be able to fly back up. But Red Amber Magenta Green has a modern all-weather runway to go with their pretensions. They have a national spaceline, you see—three suborbital transports and an old launch that might date to the Second Empire. So, not only do they have a good place for us to land, but (more important from my standpoint) they have a cradle to get us back up. Plus they're thrilled to have a real warcraft landing there."

"It's such a beautiful ship," Pikia said, lying. "All smooth silvery curves. What does its name mean?"

With chilly correctness, Adlongongu said, "I am happy to have the opportunity to tell you both what is true and what is not. The ship is actually named after the warrior hero of a Late Medieval English epic set on Mars, which was immensely popular for about two generations in Old America. But some nitwit of a crewie, knowing only that the ship was named in Late Medieval English, looked up the parts of the name and concluded that it meant 'transporter of prostitutes' customers.' Despite all of my efforts to correct this unfounded legend—which I think is prejudicial to good discipline—"

The acceleration bell rang, and everyone airswam to a safety couch. With a subtle push, the linducers activated. The ship glided along at a meter or two per second. Jak tilted his acceleration couch up for a better view; there was a subtle shimmer outside the window as air was recovered from the lock, and then the great metal doors in front of them dilated, opening to a view of the black night of space dotted with bright stars.

Jak didn't have time to spot any familiar constellation before *John Carter* rotated end for end horizontally, so that now it was moving backward on the linducer track; the nose viewports filled with the red-blue-green-white whorl of Mars.

Jak's purse tingled his left hand for a private message. He pressed to acknowledge, then looked down at his palm; letters scrolled across.

DO YOU SUPPOSE THAT THE COMMON USE FOR SPACE AVAILABLE SLOTS ON THIS WARSHUTTLE HAS

ANYTHING TO DO WITH THE PERSISTENCE OF A CER-
TAIN LEGEND PREJUDICIAL TO GOOD DISCIPLINE?—
PIKIA

Jak rested the fingers of his right hand in his left palm
and, double-keying, sent a quick response:

NAUGHTY. SHUT UP BEFORE YOU MAKE ME LAUGH. —
JAK

A slight increase in gravity made Jak look to the side; a
screen showed the linducer grapple grabbing the Deimos
loop. As the linducer gradually increased the strength of the
magnetic field, their coupling to the loop increased, and they
accelerated. For this part of the flight, they would not go
above a quarter of a g, and the couches were really needed
only as protection from safety inspectors and insurance
agents.

Tourist brochures said modern Deimos looked like a diamond ring. Jak thought it looked more like a hula hoop
glued to a smoldering lump of coal. The main recre-
ational/shopping area was in a roofed-over dome at the West
Pole; from space, the many lights under the dome, and their
reflections, littered brightly in the darkness. At the East
Pole, the loop was sixty-five kilometers across, several
times the largest dimension of Deimos itself, but barely visible because it was formed by a ribbon of superconductor
five centimeters wide and three millimeters thick.

Deimos orbits Mars at about 1350 m/sec; riding around
to the retrograde side of the loop in a very light coupling,
they could have killed their orbital velocity and simply
dropped. This would have resulted in their arrival on the sur-

face at a speed of about five kilometers per second and a temperature of around two thousand kelvins, in an excellent impression of a meteor impact. (In fact the impression might have been as large as 250 meters in diameter.)

Therefore they stayed on the loop until they were on the side moving against Deimos's orbital direction, but they coupled lightly, so as not to completely kill their forward velocity relative to Mars. As they released from the loop, they were pointed in the direction of Deimos's orbit, but moving much slower than Deimos's orbital velocity; they rolled over, and the great bulk of Deimos, a vast flying mountain, shot forward in the upper viewports, gone on ahead of them in the blink of an eye. The warshuttle's cold jets fired in a whoosh of white noise, as they course-corrected for their approach.

"I hate taking off backward," Captain Adlongongu commented. "Just seems undignified. A spaceship ought to take off on its tail, self-propelled, like in vid and viv."

For most of the four hours of free fall as they approached the Martian atmosphere, Jak and Pikia did little but float weightless and take in the view. All of the lower planets of the solar system had been drastically altered by the Bombardment a thousand years before, but none more than Mars. The softening-up rain of light-speed projectiles that had begun the First Rubahy War had pockmarked Earth with lakes and started a new ice age, battered the Venerean surface into gravel with sonic damage, and honeycombed Mercury with fracture tubes, but it had accidentally done what no Old Martian Emperor could ever have mustered the political will and the budget to do—it had terraformed the fourth planet.

Effectively, the Bombardment had restarted a case of ar-

rested development. Because Mars had been too small to develop plate tectonics to recirculate volatiles, eventually,
after a billion years or so of being a wet world with abun-
dant life, Mars had lost its water and CO_2 into the pores and
cavities of its thick crust. As its internal heat had retreated
toward the core, the kilometers-deep beds of groundwater
had frozen solid, leaving the planet with a slush-mud "permafrost ocean" underlying a thin smear of almost-vacuum
desert.

For fifty years before the Rubahy invasion ships arrived
from Sigma Draconis, the Bombardment, a spray of tennis-
ball-sized chunks of quartz moving so close to lightspeed
that only precision instruments detected the difference, had
whacked each of the four lower planets with fifty impacts
per day. On little, dense, heavily cratered, airless Mercury,
the effect had been like rifle shots fired into a ball of soft
clay, leaving a tube of shattered and melted rock right
through the planet, a deep round pit at the entry point, and a
shallower pit at the exit, with thousands of rocks raining
back for the next few hours. This had meant little, except the
occasional accidental losses of unlucky miners, habitats, or
pieces of machinery. On Venus the thick atmosphere had absorbed much of the energy into immense shock waves that
traveled around the planet several times, battering the surface to gravel, and heaping the gravel into dunes and ridges;
in the millennium since, the howling, lead-melting-hot
winds had reshaped the dust and gravel surface into one vast
dune field.

Earth's atmosphere had absorbed most but not all of the
force of each projectile. Ocean impacts had put enormous
quantities of water into the atmosphere, darkening the skies,
spreading blankets of snow on the adjoining land, and fill-

ing northern rivers with freshwater that had stopped the flow of the great warm currents in the oceans. The impacts on land had left kilometer-wide circular pocks, averaging a few kilometers apart, all over the northern hemisphere north of twenty-one degrees north, their frequency falling off until, below twenty-one degrees south, the body of the planet had shielded it. Earth was now the planet of pocks and glaciers, a pretty place if you could avoid knowing that it was also the grave of seven billion people and about three million species.

But Mars had become another world entirely.

The frozen ancient oceans, with much of the atmosphere dissolved in them, underlay most of her northern hemisphere. The thin atmosphere provided little shielding. Every impact had broken through the thin, weak soil and rock of the surface and plunged deep into the honeycombed ice, giving up its kinetic energy as heat, leaving an open channel to the surface for the great blasts of steam, methane, carbon dioxide, and ammonia, the greenhouse gases needed to warm the planet back to life.

The Bombardment had not been easy on the Martians themselves; the planet had started with two billion people and finished with three hundred million, fifty Earth years later. But during those twenty-seven Mars years, as the Old Empire collapsed, as all the nations of the solar system seceded from the Empire and convulsed in war and revolution, as the League of Polities seized control of the Imperial Fleet and Army and prepared to meet the oncoming invasion, and as refugees poured back and forth over the face of Mars in bewildered, helpless, and ever-dwindling hordes, day after day, year after year, the ancient volatiles had poured out onto the surface again.

At first the projectiles had arrived with almost no atmosphere to penetrate, giving up all their energy in the permafrost layer. The water and carbon dioxide fell out as snow, forming glaciers over the old collapsed surface. But under the thickening blanket of greenhouse gas, the surface of Mars grew warmer, and the pressure climbed. Algaes and lichens, all the microbiota of Earth whose spores had carelessly strewn the planet for centuries before, bloomed on the rocks; other living material leaked out of abandoned habitats and wrecked cities.

Photosynthesis liberated oxygen; chemical reactions and the explosions of the quartz projectiles broke down ammonia to liberate nitrogen, and burned the methane and oxygen together. Near the surface, water deposits began to melt and flow; dirt and rock collapsed to the bottom of the new sinkholes.

Due to Mars's great scale height, each year the projectiles reached the surface with less force, but still they raised dust and grit into the atmosphere, dirtying the ice, preventing the albedo from rising too high. A wet, warm world began to come back together on top of the sunken ruins of the old.

In the tenth Martian year of the Bombardment, water stood in small lakes on the hitherto dry bottom of the Boreal Ocean; in the twentieth Martian year, the Boreal Ocean did not freeze over, and the first hurricanes blew. Just after the Bombardment, when Ralph Smith, and the last remnants of the Grand Army of the League of Polities, battered the desperate Rubahy into submission on Titan, the backup plan relied, in part, on submarines beneath the Martian seas. And when Ralph Smith's grandson accepted the imperium of the Second Empire, at Chrysepolis, the Imperial Sea Guard swore its loyalty to him on the docks there.

Earth has a worldwide ocean interrupted by a scattering of continents; Mars, a worldwide continent surrounding a small ocean, with only two inland seas to help moderate the climate. Large parts of the planet broil and freeze, far from any moderating water, the thinner atmosphere responds with much greater violence to the differences, the Coriolis force per kilometer of north-south difference is about twice what it is on Earth, and the high-viscosity atmosphere delivers more of its force to any exposed surface. Martian hurricados—savage spiral thunderstorms, fifty kilometers across—rip across the Martian desert, their sticky almost-Mach-1 winds flinging gravel and mud. Waterspouts deposit whole lakes onto surrounding land. Double-length seasons bake grass dry for prairie fires in summer, and bury the black land deep with blizzards in the winter.

Jak and Pikia could see all these things from the viewport of the warshuttle: violent tight swirls of hurricados, bouncing and weaving ice clouds above waterspouts, streaks of black smoke from grass fires, big white feathers of blizzards.

Jak's purse tingled again; he glanced down, mentally preparing to tell Pikia to cut it out, but it wasn't from her. He slipped on his goggles and earpieces.

Hel Faczel looked sour. "Hive Intel has won two concessions. The first is that two stringers for Hive Intel, Sibroillo Jinnaka and Gweshira Byeloaibari, are accredited to join your party when you land. Reeb Waxajovna assured me that you would be less than pleased. I hope you can come up with something clever to keep them sidetracked and harmless."

That's a forlorn hope, Jak thought. *Oh, well, I tried to keep Sib out of things.*

"They will shortly be joined by a regular Hive Intel agent. He's low-level probationary, in his third year of probation—I am trusting you to dak the implications—"

Most Hive bureaucracies either took new officers off probation, or fired them, within ninety days. Jak's own probation had been thirty days, and Dujuv's less than two weeks.

"—and he is the Hive Intel open agent in place for the Harmless Zone. An agent's prestige, in that organization, is much higher if he is secret rather than open. Prestige also depends on the importance of the nation in which an agent operates. So Hive Intel has bounced this heet as low as they can bounce him without bouncing him out. You're getting a heet who has a knack for antagonizing the powerful and for failing his superiors.

"He will be under your orders theoretically but you will not be able to punish or fire him, because his name is Clarbo Waynong. *That* Waynong family. He will arrive in a day or two—he had to meet with friends at the Patridiots Association expats banquet."

Jak felt sick. The Patridiots were a reactionary student movement; it was the shorthand combination of patrician-patriot-idiot, young men and women from the Hive's traditional political families who favored the abolition of the Republic, the creation of a hereditary aristocracy, and an enforced loyalty to a list of conventional ideals. They proudly described themselves as "too loyal to be smart" and declared that "Leadership isn't what you do, or know, it's what you are."

Faczel shrugged just as if he could actually see Jak's shudder. "Sorry to be adding all these complications, Jinnaka, but the Assembly Steering Committee ordered this directly, and since four of Mr. Waynong's cousins were voting on the subject—" He shrugged again. "Good luck to you, sir.".

The vision clicked off. Before Jak could even decide to take off his goggles, there was another signal; an incoming call from Hive Intel's Deimos office.

Doctor Mejitarian's big warm eyes had never looked so troubled before. "Hello, Jak. You'll be happy to know that for once this is not about the Princess. I wanted to let you know that we intercepted Hel Faczel's message and he is correct in *all* particulars. Clarbo Waynong really is a fool and had no business passing the PSA, let alone being taken into Hive Intel.

"But in our business, we work with what we have. We are keeping Waynong in Hive Intel because he wants to be in Hive Intel. We give him what he wants because he is the oldest son in the senior branch of an important patrician family. He is highly electable and appointable, and therefore certain someday to be very powerful.

"We want him favorably disposed toward us.

"We need him to succeed at the present business, and we need his name to be all over the success when the story becomes public, you see.

"Engineering his success is not going to be easy. (I assure you that you will get no help from *him*.) Nonetheless, if somehow he succeeds, we will know who engineered it. So, by way of incentive, direct from Dean Caccitepe: if Hive Intel obtains control of the Nakasen lifelog through your efforts, in such a way that the public credit goes to Clarbo Waynong, then we will at once completely decondition you from your attachment to Princess Shyf, terminate your double-agent mission, and transfer you out of PASC and into Hive

Intel. Make what we want happen, and everything you want is yours.

"Any questions?" The kobold's grin was surprisingly warm.

"None at all, sir. It's a deal," Jak said. "Thank you for the opportunity."

Mejitarian's expression went flat. "I have been working with Clarbo Waynong for most of two years, and I would say, don't thank me for this opportunity until you've had some firsthand experience of it. Good luck."

"Thank you." Jak took off his eyepieces and his headphones. Pikia was looking at him curiously.

"Bad luck, not of our making, but we're going to be cleaning up after other people's messes," Jak said to her. "We're getting three backseat drivers. Two pushy zybotniks and a probable incompetent." He gave her the truth about Sib and Gweshira, and a highly edited version of the Clarbo Waynong problem. It was a chance to practice his cover story with a less-experienced person.

When he finished, she made a soft click with her tongue.

"What?" Jak asked.

"Well, at least I'm not the most useless person on the team anymore."

CHAPTER 5

If You Can Pull It Off,
You're In Out of the Cold

An hour later, they were back on the acceleration couches, comfortable enough in slightly more than two g, as *John Carter* slid down into the atmosphere. The Martian scale height is large (pressure falls very gradually with increasing altitude), and much of the post-Bombardment atmosphere is far above the surface, since the planet does not "hold it down" very hard. Martian air is sticky so that it exerts great force on any airfoil, but its thinness and high heat capacity dissipate aerobraking heat rapidly.

Thus the risk in coming into Mars's post-Bombardment atmosphere at too steep an angle was not so much of burning up as of being squashed flat; the danger of coming in too shallow was that the terrific lift of the sticky air could fling one away from the planet all too easily. *John Carter* entered shallowly, and moved rapidly down to a hypersonic glide at very high altitude. The relatively short distance around Mars—half that around Earth—the great velocity, the shallowness of the glide, and the great distance to be descended meant that they would glide right around the planet almost three times during their reentry.

The captain announced, "All right, no more aerobraking, and we're not in free fall: You two can get up."

Jak got off the acceleration couch. The grav was about a third of a g, downward, with a gentle noseward pull.

Day and night flashed by at hour intervals, twice; three times they passed under Phobos. There was something ominous about the Jovian League's major base hanging there, seemingly close enough to touch.

Every few minutes the captain talked to his purse, and the variable geometry of the warshuttle varied further. Fins grew to wings, wings lengthened, then widened, then curved. After their third swift dawn, the warshuttle, still fifteen kilometers up, took up a twenty-kilometer-radius circle around Red Amber Magenta Green's landing field. The fuselage, which had been nearly the whole ship on Deimos, was a small ellipsoid between vast wings.

At last they coasted a dozen meters above the hard-packed red sand, toward the mad jumble of spires, towers, arches, and domes that was Magnificiti, the capital of Red Amber Magenta Green. *John Carter* dipped as if bowing to the towers, the linducer grapples coupled to the maglev rails, and they had grabbed the planet's surface, like a perfect catch on the trapeze.

Around them, the wings and fins rolled, folded, and collapsed back into the fuselage, until *John Carter* looked much as it had on Deimos, with only two meters of the boarding wing extended on the right side. The linducer track carried the warshuttle on across the desert, as if it were a big, slow-moving Pertrans car.

There were five people waiting at the quai. Dujuv rocked back and forth like a small boy, and Shadow on the Frost stood with exceptional straightness, the floppy feather-covered scent organs standing so straight up that he really did look like a bunny—at least, like a very tall feather-covered bunny with a mouthful of saber-teeth. Erect posture was the equivalent of a broad human grin; the Rubahy have no facial muscles and hence no expressions.

Sib and Gweshira stood by uncomfortably, too aware that Jak would rather they were not there.

The fifth person was a tall young woman, very beautiful even in a century when genetic modification and routine body sculpting made everyone beautiful. Her gold-blonde hair and her all-but-jet skin were made more striking by her full, long white gown.

Captain Adlongongu clasped forearms with Jak and Pikia again, gripping Jak's muscles like a vise, but closing as lightly as a breath all the way round Pikia's slender arm. "Well," he said, "if (as you tell me) this mission is actually something that might someday make the history books, make sure my ship gets a footnote."

The boarding door dilated, and Jak walked out across the wing, onto the quai, and into a bear hug that could crush a pony. "I missed you too, Duj, you big goon," Jak managed to gasp. The six hours down from Mars to Deimos, and the ten hours back up, and their tight schedules, had prevented their seeing each other since taking up their duty stations.

Dujuv released him and stepped back. Jak's oldest and best tove was a panth, a breed the genies of the Old Martian Empire had intended as bodyguards: mesomorphs with ultra-short reaction times, ultra-fast metabolisms, and far more fast-twitch muscle fiber than unmodified humans. Natural gymnasts, wrestlers, pilots, or commandos, they were also modified to bond deeply—once he was your tove, a panth could hardly help being anything else. They had a bit less verbap and mathap to make room for a great deal more spatiap, and their speed at sorting out a chaotic situation was astonishing. A panth often won the fight before anyone else in the room knew there was one.

Panths were naturally all but hairless; Dujuv's only visible hair was his eyebrows, which were a mere scattering of a few coarse hairs on his deep brown skin. They had little subcutaneous fat; naked, Dujuv looked like an anatomical drawing. "It's good to see you again, pizo," Jak said.

"And to have you along on this, old tove," Dujuv answered.

"The Rubahy say that a meeting of three old friends is seven gladnesses," Shadow on the Frost commented. "Three who are glad to be with each other as three; the gladness of each one not to be away from his toves; and the gladness of each pair. I feel that saying at this moment. It honors me to stand in both your company."

"And it honors us, your oath-friends, as well," Jak said, giving the reply that he knew was correct—though even after five years of friendship, Rubahy social customs were a permanent bewilderment to him. "Let me introduce my assistant, Pikia Periochung."

Sib, Gweshira, and the silent young woman all gathered for introductions; when Pikia had been introduced all around, Dujuv said, "And you are to receive your official greeting and welcome to the territory of the Splendor of the Splendiferous Chrysetic People from Princess Kayadi Guntrasen, recognized second heir of King Witerio Guntrasen of the Gunemabuv Branch of the Kaesenedi Dynasty."

"If you call me anything other than just 'Kayadi,'" she said, "I will slap you. My brother Prince Cyx, or Heir Number One as I call him, is fond of ceremony. I have decided to let him have all of mine."

A whirling cloud of dust bounced over the nearest hillside. Turning to follow Jak's gaze, Dujuv said, "Oh, there she is now."

"She?"

"What has sprung over our short Martian horizon," Shadow explained, "is a hovercar, which is why it is kicking up such a large cloud of dust, carrying Teacher Xlini Copermisr, which is why it is late."

Dujuv shrugged. "She's very dedicated to her work, so she never leaves it till the last second. Still, no one gets around in the Harmless Zone better. She's the first one I call when I need advice in dealing with some petty king. If they had let her handle the whole deal, it would be done by now."

"She said more or less the same thing about you," Jak said.

Dujuv nodded. "She would. My predecessor told me to follow her around as much as I could, keep my mouth shut, and *listen* for my first two months. He should have said *three* months, or four."

The hopping and leaping cloud was nearly on them. The hovercar burst from the base of the great pillar of dust, slewed sideways, flared its flexible skirts toward them, and coasted to a sloppy stop beside the goal, throwing red-brown dust up toward them.

"Sorry, sorry, sorry," Teacher Copermisr said, hurrying up the walkway onto the goal, as if she were five years old and they were going on a picnic.

Introductions were repeated, and then Kayadi said, "Well, I have to go stand around uselessly at a party all afternoon. And no doubt you all need to confer. We set you up with the guest pavilion, Dujuv, with private rooms for everyone. If you like, take one of the royal taxis there."

"That will be fine," Dujuv said. "Thank you for being the

one who came out to meet us—this wouldn't have been so pleasant without you."

"You mean it wouldn't have been as efficient. With my father or brother you'd have had a brass band and a full military review, and with my mother, my grandma, or either of my sisters, you'd have all been inspected for the presence of eligible men with some aristo blood, for possible matching up with my minor cousins. But be sure you remember, Xlini, I'm counting on you for an invitation to a dig this fall—otherwise I'll be stuck going through my second social season."

Teacher Copermisr grinned. "I wouldn't let that happen to a tove. We've got some undersea excavation to do. You'll probably have to take off some of that hair for the helmet."

"Ruined for *two* social seasons! Oh, Xlini, you're a tok-tru tove! Good-bye, everyone, welcome to the Splendor!" A small robot limousine glided up; Kayadi got in and it whisked her away.

Dujuv spoke into his purse. "Taxi for seven, bill to the King. To the guest pavilion."

"Right," his purse said. "And notify guest services at the palace?"

"Please." Dujuv touched the reward spot, and his purse cheebled merrily. He looked up at the rest of them. "The plan for the rest of the day is to do nothing," he said. "To save up energy for tomorrow, when we'll be doing nothing with great grace and style."

Jak worked out three times a week in a full-g centrifuge, and Martian grav is a bit less than 0.4 g, but the difference between voluntarily working against weight for an hour, and having weight all the time, is painful and exhausting. Besides, he had been in constant motion for thirteen hours. His aching bones and tired muscles cried out for a comfortable bath and early bed. He took a muscle relaxant, and set up the conference room in his suite so that everyone could talk half-reclining.

Jak's first conference was with Sibroillo and Gweshira. They had been awakened at their hotel on Deimos after only four hours' sleep, flown down on a regular commercial launch into Bassoon, and caught a four-hour trip in a sleeper Pertrans car from there to Magnificiti, and of course they were both more than a century older than Jak; it was hardly surprising that they both looked strange. But there was something else as well.

Gweshira looked grimly determined. Sib appeared slightly hangdog and defiant, showing more of his bald crown than his face. Gweshira said, "Jak, Sibroillo has something to say to you."

"Well, it's Gweshira's idea, but she's right, and I'm working my way around to feeling that she's right. Jak, we're only stringers for Hive Intel. For them we're strictly mercs, and all that they have officially asked us to do is to make sure that we are participants in the process and that Hive Intel's interests are looked after. It looks to Gweshira and me as if Hive Intel is reaching hard for something that it would be better for it not to touch—if they capture that object for their exclusive possession, it will cause enough negative blowback to be contrary to Hive Intel's own interests—if only they had brains to see that! So . . . we will look after their interests by just riding along—unless you appear to be completely crazy or stupid." Sibroillo winced slightly.

Jak had barely seen the flick of Gweshira's fingers against his arm. She'd lost none of her speed in all the years he'd known her. Sib hastily added, "And we won't be too quick to make that judgment. Carte blanche, old pizo. I'm swallowing several tons of advice right now, you know."

"I know, Uncle Sib. I appreciate that." Jak was touched, overwhelmed really, but his feelings were severely mixed. It was good that there was no risk that Sib would snatch Nakasen's lifelog himself, or take any of Jak's credit away. Yet at the same time, Jak really had not thought about whether it was a good thing for Hive Intel to have the lifelog or not.

"Well, then," Gweshira said, smiling brightly, "we'll be going now—I know there's forty minutes left in the time for this meeting, but if we stayed, poor Sib would compulsively spend that forty minutes finding ways to *not* give you advice."

"Thank you, Aunt Gweshira."

It was nice that Sibroillo and Gweshira would be letting him run his own show, but on the other hand that also meant he would *have* to run his own show. Oh, well, weehu, Principle 129 said that "The hardest thing to understand about a balance is that both sides are equal; grasp that and the universe is yours." In a way he wished they had stayed. Jak did not need forty minutes before his next meeting to nervously arrange chairs—

His purse said, "High priority message from a high priority source."

"Screen it."

"From Myxenna Bonxiao, coded channels, and it came from *von Luckner*. Eyes only."

Von Luckner was a *Ranger*-class raider; raiders were the fastest ships in the Spatial and *Ranger*-class were the fastest, most modern raiders. A Hive Intel agent aboard one was hardly unusual, but Myxenna was also one of Jak's best and oldest toves, and for her to call him from *von Luckner* meant it was at least semi-official business.

"Can you do eyes-only protocol here?"

"It will take three extra minutes for bugsweeping."

"Then do it."

The door to the room contracted, the locks activated with a synchronous thud, and the windows opaqued. White noise roared through the speakers. That must be some side effect of his purse attacking and defeating listening devices.

The screen flickered to life. "Hi Jak." Myxenna Bonxiao had blue stars within her green irises, thick dark hair, freakishly pale skin, big high breasts, trim little waist, tight round buttocks, and beautiful legs. Any reasonably hetero male had a hard time looking away from her. She was also one of the smartest people Jak had ever met, both book-smart and people-smart and able to use the two together.

"Jak, I'm on *von Luckner* because it's delivering me to Mars, as quickly as it can. The Hive is still four months back from its next opposition with Mars, so even at *von Luckner*'s top speed, it's going to take about ten days for me to get to you. When next you see me, I'll have the happy expression of a girl who's been mashed by nine g, one hour out of every six, for more than a week, with full grav in between.

"My job is to secure the lifelog if you haven't. So if you're going to grab that thing and save Clarbo Waynong's career, you've got ten days, and it won't be easy. Did you know him in the PSA? He was two years ahead of us and always asking me out. For every course he ever passed, his family had to create a scholarship, donate a research grant, or buy the athletics program a new toy. He has a major self-confidence problem—he has *major* self-confidence and that's a problem. When Caccitepe heard who would be assigned to retrieve the lifelog, he turned gray and started shouting, and when he was done shouting I had this mission.

"Oh, and Clarbo is Patridiot to the bone, too, so the people he listens to most pride themselves on being as dumb as their genes will let them and as ignorant as possible.

"Something else you should know about—I mentioned that the Hive is four months from opposition with Mars. That means Earth is two, and since the Aerie is two months ahead of Earth in orbit, they're nearly *at* opposition."

At the unexpected mention of the Aerie, where Greenworld was (and therefore where Princess Shyf was) Jak was distracted by the surge in his heart and the cold rolling over of his intestines. He told his purse "back her message up to where she mentions the Aerie, then continue."

After half a second of silence and a white screen, Myxenna resumed. "—the Aerie is two months ahead of Earth in orbit, they're nearly *at* opposition. Ten hours ago Hive Intelligence agents reported that Princess Shyf of Greenworld, her security chief—that's Kawib Presgano, poor devil, I'm sure you remember him—and fifteen other people from Greenworld's defense and national security establishments had cleared their calendars for the next month. Eight hours ago—there were leave cancellations all through Greenworld's Spatial. And less than two hours ago, Greenworld's only battlesphere, the *Rufus Karrinynya,* departed from the Aerie, destination unspecified. It's a superannuated Hive battlesphere, it was originally the *Bowie,* and it's about four hundred years old, but if they're willing to take the accelerations and the rough ride, at opposition like they are now, they can make it to Mars in just a couple of days.

"Our guess is that because you're our heet on the spot, Shyf sees a chance to try to get Paj Nakasen's lifelog for

Greenworld. All right, that's all for now. Good luck, keep Waynong on a short string, watch out for the bitch, get that thing if you can."

The screen went blank. Jak leaned back and let a map of the situation form in his head.

Imagine the planets as runners on a circular track, with the slower runners in the outer lanes. One group of three runners trots along in the third lane in a perpetual pursuit: the Aerie, an immense space station with more than four hundred nations and two billion people, is the lead runner. One-sixth the length of the track behind the Aerie is the Earth; one-sixth farther behind the Earth is the Hive. (The distances are set by orbital mechanics; Earth and solar gravity stabilize a station in those positions, so that it need expend little or no energy to stay in place.) On the next track outward, Mars trots along slowly. On nearly every lap, the slower Mars runner is passed by first the Aerie, then the Earth, then the Hive, over and over forever. (The moment when they pass closest to each other is called opposition, because, from the standpoint of ancient Earth-based astronomy, it's the moment when the sun and the planet are 180 degrees apart in the sky.)

At the moment the Aerie was just passing Mars; the distance between them was at its minimum and a fast ship, accelerating most of the way, could make the trip in mere days, like a baton passed between two runners. The Hive was 120 degrees back around the bend, and *von Luckner* would have to travel like a ball passed across the track, swinging in very close to the sun, well within Mercury's orbit. So even though *von Luckner* was much faster than *Rufus Karrinynya,* it would be getting here much later.

Jak had barely drawn a breath and started to consider

what he might want to do next when his purse said, "A message from Princess Shyf."

"Stay in eyes-only protocol and screen it." Jak gulped icewater from the glass beside him and considered pouring it onto his crotch.

"Jak, you really are advancing in the world." Shyf was seated in a chair, wearing very brief and tight gozzies and several layers of slashed-and-pulled-through tops. As always her hair and makeup were perfect. "Greenworld Intelligence has learned exactly what you're going down to Mars for, and all I can say is that the job couldn't be in better hands. I'm so proud of you." She tossed her head and her red hair slithered over her shoulders.

"Now, I wouldn't dream of asking you to violate the security of your own nation; that would be wrong, and besides Hive Intel would be very apt to put you through a thorough permanent deconditioning and cut off all our contact, and you know how much I would miss you then, my darling." She pouted; Jak felt his heart form a warm puddle in his chest. "But I would appreciate it if you could keep me posted, perhaps, now and then. And you might receive, at a later date, a contact from Kawib Presgano—oh, you probably don't know. Kawib is all over that nasty depression he was dealing with for so long, and I've promoted him. He heads my personal security nowadays."

Jak felt ill. Kawib was a decent enough young man who had wanted nothing more than an ordinary military career or a quiet bureaucratic sinecure somewhere. But his ancestry made him a potential rallying point for the overthrow of the monarchy. Shyf had arranged to have his fiancée, Seubla, murdered, though she and Seubla had been toves of a sort; she had sent half a dozen good men to their deaths for trivial reasons, to Jak's certain knowledge, including Kawib's most trusted tove Xabo about a year ago; and Kawib had been conditioned far more thoroughly than Jak, and with no countervailing deconditioning.

The Karrinynya Dynasty, which ruled Greenworld, had a tradition of placing their rivals into important positions, where they could be watched closely, sent into danger, forced to betray everyone close to them, and, if they resisted, executed for treason. After ruining his life many times over, Shyf had made Kawib her security chief to ensure that what remained of it would be short and unhappy, with as little compunction as a python swallowing a still-struggling rat.

Yet Jak's heart leapt up at her slightest smile. Yet he flew into ecstacy from her mildest compliment. Yet he could barely perceive her as dangerous.

Cold reason clamped down on his surging feelings. Perhaps Sib and Hel Faczel and the others were right, and maybe it might not be best for Hive Intel to have control of humanity's religious and philosophic development forever. It could be that enabling a young ninny of good family to rise to high office was not good for the Hive. Nonetheless, Jak was not humanity, and he cared very little for religion or philosophy, and he was not the Hive. His own freedom and happiness were at stake. As he thought of what Shyf had already done to him, and had done to Kawib and many others, he resolved to take the deal Caccitepe offered, and take it with all his heart. If Hive Intel would fully decondition him, Jak would happily hand over Nakasen's lifelog.

Hell, he'd have killed Nakasen himself, personally and bare-handed, to get deconditioned.

With a little more iron in his spine, Jak resumed watching the Princess's message.

Shyf said, "Anyway, I wanted to tell you how proud I was of you, and how happy I am that you're getting on in the world . . . to tell you I might have a nice surprise for you in a few days . . . and to remind you who you love . . ." She raised her hair in her hands and let it fall back onto her shoulders in a soft cascade; to Jak it felt as if she were fellating his heart. "And I wanted to remind you who loves you."

The screen clicked off, and Jak said to his purse, "Trace and save. Send Hive Intel a copy." His own voice sounded excruciatingly tight to him, a squeak far back in a long cave.

"Done," the purse said. "Details?"

"Yes please."

"Source: virtual, via fully secured polychannel, not traceable. Copy to Hive Intel. The message attempted to self-destruct but I got there first."

"You're a great purse." Jak touched the reward spot.

"Do you need help from Doctor Mejitarian?" the purse asked. "Your vital signs are varying rapidly, and you often do need his help after a message from Princess Shyf. Shall I put in a call to him?"

"I don't think there will be time before—"

A faint chime. His purse said, "Pikia is at the door."

"Let her in."

She came in with a light step, but one glance at Jak sank her into deep concern. "Are you all right?"

"No, but I will be in a few minutes," Jak said. "Were you briefed about my, um, conditioned problem?"

"Yes, but Great-great-grandpa Reeb said you don't want to talk about it."

"Normally he's right, but you're my assistant and you had better know how these things work. I had a message from Princess Shyf a few minutes ago and I'm upset, is all. I'll be more or less normal in time for the meeting. If you don't mind, talk to me while I wash my face, masen?"

"Sure."

Jak felt slightly strange removing his tunic in front of Pikia—the Hive is the most modest place in the solar system, and wasps are embarrassed by things the rest of humanity barely even perceive—but she looked politely away, and the water, first warm then cold, felt good on his face. He set the dial on the towel for slow absorption and enjoyed scouring his face while leaving it slightly damp. "So this evening we get our act together for the meetings tomorrow, at the royal palace in Magnificiti. Officially I'm in charge and you help me. Unofficially, we both sit back, nod sagely, and take credit, while Dujuv and Teacher Copermisr bargain for the lifelog. I will sit, be polite, and not fall asleep. You will help me do that."

"Five minutes till the others get here. Are you going to be all right for this meeting in five minutes? You still look pretty tired and pale, chief."

"By this point it looks worse than it is."

"Can I ask something that might be really personal and rude?"

Jak considered that on his first missions—when he had been a bit older than Pikia was now—no one had told him anything. He decided that was not an essential part of the experience. "Ask."

"What does the conditioning feel like?"

"Like being really intensely in love," Jak said. "Not like love for your parents or like a long-term couple feel for each other. Like the crazy can't-think-of-anything-else feelings some people get in late puberty, but more intense. Some shrinks say it's like the emotional lives of some badly abused people, the ones they call 'natural slaves.' Right after I get a message from her, the only thing that matters in the universe is Shyf and what she wants, even while I know that she's pulling my strings as if I were a puppet. So it's . . . hmm. Degrading. Dirty. Is that what you wanted to know?"

"Yes, thanks." Her voice was soft; she seemed ashamed.

"All right, now, we want Dujuv and Teacher Copermisr to talk about what we can do to help them—"

"Jak, I didn't ask because I'm some kind of voyeur or something."

"I never thought that was why. I thought you'd tell me sooner or later."

"Well, sooner. Jak, I want to *really* be your assistant on this, so that my help really helps, and I do things you toktru need. I know that's stupid. I'm sure Great-great-grandpa Reeb told you to keep me out of trouble and make sure I was photographed next to anything important, but I want to really be some use. So I need to know what's wrong, and how you have to deal with your, um, problem, so I can help or at least keep things from coming at you until you can cope. Masen?"

"Toktru." It felt right to say "All right, then, I'll rely on you."

" 'Kay."

"Now, if I seem to be really trying to shut my uncle up, jump in and help."

"Right, chief."

"And if you call me chief again, I'm going to declare a special local exception to Hive personnel rules, and spank you."

"Toktru—uh, what should I call you? Mister Jinnaka?"

"Nakasen, no, I'll feel ancient. Stick to Jak. It's my name."

"Dujuv Gonzawara and Shadow on the Frost are arriving," Jak's purse said.

"Well, let 'em in," Jak said. "Got the seating chart?"

"Got it, ch—Jak."

The door dilated. Duj and Shadow came in. Sib and Gweshira arrived immediately after, exactly on time. Pikia seated everyone; Jak studied his notes for the meeting, which read:

1. START WHEN THEY'RE ALL HERE.
2. TURN OVER TO DUJ & XC.
3. ADJOURN.

Xlini Copermisr came five minutes late, apologizing frantically and dropping things in a confused whirl. As soon as Pikia seated her, Jak called them to order and asked Dujuv and Teacher Copermisr to fill them all in.

The two summarized quickly, supplementing, modifying, correcting, and finishing each other's points: Most important event in the Harmless Zone in a very long time. Royal Family of the Splendor exceptionally proud about it. "They're already kings and the Splendor is already a rich nation," Dujuv summarized. "The only meaningful bribe is the bribe to pride. So we will kiss them where it's good, and the way they like it. Then they will pat us on the head and let us have the lifelog."

"Witerio and Cyx are pleasant but sensitive." Teacher Copermisr added, "Let them have the slightest suspicion that you don't regard them as the full equals of the Hive's prime minister or of the Duke of Iron, and it will all turn to shit in a hurry."

They went over court protocol until everyone could recite everything automatically. Pikia asked, quietly, "What about this Clarbo Waynong that's coming in late? The Hive Intel agent? Can someone brief him?"

Jak said, "He's supposed to arrive—um—"

"Tomorrow, right in the middle of the scheduled second meeting of the day," Pikia said, consulting her purse.

"Can anyone catch him and brief him?" Jak asked.

"I can try," Shadow said, "but I've met him, and whether I can brief him or not will depend on whether or not he is willing to listen, and I do not think he will be. He is rather a fool."

"I've dealt with him too," Dujuv said. "Nothing 'rather' about it."

"Fools often get into awkward situations," Shadow said, "which prevent them from fulfilling their duties, leaving their duties to be carried out by more capable people. It could be reasonable to hope for this."

Dujuv nodded vigorously: "It might be better if Shadow got into a fight with him and they both were jailed for a few days."

Teacher Copermisr was nodding too. "I've met him several times, and I'm sure that since he tends to offend nearly everyone, and Shadow is after all a Rubahy warrior and easily offended—"

Jak did not see any way that he could get the credit for the negotiations to go to a man in jail, and anyway, ideally, that lifelog ought to be carried back to the Hive by Waynong. He tried to sound both casual and absolutely commanding. "Just meet him, tell him what's going on, and bring him to the negotiating session, Shadow, that's an order."

The Rubahy's facial expression never changed—it couldn't—but he sighed with his whole body. "You have a vital mission, a known bumbler is going to bumble right into it, and you are worrying about propriety. I have lived among your species for many years now, and I am still forced to say that you make no sense at all."

"I know," Jak said. "And I may be wrong in this. But I want to stay by-the-book, at least officially."

Shadow sat back. Jak, his oath-friend and mission commander, had made a decision, so Shadow on the Frost would not question it further.

"Well," Jak said, "other than a problem I have ordered the most competent person here not to solve"—they all laughed, and Shadow made the sound of big slow bubbles inside a metal bucket, the Rubahy equivalent of laughter—"what else do we have to cover? Shall we adjourn?"

There was nothing more. Xlini Copermisr, Gweshira, and Sib departed at once. Jak was trying to think of a delicate way to—

Pikia said, "Let's see, three old toves, one over-eager subordinate. Let me guess who ought to take a walk."

Jak said, "If there's any actual business or anything—"

"Close toktru toves who haven't talked face-to-face in a year? You won't talk business." She smiled and left.

"Jak, you have a better assistant than you deserve," Dujuv observed.

"I was just noticing that. So, now that we're in a bugswept room, what do you two think and how's it all look to you?"

Dujuv held his hand out and wobbled it from thumb to

little finger, vigorously, several times. "Might go perfectly, still," he said. "But you know, old tove, here on Mars, the Great God Murphy is still alive as a belief, and there are Murphyites everywhere, even among those who claim to follow the Wager. And there is that old proverb, 'Murphy rules the universe and he is a malign thug.'

"After a year here, pizo, I believe in Murphy. We have one of the most valuable objects of all time, protected by nearly senile ceremonial guards. We have a king who is a nice old gwont but also deeply in love with himself. We have the prince . . . this place was bugswept?"

"Bugsweep this entire suite again, give it all you got," Jak said to his purse.

Another wave of crashing thunder rumbled through the room, dotted with little squeals and screams as the purse hunted for anything that might be listening. Then, speaking in Jak's voice, the purse loudly said, "Stolen plutonium fifty tons of *xleeth* coming in tomorrow tunnel under the palace kidnap the prime minister's daughter concealed Casimir bombs Rubahy mercenaries." About ten seconds of silence followed, and the purse said, "All clear. Everything that was found is confirmed destroyed, no evidence that anything wasn't. The trigger phrases produced no response at Red Amber Magenta Green's central intelligence systems."

"Now, Dujuv, what's your candid assessment of Prince Cyx?"

"Well, either putty in our hands, or a thorn in our side," Dujuv said. "Or any other cliché you like, depending on the day."

"You've pinned it down in pure clear quartz," the Rubahy warrior said. "I have seen Prince Cyx three times, and I have seen this Clarbo Waynong too many times, and if it were the

religious heritage of *my* species hanging on the slim possibility that the eager, hasty fool will not offend the proud, su-
percilious fool, I would tremble for us. One less fool in the
picture would brighten everything considerably."

Jak pretended to think about it; but still he needed to
make it appear that Waynong had succeeded. And Mejitarian had already told him it wouldn't be easy. "I don't like the
situation much," Jak admitted. "Maybe if I were older and
colder-blooded I'd merely mutter something about how in-
convenient Clarbo Waynong is, and 'let things happen' and
thereby be able, if they found out who did it, to claim there
was all a cultural misunderstanding. But . . . I can't take that
step."

Dujuv sighed. "Old tove, I'm glad to see you have scru-
ples, but what a time to develop them!"

"I know. I don't believe it either." Jak leaned back. "How
about telling your toktru tove everything about your life?
Your messages are great, but people always leave a lot out
of messages."

With a billion people, the Hive had more than enough to
provide an ambassador to everywhere, and a staff for the
embassy, but that did not mean the diplomatic work got
done. Harmless Zone diplomatic posts were magnets for patricians who liked all the recreational opportunities but ob-
jected to doing anything other than attending the more
entertaining receptions and playing outdoor sports with the
better class of Chryseans.

Since all embassy slots were allocated to political ap-
pointees and their friends and relatives, the Roving Consuls
were created to do the actual work. Theoretically a Roving
Consul was not much more than a traveling clerk who
arranged everything a Hive citizen might need: legal repre-

sentation, medical care, extradition, corpse-transportation, out-of-polity marriage licenses, intellectual property liens. Roving Consuls also negotiated "boilerplate" treaties as they were expired or canceled or suspended, and did the endless face-to-face talking for, to, and about the Republic of the Hive to 1200 puny principalities and powers. Dujuv's description of the job was "half file clerk, half kindergarten teacher."

"I can see you've got parts of that diplomat job down cold," Jak said.

"They tell me I'm good at this," Dujuv said. "Who'd've thought I'd turn out to have either the brains or the talent?"

"Uh, me. Your oldest tove. Myxenna wasn't surprised either, you know."

"How is she?" Dujuv smiled at the mention of her name, which relieved Jak no end. Panths bonded strongly in midadolescence, and Dujuv had bonded to Myxenna, who had been his demmy all through gen school; it had taken him years to be able to see her as just a friend.

"She's on her way here. Supposed to take over from Clarbo Waynong. I got a short note from her earlier. Same old Myx." He was afraid that his toves might ask him for details (strange, now, that with so much at stake, lying and covering up was bothering him more than it ever had before) so he hurried to change the subject. "I'm afraid I don't have anything like your stories to tell, Dujuv. I've been keeping track of Forces dependents arrested for shoplifting, and permits for roast hamster stands, and so on."

"They seem to think you've done a good job of it," Dujuv pointed out. "You're the one that they put in command of this mission."

"Does that bother you?" Jak asked. "Because it does me."

"Yeah, it bothers me." Dujuv's expression was utterly flat. "Like the thing on Mercury, three years ago. You have a gift for being noticed . . . and I have a gift for being your sidekick. The heet who was there with Jak Jinnaka."

Jak nodded, and said, "I speck you might feel that way. You deserved to have this as a solo mission without all the rest of us horning in. It was not my choice, Duj."

"Yeah, I know, old tove, but who else am I going to complain to? And honestly, it's not just your getting the credit; it's the fact that I spend all my time doing the actual work for all these people who just picked their families carefully. And creating credit for my superiors to claim. I feel like a chump and a stooge." He leaned back and stared into space. "I haven't really known what to do with myself since Mercury, Jak."

Three years before, in a complicated many-sided web of betrayals and exploitations, Jak, Dujuv, and Shadow had been sent to Mercury to look into the supposed mystery of emerging labor trouble in the vast mines on which the whole solar system's industry depended. In fact, they had found Jak's mortal enemy, Bex Riveroma, the man who most wanted Jak dead. They had also found a system of brutal oppression, known to everyone in the solar system, discussed by no one.

The three toves had been lucky to escape with their lives. Jak had wronged toves and done things that had shamed him in ways that he could not have imagined, before, that he was capable of; he had faced Riveroma, who had beaten him once before, and this time had gotten away with his life and pride, but without his once-secure and once-automatic sense of having his honor; he might die for some things, but not that. If there was any Principle of the Wager that Jak believed in, it was 116: "The dead can have honor, but *they* can't eat it, either."

But as much as Mercury had changed Jak, it had changed Dujuv more. The happy-go-lucky athlete-adventurer had been shocked and horrified by what he had seen, and had come back as a painfully serious young man.

Jak himself had been shaken by the conditions on Mercury. Even with longevity treatments, most people there lived only a bit past age one hundred, as opposed to the common 350 on the Hive, the Aerie, or in the clean parts of Earth and Mars. Mercurials had a word for it—*razdund-slag*—the mix of high radiation and background toxicity that aged them prematurely. Mercury had the nearest thing to real poverty to be found anywhere in the eighth century AW, hereditary peonage, uncontrolled corporations, and the last actual banks in the solar system. After having been there and lived among Mercurial miners, Jak knew that they had nearly every other ancient evil, no matter how long it had been eradicated in the rest of human space. He had heard tales of torture and meat-puppetry, and would not have been shocked to hear of cannibalism. The Mercurials' worn and stressed faces, unmodified by even the simplest cosmetic work, looked like bags of old leather hanging clumsily on the front of a skull, broken by rows of crooked teeth and surrounding eyes blank except for mistrustful sadness. This on people not much past fifty. It still haunted Jak's dreams at times.

Jak had come back to the Hive angry and half-willing to join the Reform Party, but Sib, and Gweshira, and Dean Caccitepe had straightened him out with a few short lectures. The free, peaceful societies of the Hive, the Aerie, Earth, Mars, and all the upper-planet satellites depended on cheap raw materials to keep people quiet, contented, and un-rebellious. One substantial revolution would cost genera-tions to pay for, even if it was defeated, and would unleash violence and terrorism throughout the solar system, as other malcontents tried to imitate it. The peace and safety of every free, affluent citizen, of all the people Jak had grown up among, depended on Mercurial metal staying cheap.

Resources from Mercury were cheap because it had no government to impose taxes or regulate production; every mine and quacco on Mercury bid against every other, with the banks against all. Four thousand years of well-recorded history showed that people didn't rise up until conditions improved; misery meant no revolution on Mercury, no rev-olution meant no government, no government meant that the solar system would continue to be the pleasant place it was for most of its eleven billion citizens.

Compared to that, the unhappiness of a mere seventy mil-lion Mercurials was nothing. Besides, Mercury was where the human race dumped its chronic criminals, debtors, wastrels, and all the other sludge off the bottom of the ge-netic pool. Mercurials were a small minority of worthless people who suffered, so that the great majority of the solar system could live in a garden. No doubt it was bad for the few, but who could demand that the great majority sacrifice the best standard of living ever achieved?

It had taken Jak only a few days to dak that.

Dujuv, however, was incapable of realism. He had bonded to the Mercurials as only a panth could bond, and stayed on for two more oppositions—230 days—after Jak and Shadow had left, helping the Mercurials to deal with all sorts of legal repercussions from Bex Riveroma's brief coup and to collect what the insurance companies owed to them.

He had lived and worked among them for a long time, coached their children in slamball, attended group sings in dozens of kriljs, visited mines and processing plants everywhere, and he identified utterly with that impoverished mob of irradiated and poisoned convict-spawn.

Tonight, when they were visiting for the first time, face-to-face, in more than a year, Jak didn't want to hear about kids with dental caries or young women sterile before they were thirty or any of Dujuv's favorite horror stories. "Are you still getting calls from slamball recruiters?" Jak asked, in a complete non sequitur.

"Yeah. On days when being a Roving Consul really, really stinks, I think about taking them up on it. I was a higher draft pick for slamball than I was for the bureaucracy, after all, and I know, deep down, I could be one of the great goalies of all time. Call me crazy but sometimes I would rather get rich playing a kid's game that I love than listen to a petty king explain that five generations ago the king over the next hill stole the sacred water buffalo statue and that that's why they have to go to war and kill fifty young men."

The evening went late, with much to remember, much to laugh at, many absent friends to salute, many gossipy stories to share. As Jak finally said good-bye to Dujuv and Shadow at the door, he knew he would be a bit short on sleep tomorrow, but at least the first day of the negotiations would be mostly ceremonies.

"Get me Mejitarian," he told his purse as soon as the door contracted after his toves.

Hive Intel's doctor actually looked as if he might really be sympathetic this time. "Well, that was quite a message she aimed at you. Your purse tells me you functioned through the whole meeting afterward just fine, though."

"I think so, sir," Jak said, facing the camera and talking to his superior's projected image on the wall.

"Well, you've got some resources and strength that you probably don't know you have."

"Sir, just to make sure—if I succeed at all my assignments—"

"The deal remains in place, Jak. Get the Nakasen lifelog for Hive Intel, make sure that Clarbo Waynong gets the credit, and we will have you deconditioned from Princess Shyf and give you a full, regular appointment with Hive Intel. It's a tough job, but if you can pull it off, you're in out of the cold. Good luck."

CHAPTER 6

Don't Expect My Call
Anytime Soon

The next morning was taken up with the ceremonial preliminaries. King Witerio was a pleasant-enough-looking man, built like a weight lifter, with a waist-length thick iron-gray beard that was combed, clean, and smooth, deep warm brown eyes, and surprisingly delicate brows and nose. He performed his parts in the ceremonies like a meditative exercise.

Prince Cyx's skin was smooth, soft dark mocha, and his short curly hair and wide-set eyes were jet-black. His forehead was high rather than broad, and his clean-shaven jaw formed a strong, hard, angular line. Witerio's court robes reminded Jak of old theater curtains; Cyx wore a conservative version of the clash-splash-and-smash style of a few years ago, what a well-groomed but not fashionable student might have worn to a school dance on the Hive. He looked eager, bright, focused, and excited, but during breaks he talked only about clothing, viv, and sports.

Jak was glad to have his purse supplying him with continual coaching via earpiece; the ceremonies were complicated. They took tea in four different pourings (the first and fourth with food, the second and third refusing food; the second and fourth from tall narrow porcelain cups, the first and third from wide shallow glass cups). They gave the King a Hive-certified copy of the Principles, and received in exchange his scholars' annotations on the Suggestions. They presented him with a palladium tiara (he surely must have had a hundred of those already) and he offered them a crown, which as citizens of the Republic of the Hive they were required to refuse, accepting instead the King's embrace and handshake. They inspected each other's weapons.

They broke from all that intense work for a midmorning meal: yogurt, figs, and pomegranate with lemon. They were required to eat three small portions, refusing twice before each acceptance. Then the King and Prince went off to change into their military uniforms.

The costume change was followed by frank but entirely ceremonial statements of the strength of each nation. The very disparity of power made the ceremonial gestures of respect all the more important, Jak reminded himself. He declared, seriously and forthrightly, that his nation, the largest in the solar system and the greatest military power in human history, with fourteen battlespheres and five million troops in active service, felt fear and dread at Red Amber Magenta Green's nine hundred light infantry and single museum-piece warshuttle.

For lunch break, the Hive negotiation team went back to the pavilion, bugswept a conference room, and ordered sandwiches in. Everyone agreed that it was going well and no one had perceived anything unusual. Jak called Shadow, who said he had not yet seen any sign of Clarbo Waynong.

When they reconvened, they at last began the process of talking about how the Hive would get Nakasen's lifelog. Over the course of about an hour and a half, the Hive delegation—mostly Dujuv and Xlini Copermisr, with Jak occasionally agreeing that yes, that was right, and yes, that was important—managed to communicate many things that both sides already knew: That the Hive wanted that lifelog. That the Hive wanted the Splendor to be happy with the deal. That title to the lifelog and official credit for its discovery were fully negotiable (Teacher Copermisr had explained to Jak, at lunch, that every archaeologist who mattered would know that the find had been her work; therefore the official credit could go to Prince Cyx, or to whomever it did the most good).

Then it was the turn of the royalty of the Splendor to communicate: That the spot on which Nakasen's lifelog had been found was unquestionably within the rightful territory of the Splendor. That ancient artifacts belonged to the state in whose territory they fell. That this rule was important. That Witerio and Cyx knew that they did not have, and could not afford to hire, adequate facilities to care for such a find.

Both sides agreed that the lifelog, being as yet unread, might include material that might be seized upon for misinterpretation, and therefore any scientific, philosophic, or philological project—really, any analytic project of any kind including methods of analysis not yet devised—must be subject to a thorough scrutiny of its results, by responsible and competent political authorities of both governments, prior to any sort of publication.

Half an hour after the meetings resumed, the moment came when all ceremonies were exhausted, and it was not yet time for a break: the moment for actual negotiation. "Well," King Witerio said, "let's begin by stating the obvious. I have in my possession an extraordinarily valuable artifact, but the lifelog of Paj Nakasen does not add to the glory of the Splendor, sitting under guard in my palace."

Jak nodded. "We need to find a way for the Hive to properly show the deep respect and gratitude we feel toward the Splendor, and to bring the lifelog into its full and proper place in the history of human beings in the solar system."

Witerio inclined his head in agreement. "The difficulty is that because the Hive's generosity is so well known, my political enemies will say that I *sold* the lifelog. So it must be clear that we do not give up the lifelog permanently."

"Exactly," Jak said. "And let me express here and now, for the record, that the confidence of the Hive in your ability to care for the lifelog is total. Our regard for the honor of a friendly power is such that we would in no circumstances ask you to transfer title to the lifelog in any permanent way. We do have the finest laboratories and facilities in the solar system, on the Hive itself, and therefore we think the Hive is a suitable location for analysis and copying of the lifelog. We should therefore very much like to arrange access to the lifelog so that it may be open-ended with regard to time because we cannot possibly know how long it will take the large group of scholars, sure to be involved, to fully analyze and understand anything of this consequence—let alone the fact that eighty-nine years of diary entries, together with multiple drafts of several important works, all in Early Postwar Standard, will take considerable time to be fully understood and appreciated."

Witerio smiled slightly. "That consideration is well thought of. Though should it prove politically desirable to set a fixed term for the period in which the lifelog will be on loan to the Hive, there should be no problem so long as the fixed term is indefinitely renewable. I do not see that this is a matter which we must dispute."

Jak held up his hands in the ancient gesture of concession. "An indefinitely renewable fixed term would be acceptable to the Hive, of course, as would any other term you choose to set. But of course we will seek an open-ended loan because we know that politics and government are an uncertain business; our thoughts are that while we can rely upon King Witerio, and upon King Cyx after him, the fortunes of war or treachery might someday cause a nonrenewal. But let us not speak of such unhappy things. If the renewable term is necessary, we shall feel perfect confidence all the same."

"Well, then," the King said, "I think that the compromise is that renewals be automatic, and the term be as long as honor will comfortably bear. That can be worked out by our people meeting together to draft details. Shall we move on to the next point?"

"Let us do so, Your Splendor."

"Well, then," the King said, "we should discuss whether any part of the lifelog actually is intellectual property—"

The door swooshed open. A court guard leapt through, came to attention, and shouted, "Mister Clarbo Way—"

But by that point Clarbo Waynong was already advancing on the negotiation table, having paid no attention. Jak heard a soft ululating hoot, like a dying bassoon audiomixed with the bibby-bibby finger to the lips sound—a frustrated-to-the-point-of-exasperation Rubahy. Shadow came through the door and came to attention.

"Hi, I'm Clarbo Waynong, Hive Intelligence. Which one of you is the King?"

Only Witerio was wearing a crown.

"Well, which one's the King?" Waynong came to a halt at the edge of the table. He was a breathtakingly handsome young man. If you had been looking for a model for the cover of an intrigue-and-adventure viv, clutching his best girl with one hand and his weapon with the other, this was the heet you would have photographed. He had café-au-lait skin tanpatterned in this year's heliopause of clash-splash-and-smash, Fractal Leopard Remix. His hair was a rich yellowish blond, his eyes deep ocean blue, and one sight of the jaw told Jak that this was a true patrician. Centuries of genetic sculpting, crossbreeding, and trying again had created the chin that anyone from the Hive could recognize—the chin that was on every poster at every election, the sort of chin you would trust to tell you that war had broken out or that economic productivity was falling off.

Jak drew a slow breath through his teeth, glared, and said, "Yes, you are Clarbo Waynong. And your ill manners and aggressive rudeness clearly indicate that you are a member of Hive Intelligence. I am Jak Jinnaka. Your orders are that I am the commander of this mission. Therefore—this is a direct order, Clarbo Waynong—sit down at this table immediately and remain quiet."

Waynong remained standing and said, "Oh, yeah, weehu, I know, I know, they told me that you were supposed to be the person in charge and all that, but you know and I know that as soon as they can Hive Intel is going to take this away from you, and they've got some big-deal agent coming out to take care of that, and if I'm going to get anything good on my record then we need to get this deal wrapped up. We can do all that respecting and bureaucratic stuff later, after we get that Nakasen thing bought and paid for, Mister-Bureaucrat-Sir. Now, which one of these heets is the King?"

There was the sort of silence that occurs when a four-year-old describes his latest bowel movement, loudly, in public.

"Shadow," Jak said firmly, "thank you for bringing Mister Waynong here, per your instructions, and please stand by in case I need him removed. Article Eighty-eight, conduct in diplomatic settings. Section Ten, overt misbehavior, and Section Seventeen, open defiance of a superior, are relevant here." Still ignoring Waynong, Jak turned to address the rest of his delegation. "I'm sorry to cut into your time off this evening, but it may be necessary for us to hold a formal conference about Mister Waynong's behavior—"

"Cyxy! Weehu, hey, Cyxy!" Waynong whooped.

Prince Cyx had bound out of his chair—about head high, in the Martian gravity—and leapt across the table to embrace the Hive Intel agent. The two of them pounded each other's backs, then stepped back and formally grasped each other's forearms.

"You know this . . . man?" King Witerio asked.

"Know him? We were roommates and toktru toves, Dad! Clarbo was the lightest of the light! He taught me everything I needed to know to come back here and get fashion turned around. (Not that some people get it—look at these robes! But we've argued about that before.)"

Witerio glanced sideways at Jak; Jak raised an eyebrow, not sure how to express the sympathy he felt.

Xlini Copermisr's hand was plastered across her face as if it were an octopus trying to eat her nose. Pikia appeared to have only just discovered that the wall was vertical, and was rapt in the implications.

Prince Cyx burbled on. "You remember that wonderful, incredible vacation on the moon, during Long Break of ju-

nior year, when I got to try big-slow-wave surfing in the
aquadomes? Remember how excited I was about it and what
a long message I sent you about it? Well, I went on that trip
with Clarbo's family. This is the Clarbo that I'm always
mentioning for maybe someone to marry Kayadi, if you ever
decide you do want to mix some commoner blood into the
line, because even though his pedigree is commoner, he's
just—well, look at him, Dad, a natural aristocrat."

He does have a light smile, Jak thought. *What was the
name of that ancient heet, one of the Al-fredis? Al-fredi-
Packer? Al-fredi-Boom-Boom-Cannon? Al-fredi-Nomen,
that was it. Anyway, it's the same smile. No wonder people
will vote for anything named Waynong.*

Cyx turned back to Clarbo and said, "So how have you
been?"

"Oh, you know, you know. Have to work a job, get some
of that experience and those credentials before they pick out
a seat for me in the Hive Assembly or appoint me to a cabinet post. That earning your privileges thing, Principle 133,
you know. Doing things for Hive Intel since graduation. A
little work here, a little work there, just haven't quite found
a place where I fit in yet, you know. Lots of misunderstand-
ings. Need to find some toktru sympatico toves in the leadership, haven't quite done that. Always having to deal with
these petty bureaucrats and all these officious formalities."
He nodded in a way that he doubtless thought was subtle, directly at Jak. "So here's my big chance, you know, to get
something worthwhile done for Hive Intel. We know you
have that wonderful book or tape or whatever it is, and here
we are with a lot of money, and here you are, a little tiny nation on a dumpy old poor planet, and it isn't the kind of thing
that you folks ought to have—it could fall into the wrong

hands, masen? The wrong sort of people could read it and get ideas. And with your feeble little army, who's going to guard it? So it's time for me to make you the offer and for you to accept and then we'll be leaving with this Nakasen thing. Now how much do you want for it, old tove? The treasury's loaded; don't be shy about naming a big number."

He was still grinning, holding Cyx's forearms with his; Cyx withdrew his right hand and turned his left over gently, then yanked hard on Waynong's forearm and jabbed hard with his right fist. The sucker shot flew directly into the young patrician's nose, sending him reeling backward, trailing blood from his nostrils, to lie supine on the floor of the conference room.

"Your Splendor is too kind," Jak muttered, then added aloud, "I believe both delegations will want to regroup."

"Agreed," Witerio said. "Let us adjourn sine die. I'll communicate with you privately about when we'll resume talks." As the two of them shook hands for the camera, the King murmured, through clenched teeth, "Don't expect my call anytime soon."

Clarbo and Cyx had been toktru toves, and neither of them was the sort to hold a grudge (or any other idea) for very long. Gradually they were making it up; Xlini dedicated herself to the task of getting the problem explained to Cyx, trying to help him see that Clarbo had not intended any of the grave insults he had spouted, and that the two of them could settle the whole matter in no time, stressing how much it would impress the King. "Cyx is perfectly representative of his class," she said at lunch with Dujuv and Jak. "A big kid with a small army. We'll get him around. How's it coming with Clarbo?"

Jak shrugged. "The person who's really having an effect is Pikia. I have to say that for someone I was ordered to bring along and keep out of trouble, she's been worth her mass in plutonium. And about as dangerous if she got mad, I think."

"My boss always gives me the loveliest compliments," Pikia said, coming up behind them. "May I join you in this dining room? My eyes are getting tired from all the batting and I need people who will give me sympathy if I decide to scream."

Dujuv reached for the button; a chair rose out of the floor. "Of course you're welcome, Pikia, join us and tell us all about it, and don't leave out a single ghastly detail."

"I ought to take you up on that and repeat everything that man has said to me while I sat and looked adoring," Pikia said. She plopped down, grabbed a burrito from the platter, and tore into it. "Armph murph."

"'Armph murph' indeed," Xlini said. "Eat, then talk. We'll hang around. None of us has anything urgent to do."

While Pikia wolfed the sandwich, two bowls of noodles with scallops, a large orange-and-spinach salad, and half a pot of tea, Dujuv had three desserts to keep her company. Jak and Xlini watched the race between the panth and the unmodified teenage appetite with awe.

"What's silly about Cyx and Clarbo," Xlini said, "is that they're toves. They like each other. The deal would already be done if they didn't fuss so about honor. If Clarbo would just act impressed about Cyx being a prince, or if Cyx would just act impressed with Clarbo's brilliance . . . how's the King taking it all?"

"The King and I see a lot of each other, but we don't talk much. Mostly we play Maniples," Jak said. "At least he's really good and it's not difficult for me to lose." Jak had been the PSA's school champion, setting several records, and in his senior year he had attained the rank of Master. "The King doesn't have the time to practice as much as he would need to, but he could easily be a Master."

"About the same way that you could be a Great Master if you did nothing but play Maniples?" Dujuv asked, between bites of papaya puff pastry. He seemed to be winding down, while Pikia was still going, but then he'd had a head start.

"About like that," Jak said. "Not like you and slamball."

"Ubrade slabble?" That was all that escaped of "You played slamball?" through Pikia's salad.

"When you get to the PSA (and I think you will, Pikia, you belong there, and if the Admissions Committee has two brain cells to rub together they'll find a way to get you in)," Jak said, "anyway, when you get to the PSA, check out the athletic trophy case in the Hall of Honors and count off how many times you see Dujuv's name next to a record or an award. He could've turned pro."

Dujuv shrugged. "Still could. And if I were a second-stringer on a minor league team, I'd be making twice what I make as a Roving Consul. Then I consider the pleasures of spending a lot of time in the little capital towns of all these little nations, trying to keep petty kings and minor republics from doing stupid things that get people killed, and I ask myself, 'Is there anything to that stereotype about panths being stupid?' "

Pikia swallowed the last of her salad and belched. "Excuse me. 'Such a lady,' as Great-great-grandpa Reeb would say. Weehu, it's a relief to eat without being constantly corrected."

"Your great-great-grandfather does that?" Jak asked.

"Clarbo Waynong does. He tries to fix everything in the universe around him." She belched again. "Oh, that's better. Not the belch, being able to do it."

"Good, because the entertainment value is wearing thin," Xlini said. "So how is the attempt to culturally sensitize him going?"

"Well, I listen. He tells me about what fine people his family are and how he's expected to be promoted quickly to senior agent and then be in the Assembly and in the Cabinet and be prime minister someday. I don't think he realizes that any of those jobs involve doing anything; he's supposed to collect jobs the way scouts collect badges. And then everyone will love him and think he's a good boy. Because that's what the universe is here for.

"As far as he understands things, he's supposed to bring back Nakasen's lifelog and be a hero for it and then everyone will love him and his career will be back on track. And he doesn't dak why people don't understand their place in the script.

"He does grasp that Prince Cyx's feelings are hurt, but I think he thinks that if they play golf together, or perhaps go out and shoot a couple of animals, everything will be fine.

"I listen and smile and bat my eyes.

"As far as he grasps the world, you ask for what you want, and the world gives it to you, and that makes you a hero."

"So," Dujuv said, leaning back and gazing up at the ceiling, "at least the food's good here, masen?"

Dujuv said, "Let me just point out that your old demmy has a gift for being a pain in the ass."

Jak managed a sad chuckle. "When have we ever known her to be convenient about anything, masen?"

"There's the Princess's yacht," Pikia said, pointing. The winged dot, like a distant hawk, cut a great swipe across the vibrant blue sky.

"Hard to imagine that sky was ever red," Jak said.

"If it still were," Dujuv pointed out, "that yacht would drop like a rock. Pity it's not."

They were standing on the quai. Red Amber Magenta Green's landing field chief had been ecstatic to have a visit from a Hive warship followed by a royal party, within a week. The chief, and Clarbo Waynong, were probably the only people happy about this, and Clarbo tended to be happy about everything.

The just-rising sun was dimmer and smaller than it was from the Hive and less sharp-edged than it was from Deimos. The huge-winged launch finished its last circuit and started its descent to the landing field.

On the platform, the arrangement of people had been carefully worked out by protocol officers. Jak had to be there, as the Hive's ranking officer in the Splendor. Jak had insisted on having Dujuv, Shadow, and Pikia with him. Clarbo had insisted on being as important as Pikia with a clear implication that he should have been as important as Dujuv.

Since it was a visit from the Crown Princess of a major nation, the King and the Prince both were there. Witerio was in full outdoor regalia and looked as if he were going to a costume party as Barbarossa. Prince Cyx was as close to fashionable as he dared. Jak specked this had to do with the many stillpix of Princess Shyf. He could have told Cyx that if Shyf was interested in anyone besides Shyf, it was in Psim

Cofinalez, the Duke of Uranium, not so much for the Duke himself as for the chance to tip half the lower solar system into war.

"Stand here," Jak said, not turning his head, but sensing that Clarbo Waynong had once again bounced out of the position dictated by protocol and was on the brink of being somewhere offensive. Pikia towed the temporarily obedient Hive Intel agent back into position. Jak reminded himself that when she finished gen school, he owed her a hell of a graduation present.

The Princess's yacht, a large modern launch, came in straight and level, its vast wings flexing in the sticky thin air. They curled under at the trailing edge, and the ship glided onto the linducer track. The wings scooped forward to lose speed, then rolled in from the tips and slipped into the fuselage. The Princess's yacht stopped before them like a dancer finishing a difficult piece by simply dropping her arms.

The boarding ramp dropped from its side onto the quai. At Witerio's nod, the band struck up a march.

The band had played through the march three times, Pikia had discreetly sheep-dogged Clarbo Waynong back into position two times, and Witerio was beginning to tap his foot—not in time—when the Princess and her party emerged from the launch.

Pikia murmured, "Oh, weehu, Surrealist Safari." Dujuv strangled a barely audible laugh.

Clearly Shyf thought of the Harmless Zone the way many people did, as a playground for the weird and a land of indulged fantasies, inhabited by bizarre savages. Doubtless hoping to make an impression, she had arrived in something that looked very much like a costume for "Memsahib at Amateur Strip Night." Where there was fabric, the fabric was crisp, pressed, blindingly pure white, and very starchy. Where there wasn't fabric, which was often, black lace and bits of Shyf peeped out.

The costumes she had chosen for the Royal Palace Guardsmen around her were similar, though they covered more in most places, and there didn't seem to be any black lace under them. Jak and Dujuv had briefly served in the RPG, sometimes all too accurately known as the Rutty Princess's Gigolos. Ever-changing degrading uniforms had been part of the whole degrading experience, but *these* uniforms were truly something special, even for Shyf.

The Princess strode forward to bow to King Witerio, and delivered a prettily worded compliment about the five times that members of their royal houses had officially met before. By carefully concentrating on the exact words, Jak figured out that this had actually been three shopping trips to Greenworld and two overland walking tours of the Harmless Zone that had happened to pass through Red Amber Magenta Green, and that all five visits had been honeymoons, going back about three hundred years. In Shyf's phrasing, they sufficed to establish that the monarchs of Greenworld and of the Splendor were the most toktru of toves and closest of cousins.

Jak's heart hammered; perhaps her scent drifting this way, perhaps the mere sight of her.

After she finished flattering Witerio, and the band played a short march in honor of that, she had to spend nearly as long greeting Prince Cyx. Witerio had been polite and correct; his son was just as correct but appeared to be thunderstruck.

When she had finished with the Splendor's delegation, she squealed and threw herself into Jak's arms. "Jak, so good to see you again, Jak!" A good performance, even if Jak had seen many like it. His conditioning responded.

Over her shoulder, Jak could see his old tove Kawib Presgano, decked out in the full Royal Palace Guard Surrealist Safari rig, barely controlling his rage. Kawib was much more thoroughly conditioned than Jak; his whole adult life had passed as the Princess's sex toy and object of torment.

Shyf's hands trailed down the outside of Jak's arms from shoulders to wrists, the backs of her nails brushing him through his sleeves, to keep him painfully aware of the contact.

He wanted to kneel at her feet and pledge eternal obedience. He wanted to hit her in the face, straight from his shoulder with everything he had. He wanted to shit his pants. He did none of these things.

She turned from him to Dujuv. "You handsome man, you haven't changed at all."

The panth, who she had more than once referred to as a "half-animal" and worse, smiled as if he liked her. "I can see you haven't changed."

"And Shadow on the Frost."

"Princess Shyf, you have long been the tove of my tove." He bowed deeply and correctly. Jak envied the Rubahy his lack of facial expression at that moment.

When she focused on Clarbo Waynong, Shyf's eyes glinted and her delighted smile was so deep and real that Jak automatically wondered how much she had rehearsed. "And *this* has to be a Waynong. Look at that chin and eyes."

For the first time, Jak Jinnaka saw Clarbo Waynong impressed with something that was not Clarbo Waynong. He looked so bewildered that perhaps this had never happened before. "Um, arr, yes. Waynong. Clarbo Waynong. Um yes,

Clarbo Waynong, Your Princessness." Waynong stared at her in a way Jak Jinnaka might have found funny if he didn't have all too clear an idea of what Waynong was feeling.

That afternoon, King Witerio held a reception for his visiting royal cousin. It was even worse than Jak had anticipated. The lively torment of Princess Shyf's inaccessible presence, a scant two meters away, was exquisitely balanced by the dull torment of going through the same ceremonies that had so bored him before, this time not as a participant but as an observer. While ceremonial utterances were uttered, gestures gestured, and drinks drunk, Jak had to watch attentively, his face a mask of rapt fascination. He had plenty of time to watch Shyf obsessively, an experience a bit like eating when you are already full and a bit like picking a scab.

When the door finally constricted behind Jak and he was at last alone in his quarters, he needed deconditioning, and he ached and longed to sit dejectedly on the edge of his bed until Princess Shyf came to declare her eternal and exclusive love for him. With a groan, he made himself raise his left palm to his face, and say to his purse, "We're going to run through the deconditioning exercises. When that's done I want a hot bath (muscle relaxation temperature) strongly scented (my regular mix). We're in for a rough one."

"Ready for pills?"

"Yes please." Freshly formed pills dropped out of the bedside dispenser. Jak slapped them into his open mouth, clamped his jaw, and fought down the urge to spit them out. He undressed, pulled on his skullcap, and stretched out on the bed. His purse opaqued all the windows and turned off all the lights, leaving the room perfectly dark, and then projected a single, dim, blue, slowly blinking light on the ceiling.

The little whirs and thump-thumps of countless machines nearby faded into a soft blur of white noise. A deep throb came in under the white noise, in time with the light, synchronizing to a multiple of Jak's pulse. The purse gradually, gently slowed the blink-and-throb. Jak matched his breathing to it, four beats to inhale, four to exhale, filling and emptying his lungs completely. The beat slowed. The blinking light dimmed. The throb faded.

He was alone.

In darkness.

At peace.

For some time he slept until his purse judged that his brainwave activities showed him to have healed enough and NMR of the blood passing through his hand showed the drugs were present and active in adequate quantity. Then his purse started the stimuli:

And he was frozen and paralyzed on a table. Uncle Sib was beating him, slamming him harder and harder with the fists and feet of a trained athlete, screaming all the time for him to defend himself, that he was unworthy of his training . . .

And he was at the club, dancing slec with Dujuv and Myx and Sesh, the very moment all the adventures of his life began, and then Sesh looked at him with Princess Shyf's eyes and said, "She's gone and you're a fool . . ."

And he was screaming, inside a dark bag, and no one could hear him and they were about to jettison it from a sunclipper, and he knew they would throw it through the cables so that he would be sliced open just at the instant he saw the stars, nothing to breathe but vacuum, his face a screaming freeze-dried mask of horror for many centuries as he orbited past Pluto, out where the sun is a bright star . . .

And he was in the Rubahy nightmares of his childhood, when he had hated and feared them in his ignorance. Madly cruel feathered monsters who lived only to eat human flesh, and their teeth were closing around him, and he turned to his left and they were eating Shyf alive, and to his right and they were eating Dujuv, and a calm voice said, "You know better."

Jak looked up to see Uncle Sib walking among the fearsome monsters, just before they turned and began to eat him, but Sib seemed very calm about it all.

Jak awoke, his skin as clammy with sweat as if from many hours of fever dreams, his guts clenching and squirming, his face a sticky mess, his muscles sore from the savage contractions. The lights were coming up and the purse had selected soothing music. Jak drew a deep breath, and recited the Short Litany of Terror, as he made himself settle into the neutral posture that begins the Disciplines. "'144: Death happens, anyway.' Therefore '62: Since it doesn't change anything, go ahead and fear death if it makes you feel better,' because '9: Fear is an excellent way to pass the time when there's nothing else you can do,' but remember that '171: Courage is fear without consequences.'"

The comfort and courage began to flow down his spine from his skull, and Jak, far from the first time in his life, thanked Uncle Sib silently for having taught him the Disciplines when he was so young that they had become automatic and so much a part of him that he could not imagine not having them. Strange to think that Sib was probably only a kilometer away at the very most, and that Jak could shake his hand at dinner and tell him directly. He made a mental note to himself to do that; Sib was proud, even arrogant, about the way Jak had turned out (sometimes enough to be irritating—to hear the old gwont natter on, you'd think that Jak hadn't done any of the work!), and he'd get so much pleasure out of being thanked. (Enough to compensate Jak for the annoyance of Sib's preening.) Besides, if the horrible old gwont started puffing up with too much pride, Jak need only say "Bex Riveroma" and "sliver in my liver" to deflate him like a bad tire.

Jak climbed into the warm, scented tub. The muscles between his shoulder blades eased; he no longer felt as if he were pinned back like a bug in a display case. The cold that seemed to flow out from his lower belly to the rest of his body warmed and dissolved in the gentle slosh of the warm water in low gravity. The pressure of his scalp muscles on the back of his head diminished into the ordinary ache of overwork.

"Princess Shyf is at the door," his purse said.

"Put her on voice."

Shyf's voice was the warm kitteny purr he remembered from when she had been Sesh, back when it had seemed natural that an elegantly beautiful girl should want to be with him all the time. Now it was like a spike through his heart— a spike he couldn't help wanting desperately. "Jak, open the door."

"Purse, let her in."

Jak heard the main door out in the living area sigh open—or was that his purse sighing?

When Shyf walked into the bathroom, she had already taken off her clothes. "Don't get your hopes up today, silly boy. I'm going to wash your back and give you a nice huggy. I just didn't want to get my clothes wet. Lean forward."

Her hands on his back were soothing, lovely, perfection in touch in the way that her appearance was perfection to sight. He relaxed utterly, all the pain and stress gone. If time could be frozen so that Jak would live in this second, forever, he'd have stayed right here and now till the sun burned out.

For someone who seemed to treat the rest of the human race as either audience or servants, Shyf gave a surprisingly "good backrub" as Jak trusted himself to grunt, after a long period of utter heaven.

"Are you content with your life?" she asked, her voice as low and even as if she had asked him if he wanted the water reheated.

"I guess. Maybe. I don't know." He stretched, bringing his face down almost into the warm, scented water. The steam-thickened air opened his sinuses and felt good on his rough, overstrained throat. Her hands were working his lower back. "That must sound stupid," he added.

"Maybe. Or maybe you're just trying to please me (you're so toktru good about that, masen?) or it could be just honest confusion. Keep talking." Her voice was as gentle as a peck and hug, but as firm as an order given with the crack of a whip.

"Well, I guess I really don't know if I'm content. Right now I have a mission to complete. That's what I think about. It's good to have that to think about. I don't like the job on Deimos much, but it's better than not having a job. and I won't be a vice procurator for very long."

"Oh." Her hands kept working but though they were as gentle and accurate as before, they were indefinably less tender and eager, as if Jak could feel her falling out of love with him directly through the palms, heels, and fingers of her lovely graceful hands. Melancholy gnawed through his heart like a ravenous blind worm.

At last she said, "It's just . . ." and sighed before starting again. "It's just that, well, five years ago you seemed so bright and promising. Everyone said so. *I* was really in love with you. And you pulled off that amazing rescue mission for a captive princess—me, you no doubt remember—and you were in all the media, maybe the most famous teenager (well, at least the most famous one that didn't sing or dance or suck dicks on viv or wear a crown) in the solar system for at least ten days. And. Well. You . . . you just really—you stood out in a crowd, you were kind of . . . magnificent, masen? If you see what I mean."

"Five years ago I was an ignorant kid trying to live my life by the standards of intrigue and adventure vivs. That meant I was walking around with a ready-to-grab manipulate-me handle, which was grabbed and used by more people than I could count, friends, enemies, everybody with more of a clue than I had (which was pretty much the same thing as everybody). And I was proud to be that kind of gull, dupe, gweetz, whatever you want to call it. If there was anything magnificent about me, it was like being the best-looking pig at the slaughterhouse."

"Hmmmph. 'Principle 149: Real beauty is whatever is loved by people more important than you.' You were beautiful then. More beautiful even than that beautiful Waynong boy is today."

Jak shuddered. She was deliberately stimulating his jealousy. He knew why, of course. But his recent deconditioning was overwhelmed by the intensity of her presence, so that he did not even move before he felt the slight sting of the injector on his back. She waited a few minutes, continuing to rub his back. He felt more and more in love.

"'Hard.'"

It had been years since she had used any of the conditioned commands on him, but this one had certainly not faded. She pressed Jak's knees together and pushed back gently but firmly on his chest, so that he was neck deep in the warm bathwater. She straddled him. "Now watch the show."

Afterward, she sat on the edge of the tub, gazing with a fond little grin at the sobbing, gasping, aching Jak. Her voice was barely above a whisper when she added, "Now, if I make it a command and say, 'Calm love,' you know how you'll settle very quickly and easily into that state they call the 'Sunday Morning Bliss-blur,' masen? That warm, comfy, cozy, loved-all-over-forever security? You do remember that?" This seemed to be more like an interrogation than an afterglow.

"Toktru." Jak splashed a little water on his face and smeared his hand around.

"Well, if you really want me to, I'll give you the 'Calm love' command, but I think you'd be wiser not to take it."

"Why?" Jak asked.

"I don't really know, exactly." She squatted into the bathwater and washed for a moment. "If this seems a bit confusing, and I'm sure it must, that's mostly because I'm making all this up as I go along."

She borrowed his spare towel, programmed it for extra warm and fluffy, and dried herself, while Jak lay in the cooling bathwater, feeling the cold black vacuum where his heart had been.

"Why?" he finally asked, again.

"I told you," she said, quietly, sorting her clothes into order. "Self-press," she said, and they smoothed. She turned and flipped the manual control on Jak's tub, setting it to re-warm.

"You told me that you didn't know why, yourself."

"That's what I told you. I am making everything up as I go." She loosed her hair from its clips, flopped it forward into the towel, wrapped it into a turban, and then unwrapped it; her hair fell dry and clean down her back, and she pinned it back up. "Jak, if you try to dak what I'm doing as part of a plan, you won't—because I don't have one. And if I tried to tell you my intentions, you'd only be more confused, because I don't know them myself." She tugged on her clothes, gave Jak a quick hug and peck on the cheek, and walked through the dilating door, which constricted behind her before Jak could think of anything to say.

He slowly climbed out of the water. "Purse, get me Doctor Mejitarian. Did you record my conversation with Princess Shyf?"

"Yes, per your standing instructions. I also got a view from several cameras."

"Good, integrate that as well." This was hardly the time to be modest. "Relay the recording to Mejitarian, ask for his immediate review, and then put him right through to me as soon as he calls. Meanwhile, set up a light hypnosis protocol and knock me out till Mejitarian calls, or until it's time to go to bed for the night, whichever comes first." Jak lay down on the bed. The room became pitch-dark, the low thrum came to him through the white noise, and the blue light on the ceiling pulsed. It seemed to Jak that he rose toward it, and floated gratefully upward into unconsciousness.

CHAPTER 7

Utterly Contrary to Policy

"Doctor Mejitarian asked me to wake you for a conversation with him in five minutes." The lights came up, simulating a swift local sunrise, though in fact it was close to nightfall.

"All right." Jak got up, washed his face with a single big splash of cold water, patted his face once with the towel, and shrugged on a robe. "Ready, I guess."

When the kobold's face appeared, projected on the wall, he didn't seem even to be trying to hide how precessed he was. "I can't believe that she did that to you—or that we did such a poor job of deconditioning that you couldn't resist." Mejitarian had obviously not brushed his facial fur since getting up to look at Jak's message; one side was matted flat and the other stuck up in tufts. "The instant that you have obtained the lifelog—and the credit for Clarbo Waynong—we will have you completely, permanently deconditioned."

"Sir, I've already accepted that deal. But I should tell you, Clarbo Waynong is a far bigger idiot than anyone seems to realize, and he is absolutely the only reason this mission wasn't completed successfully long ago."

Doctor Mejitarian looked even more sad and tired. He stared at Jak for a surprisingly long time, and finally said, "You're right, of course, and all of us know that. Now, I am going to tell you several things that it is utterly contrary to policy for you to know. Do you know why I am going to do that?"

"No, sir."

"Neither do I." The kobold shut his eyes briefly and seemed almost to fall asleep. "First of all, whereas King Scaboron of Greenworld has been an ally and friend to the Hive, he is getting old and his longevity treatments are not taking as well as they should, and he has no more than eighty years left, perhaps as little as twenty. And it has become apparent that Queen-to-Be Shyf will be neutral, or may even slide over toward a hostile side. Our one best chance was foiled, very unfortunately, by yourself and Dujuv Gonzawara some years ago; if she had assassinated her father successfully, and pulled off the coup with our help, we might have gotten her into our pocket for at least a long time."

"I'd rather have a rabid ferret in *my* pocket, sir."

"I'll give you no argument. Nonetheless that was the game we intended to play, however unwisely. We also know that like any smaller ally associated with a greater one, Greenworld needs to penetrate the Hive and to exert as much influence as possible within our politics. This brings me to my real reason for wanting you to stay in close connection with Her Utmost Grace, and you won't like it at all.

"Whatever we may think of Clarbo Waynong, he is in the right position in the right branch in the right generation of his family to be the prime minister of the Hive in another few decades, and what we who know him think of him will not matter. All that will matter is that he is acceptable to patricians and marketable to the average voter. So I want to leave you in place to soak up attention that the Princess might otherwise put into Waynong, because he is already showing signs of infatuation with her, and he is going to be the prime minister, sooner or later, after holding portfolios like Defense, Diplomacy, Wager Orthodoxy, Energy, and Transportation—very likely after holding *all* those portfolios. He is a perfect target for the Princess; if she gains significant influence over him, the tail will have gained the power to wag the dog. You, on the other hand, are merely a very promising young agent of the type whose deaths we risk constantly. Your sanity against the independence of a future prime minister looks like a good bet. But it is not a very nice thing to do to you."

"Toktru," Jak said. "Toktru masen." He could think of nothing to say that would not make the situation worse. "And there's no problem with a complete idiot being the prime minister?"

"Jinnaka, I've done tours at headquarters. Working down the hall from the PM's office. Not only is it not a problem, it's nearly a qualification. The PM is really just the spokesperson for the staff that runs things, and there's only a dozen families that can produce an acceptable PM—the voters want that chin and those eyes and that confidence." The kobold looked down for a moment. "We will try to push things along with Clarbo Waynong so that this mission doesn't last too much longer, and anyway Myxenna Bonxiao will be there to take over in nine days. I will transmit a new deconditioning protocol, and then I suggest that you get some extra sleep. Besides being your controller, I am a neuropsychiatrist, and you've had a series of nasty shocks. A good rest is more than called for."

*   *   *

Jak awakened when his purse said, "Incoming message from a high priority person." He stretched. "What time—?"

"Twenty-two oh eight, local." Jak had had a three-hour nap. "Put it on a screen on the ceiling, no camera, display modesty notice."

"Coming up."

A white square appeared on the ceiling. Dujuv grinned at him. "Hey, old pizo, if you're in the tub or banging Princess Slut or something, finish quick and catch a Pertrans into Magnificiti, tell it you want to go to the Wednesday Rug Café. Kawib and I are going there to split some pizzas and wine, and you know we can always use another old tove to help us split the bill."

"I'll be there as soon as I can—just have to dress—the Wednesday Rug?"

"There was a fad here a few decades ago for naming businesses after any two random nouns. It's all there in the educational and informative guide file, *One Thousand Reasons Why Magnificiti Is to All the Cities of the Solar System What the Splendor of the Splendiferous Chrysetic People Is to All the People of Mars*. Which is right there in your orientation materials. Of course, what with having a major diplomatic function to attend, you probably didn't have time to properly peruse it, old tove, whereas Shadow, Pikia, and me got up to reason three hundred twelve reading it together. Then Shadow and Pikia went off to see a museum over in Freehold—it's only eighty kilometers away. She had some independent study thing she could finish for school by doing that, the museum was in the anything-goes part of that city, and Shadow suggested that she needed a bodyguard more than you or I did. (I think Shadow on the Frost is pretty badly bored, and he's hoping to use her as bait.)"

Jak laughed aloud at that. "I'm sure that's it."

"Well, it's just as exciting for all of us while the elite hold their ceremonies. Kawib, of course, got to spend his day making everyone repolish all the stuff that was already polished. I bumped into him in the cafeteria, and we started to talk, and we discovered that we like shared boredom better than isolated boredom. And so, to recover from all of this excitement and stimulation, we're going to go stupefy ourselves on wine and pizza . . . see you there?"

Jak was still laughing; it was good to have something normal and sane happening. "All right. Diplomatic receptions aren't exactly lively either."

"Attending them is usually about half the time I spend on my job, Jak. That's how I specked you wouldn't mind a little recreation, either. See you there?"

"Toktru masen."

"No need to hurry. We're going to be there for a long time. No reason to be up early. If you haven't checked the docket lately, apparently tomorrow Waynong and Prince Cyx are going golfing with Shyf, and the rest of us are hanging around."

Jak shuddered. "Tell me they aren't going to be looking for a fourth."

"Possibly the King."

"Nakasen be praised." On Mars golf was a mania, because it was more challenging than on Earth; low gravity meant long drives but sticky air meant shots curved more easily and the lightest of breezes had a profound effect. A slightly off shot that might have cost a stroke on Earth was a disaster on Mars. "I'll get dressed and be right with you."

Jak took the surface, scenic route rather than shooting through the subsurface tunnels. The Pertrans car glided through Magnificiti, a pretty little town that looked like a random collection of European architectural ideas from all the prespaceflight centuries; towers and spires, pseudotemples with friezes, rows of statues, balls on plinths, and cathedrals with imposing fronts, all packed around a star-shaped pattern of boulevards.

Twilight was still lingering. Since Mars's atmosphere was so thick so far above the surface, sunset was followed by a very slow dimming, bluing, and purpling of the sky that went on for more than two hours before full night fell. The stars twinkled more here than anywhere in the solar system, but the air dimmed them less than it did on Earth; the effect was of a great scatter of glinting diamonds on an imperial purple cloak.

At their table on the patio at the back of the Wednesday Rug Café, Kawib and Dujuv had two large pizzas surrounded, one partly and one mostly consumed. Kawib was ignoring the partially eaten piece in front of him in favor of his wine. Dujuv was rolling a slice lengthwise, his usual method for eating one in the minimum number of bites.

"Playtnaglazfya," Dujuv said, pointing to his left with his thumb at the plate and glass waiting. Jak pulled out the chair and sat, dropped a napkin onto his lap, filled the glass, and grabbed a piece of the pizza. He was surprised at how good his appetite was.

With a mighty gal-*lulp!* Dujuv bolted the rest of his gigantic mouthful of pizza, and washed it down with half a glass of wine. "We're just getting started."

"Er, actually, *I'm* finished, with the food, anyway," Kawib said.

"With Duj figured into the average," Jak assured him,

" 'we'll' be just getting started for hours yet to come. How have you been?"

Kawib Presgano was wearing a plain, unornamented coverall, appropriate for military or security people in foreign territory. He was still slim, tall, a long-and-lean natural athlete who had stayed in training, just as he had been three years ago when Jak and Dujuv had first met him.

Jak, Dujuv, and Shadow had witnessed the Princess's way of operating firsthand: like all Karrinynya, to appoint her most dangerous rivals and opponents to positions of great trust, so that the moment they failed her in the slightest regard, they could be executed for treason or sedition. Jak had been there the night that an agent of Hive Intelligence, in a "mistake" arranged by Shyf, had shot and killed Seubla Mattanga, Kawib's fiancée and a potential pretender to the throne in her own right. He had seen the things Shyf had put Kawib through as commander of the Royal Palace Guard. And now he was her personal officer for intelligence and security . . . charged with keeping her safe and liable to be killed as soon as his efforts did not seem quite perfect. "If it's painful, you don't have to tell me."

"Well, it's been pretty much what you would have guessed. I watch everything. I look for anything that might look even a little suspicious. I get reconditioned twice a week, and I don't get to take a break the next day. It's all a silly, weird game, Jak. I try not to make a mistake, since I'll die for the first one . . . and I wait for the first one to come." He shrugged, drained his wineglass, filled it again, and took another sip. "It's good to have a leave and people to spend it with."

"Glad we can help you," Dujuv said, carefully rolling the next piece of pizza. "Nakasen's hairy bag, what a waste of

talent, Kawib. You could have been anything. It's a pity you
didn't run away when you were sixteen, before she ever
came to Greenworld. I take it there's nowhere you could run
now?"

"Sooner or later a bounty killer would come and get me.
I suppose I could live free for a while, maybe in the Jovian
League somewhere—if I didn't mind living in a police
state—or maybe assume a name and go to Triton or Mercury
like any bankrupt or petty crook."

"You could do worse than Mercury," Dujuv commented.
"Like I was telling you before Jak got here, they're decent
people. Poor and beaten down and everything else, but if
you joined up in a quacco, you'd have toves who would die
for you and a place where you were needed."

"For what?"

"They can always use another strong back there. Better
still, you're educated. You could read and write for the
adults who can't, help with the technical side, even teach the
kids. And nobody in your quacco would rat you out. You
wouldn't have to watch your back, and you might get a
chance to quietly go sane."

"Recover from the conditioning."

"That's what I mean."

"You know that for someone like me that's years of misery?"

"That's what they tell you." Dujuv stretched. "Look,
don't let me get you in trouble. I suggest that you reject
whatever I say, just in case anyone is listening in, masen?
But if any of it makes sense, remember it. If you once got to
Mercury, with a few hardchips of currency, what you'd do is
throw away your purse and your ID, buy a temporary-on-
planet permit from one of the city governments, under any

old name you like, then walk down to the hiring hall and use the rest of your cash to buy a starter membership in any quacco that needs an educated hand. That's not traceable. As for the conditioning, hell, yeah, you'd be in withdrawal. I went through that myself, twice, panths bond naturally and get the same effect. Thought I was going to die. Thought it wasn't worth it. Thought I'd never make it through. And when I did make it through, on the other side, it was. Well, what kind of people end up on Mercury? Trust me, every quacco has a lot of experience with drying out drunks and detoxing druggies and working the control programming out of various kinds of slaves. They'd take care of you, and you'd live."

"As a shattered mess."

"Maybe an example to make myself clear? While I was at Eldothaler Quacco, we got a new heet in who'd been a professor, once, and ended up on Mercury because of a little problem with *xleeth*. On *xleeth*, he was happy all the time, just too inept to be trusted to flush a toilet. Off *xleeth*, he was well aware that his IQ was down to about eighty-five, that he'd once been somebody and now he was a shovel propulsion unit. And his pleasure centers were pretty burned down, so he didn't enjoy even the simple pleasures much. For some reason, it was worth it to him to be free, stupid, and sad." Dujuv hefted the piece of pizza, apparently decided the balance was right, and took it in three bites. "Look, I'm not your judge and I haven't been through a tenth of what you have. But people who really want to be free are free, or dead."

"And if I'm not free or dead, I didn't want freedom that much?"

Dujuv swallowed without chewing. "Let's talk of more pleasant things."

"Is there anything else much to talk about?" Kawib asked.

"I guess not. Want to just eat and drink?"

"Maybe . . . Dujuv, how can you be so sure that I'll be happier on Mercury, or Triton—the choice between broiling and freezing—where I'll be nobody but a false name on the right front of my pressure suit?"

"I didn't say you'd be happier. You'd just be able to use more of your abilities, stop looking over your shoulder, maybe sleep at night, have stuff to do that mattered. That kind of thing. But being happy? I didn't say anything about that."

"But you think I should go." Kawib drained his glass again.

Trying to lighten the mood, Jak said, "Sometimes I think Duj believes we all should go to those places."

The thoughtful expression on Dujuv's face would have confused every bigot in the solar system—a panth obviously lost in contemplation—but when he spoke again, Jak and Kawib were just as confused. "Oh, I don't think the really terrible places are good for the people who are there. I wish they could all get out of there. The *radzundslag* on Mercury has most people only living a bit past a hundred years, and Triton's a pretty brutal place too. I think I'd go mad living in a Venerean resource crawler, and I'm not planning to vacation in any of the asteroid mines. No question, decent schools, and enough rest, and exercise that works your whole body, and food and air without poison are good things—just look at the people in the Hive and the Aerie, or on Earth or Mars. And most ways there's more freedom for most people out here in the good parts of the solar system; I can just open my mouth and say that it's a disgrace to our species that on Mercury there's still slavery and banking, and nothing happens to me. Say that on a street corner in Chaudville or Bigpile and several private companies will be putting a price on your head within minutes, and some bounty hunter will collect it within days. No, I don't think the resource extraction areas are good places and I don't think everyone should go there.

"But they are a good place to vanish, and that's what Kawib needs to do if he's ever to have his freedom.

"And—this sounds so stupid that I don't want to say it, but I guess I should—they're more real there."

"That doesn't sound stupid," Jak said, noticing that the wine was beginning to take hold of him.

"Maybe I should say it sounds like a lot of stupid people sound, so it's sort of stupid by association. I don't think that being uncomfortable, overworked, and exploited makes anyone more real. I don't think misery creates wisdom. Really the opposite. But what working hard with the physical world, for not much reward, does do for a person, is it keeps them from thinking that little games that happen in the brain *are* real. A heet who spends all his time setting probes or running a separator, so that his quacco won't be seized and he won't be sold off as a peon, doesn't necessarily know much about what is real (his perspective is too narrow and he may not have time to think about it). But he does have a singing-on sense of what's *not* real—like most of politics and practically everything that's reported on the news: He does know that most of the jockeying between aristos is no concern of his."

"You're sounding heretical," Jak said, "and verging on republican."

" 'Then make the most of it,' " Dujuv said, obviously quoting someone (Jak didn't know who, but since Duj was an enthusiast for dead languages, it could have been any of a very large number of obscure dead people). "Ever notice you can recite all two hundred thirty-four Principles, and read all through the Teachings and the Suggestions, and you still won't find a single word about kindness, or gentleness, or keeping your honor? One of the best things about a heet busting his tail down in a mine, or out on the lines of a sunclipper, is that he knows that kind is better than cruel, and that he'd rather be around people who told the truth than people who didn't. Most of the affluent people in the 'better' parts of the solar system seem to have missed those points. So yeah, I guess I lean republican these days. Maybe even Socialist, which will get me fired, of course, but I can always go play slamball or sign on a sunclipper. It just seems to me that we've got nearly unlimited resources at hand and we've been in space for fifteen hundred years; we ought to think about getting rid of at least poverty and slavery, and on nights when I've had enough wine, I sometimes think we ought to get rid of torture and political repression too."

Jak snorted. "And if people weren't forced by poverty or prods, who would do the shitwork?"

"People who were paid enough."

Kawib jumped in. "Oh, toktru masen. What are you going to do, pay a resourcer on Venus more than you pay an orchestra conductor on the Aerie?"

Dujuv shrugged. "As a whole, humanity could afford to pay everyone like a king. And there are a lot of jobs that could and should be done by robots anyway. What's two hundred years of a human life worth? That's how much most miners on Mercury lose out of their life spans."

"Most of them are criminals. Mercury was settled by prison ships—" Jak said.

"See, this is what mystifies me about the way people think, Jak. Anyone who asks his purse can confirm this in about three seconds, counting your talking time: most prisoners who went to Mercury went for debt, not for crimes, and anyway the present population is mostly their descendants, not the original debtors or criminals. Even if you actually do think that overspending your credit rates a century off your lifetime, and living as a slave in a tunnel in hell, should that happen to you because of what your grandfather did? Come on, you were on Mercury too, would you send somebody into a krilj there, as a peon, because his mom was a compulsive shopper?"

"If you made any changes like what you're talking about," Jak said, "the great majority of people in the solar system—who are well off and comfortable—"

"Now why is it that before there can be any improvement for people who have nothing, the people who already have too much have to get more?"

"Because," Sib said, sitting down beside Jak, "they like what they have and if you want them to change you have to offer them something they will like better. Your alternative would be robbing them at gunpoint, which I assume you don't favor."

"That's why I spend a lot of time thinking," Dujuv agreed.

"You should spend more. Some professions and some philosophies just never work together—and with your talent, you shouldn't lose track of your profession." Sib's voice was curiously hard-edged and insistent for casual conversation, but he sat down and poured a glass like anyone else and said, "Kawib Presgano, we haven't met before, but I'm Sibroillo Jinnaka, Jak's uncle, and also a stringer for Hive Intel. Which post, I hope, will not last much longer, because a regular agent should be here in a few days, and they really need someone who outranks the agent they've got in charge."

"Yes, they do." Kawib made a face. "I don't speck what you're saying about the philosophy and the profession not going together—"

"Very often it's not what attitude you take, or what beliefs you hold, but the fact that you try to do anything about them that makes a mess. 'Follow your sword through life, for if you are behind your sword, and it moves forward, and you wield it with alertness, you are in the safest place you can be.'" Sib tasted his wine and nodded.

Though politics was Jak's profession, he didn't want to talk shop right now. "I *like* the idea of following the sword."

"You were raised to it," Sib pointed out. "But it's a viewpoint that only makes sense if we never question the people we follow the sword *for*." He tugged at his goatee. "Get used to the idea that even their vices are virtues. Cruelty and aggression enhance their power. Incompetence and silliness enhance our loyalty. I've had a very pleasant and interesting life, all spent following my sword, metaphorically speaking of course—and that's because my sword always had the common sense to go where it did the most good for the aristos. They're the ones who have the money to pay for us."

Dujuv sighed. "I speck you but I don't want to dak it, masen? It all seemed much simpler on the ground."

"That's because on the ground your main concerns are staying alive and carrying out your mission," Sibroillo said, and this was the first time this evening that his tone to Dujuv was polite and gentle. "Because you just followed your sword, and left the question of who to fight (and why) to the people that the question belongs to. Now, tell me about this draft for slamball players that you've been caught in?"

Accepting the peace offer, Dujuv sipped his wine and said, "Well, it happens every few months. I'm not sure why it made the news this time. I had a real good record at the PSA. I guess it's not too immodest—more just the truth—to say that I'm probably the best player around who isn't in school or signed to a pro team. So every time a minor league team gets into trouble and the head coach is trying to keep his job, they use some of their draft points and claim they're going to get me; because usually if you're trying to turn a team around in a hurry, and you can only afford one real change, a young hotshot goalie is what you want. I'm not sure why this time it made all the vid and viv sports channels; usually it's just a little flattering attention in the low-priority 'other news' category."

"You may have more friends than you think," Sibroillo said. "You seem to like your present job, but there are those who would say that when people are good at one job and magnificent at another, they shouldn't be allowed to be merely good. And therefore some busybody may have planted the story—perhaps Venus National, since they're the ones trying to draft you."

"Could be," Dujuv said. "And there are times when my mood tips toward just going and doing it."

The conversation wandered off into Disciplines technique, the new tactics in Maniples that had made Pabrino

Prudent-Reckoner (a crewie pizo and tove of Jak's and Dujuv's) the youngest Greater Master in more than a century, what the perfect all-night drunk required, why the Uranus System moons remained quiet backwaters compared to everywhere else (Sib thought it was that their culture was programmed to fail, Dujuv thought it was caused by poverty, and Kawib and Jak thought it was important to get the two of them off the subject).

When they were very drunk, Sib started on the subject of adolescent pranks for which he had had to pay bribes to keep Jak out of jail. "Going climbing in the light shaft got the most press and might have been the most impressive," Sib said, "but it was relatively cheap. And the ventures into commercial pornography and intellectual piracy were almost amusing. The one that cost me plenty, and most of it spent keeping Jak's name from getting into the media so that there wouldn't be angry mobs looking for him, was that nasty trick with the Pertrans cars."

"I told you not to do that one, old tove," Dujuv said.

"I know," Jak said.

"I haven't heard this story," Kawib said, slurring his words; he seemed pretty drunk.

Sib said, "Not much to tell—"

"—but if we make Jak tell it, he'll be much more embarrassed."

"Thanks so much, Duj."

"What're toves for, old tove?"

"Am I gonna get this story?" Kawib demanded.

"I guess so," Jak said, pouring another glass he didn't need (the room was already slowly rotating) as a way of delaying it just a few more seconds. "It was pretty simple, really. I hacked into the Pertrans message control database, the thing that tells a public Pertrans car what to say to you. The Pertrans car confirms your ID so it knows who to bill, and that also means that it knows everything else about you. So it knows which people have a fear of enclosed spaces, or which ones are bothered by the fact that those cars go at up to three thousand kilometers per hour, and so on, and it has extra-reassuring messages for them, for any time acceleration goes above point seven g for example. I just programmed it so that every so often instead of saying, 'This high acceleration is routine,' it would crank the volume way up and scream, 'The line broke! We're all going to die!' Now if those poor gweetzes thought about it for a moment they'd know that if a linducer track breaks or depowers, all that happens is you glide to a stop, and anyway they never break—"

Dujuv shook his head. "Phobias aren't rational, and you were scaring the piss out of people who already have more than enough fear in their lives. Not adventurous, not funny, that's why I bowed out."

"And that's why I thought about adopting Dujuv," Sib added. "And having you neutered and keeping you as a pet. But there is a funny part coming. Tell Kawib why you got into trouble—it wasn't merely because you frightened some unfortunate people so badly that some of them had to have medical treatment."

Jak groaned. "Oh, all right, it *was* mean. But the other thing was really stupid, and that's much more embarrassing."

"Really?" Dujuv asked.

"Really what?"

"You're really more embarrassed about having been stupid than you are about having been mean?"

"Well, yeah. Toktru masen."

"My fault, I suppose," Sib said. "I raised him that way. Let's not let him wriggle out of telling the story."

"Toktru."

Seeing no way to avoid it, Jak explained, "So, I was very involved with hacking at that time, loved it more than any other part of tradecraft class, spent a lot of my spare time for a couple of months getting good at it. And there happened to be this Dean of Students who I hated very much."

"Dean Caccitepe," Dujuv filled in. "Philto Caccitepe. You may know the name—"

"The head of staff for Hive Intel's counterintelligence unit? Yes, any security heet has heard of him," Kawib said, and began to giggle, partly from seeing where this was going and mainly because he was exquisitely, excruciatingly drunk, even more so than the rest of them. "Oh, Nakasen's furry pink bottom, Jak, don't tell me you hacked into his home number."

"Nothing that painless. I found a number associated with his account that wasn't marked for any purpose—"

"And even though Genius Boy here knew that Caccitepe was involved in Hive Intel—" Dujuv added.

"Oh, Nakasen, *because* I knew. You know, that spirit of you're going to commit a crime and get caught, why litter or shoplift or park illegally when you can get caught raping the president's pets in a secret weapons plant on top of a bag of *xleeth*? You know, that go-for-the-record spirit. So I took this number, which I knew must be something, but did not realize was the hotline for urgent counterintelligence calls, and I put it into a special message that played in that Pertrans message database. If it gave anybody the 'We're going to die!' message, one minute later it would say, 'This joke was brought to you by the Pertrans company to brighten your day. If you'd like to thank or compliment us, or if you're a humorless crybaby sissy who wants to complain, please call . . .' and gave them that number.

"Dean Caccitepe was sub-impressed and infra-thrilled. Especially because he had five ordinary law-abiding citizens in jail for calling him on a high-security line and making threats—and thirty agents investigating—before they got hold of someone coherent enough to tell them what had happened, and checked the database, and figured it out."

"It cost a small fortune," Sib said. "Only a small one because the Dean and I are old friends and colleagues. As for what consequences it might have for Jak . . . hmm. Well, as long as I'm alive, and able to keep an eye on things, limited consequences. But if I die before the Dean does, Jak, you could do worse than to defect."

"I thought you believed in absolute loyalty," Dujuv said. It came out as "Athaw yabeleeved nabsloo loytee," but after a moment, everyone pieced it together. He pulled himself up straighter said, "Shouldn't Jak 'follow his sword'?"

"Absolutely. For as long as it makes sense. Once your employer has decided to kill you or throw your life away, well, that's when you follow your sword over the wall and down the street to find another employer—and be just as loyal to that one. A smart aristo won't throw a good merc or op away—and a smart merc or op won't make himself ripe for throwing away."

"Even though I do feel sorry for those poor people that Jak did that to—especially for them being arrested afterward—I have to say, it's kind of hilarious," Kawib said. "I still can't quite see what you were thinking. That has to be the stupidest stunt I've ever heard of."

"People always laugh at record-setters," Jak said.

CHAPTER 8

How Is Up to You

Later, it seemed like a good idea to all walk back to the pavilions together, about five kilometers in the mild night along the Phobos-lit road. Kawib and Dujuv got involved in some obscure race that probably wouldn't have made sense to them, either, sober. After they had bounded around the bend in the road ahead, Jak said to Sib, "You used to seem to really like Dujuv, and be very pleased that he was my best tove. Now I think you really resent him. What is it that precesses you about him?"

"Nothing except that he's gone from being a fine young fighter and op—Nakasen's hairy bag, he still is—to being the sort of high-minded young turd who is going to make everyone else miserable forever. Just another stupid idealist out to ruin everything that is good and right and beautiful about the world, just because it isn't perfect for everyone. Would you want a world where there was no one as beautiful and terrible as Princess Shyf? Would you want a world where there was never the kind of magnificent pagentry we see every day here at the palace? Would you want a world where there were no high, wild adventures to be had against all odds, because there was never a desperate aristo to give you a glory-or-death mission? Because that's the kind of world that a young high-minded cretin thinks he wants. The kind of world that the socialists and the republicans, and the free-marketers and the democrats, put together back in the middle of the Red Millennium, which took centuries to undo. Nakasen and every Principle be praised that there was still enough red blood and high courage in the human race so that after we got into space, there were enough pirates, filibusteros, freebooters, and adventurers to create the new aristo class.

"A thousand years ago, if things had gone the way that your friend Dujuv and his pink-and-red pizos would have preferred, everybody would have been living in their comfy little cubes thinking comfy little thoughts, and there would have been no Ralph Smith, nobody even faintly like him, to win the war against the Rubahy. And why *should* the kings and the parades and the adventures have to go away, or fade to shadows of their former selves? So that ugly little children on Mercury, tenth-generation social scum, can have orthodontia? I've heard your silly tove getting emotional about how tough the little kids have it there. Well of course they do. Look where they live. Look who their ancestors were—prison sweepings, masen? Look who Princess Shyf's ancestor was—a magnificent brilliant beast of a man—and look where she is. Everything is as it should be."

"Uncle Sib, you're practically shouting. Are you all right?" His uncle turned back to him and said, "Yeah, old pizo, I'm all right. Just getting old on you, is all. I'm exhibiting some of the diseases of the old—like thinking that if young people aren't immediately, vociferously agreeing with me, I can fix the situation by repeating myself and shouting."

"By that standard of evidence, you've been old as long as I can remember."

"Why you insolent cub—" Sib aimed a mock kick. Jak ducked and ran, his uncle pursuing. "Impudent puppy!"

"Silly old man!" Jak said over his shoulder, slacking his pace so Sib could keep up with him. They covered the better part of a kilometer before they slowed down, laughing because running in low gravity is fun. As they stood, bent over, gasping, feeling alcohol, CO_2, and oxygen levels fight it out in their bloodstreams, Sib said, "Jak, I am serious. The beliefs and ideas that Dujuv is listening to are putting him on a road that doesn't lead to a successful career for a commoner with ambitions—like you, or like him."

"Sib, I don't willingly lose a tove," Jak said. "Too many past experiences taught me not to do that."

"Then don't lose him. But don't join him, either. If you turn aside from the paths of glory, you don't avoid the grave; you just waste yourself on a lesser path. If you follow the tepid pink flag, and throw away all your training and your family destiny, it will make me sick—and break my heart."

"I'll remember that, Uncle Sib."

"Thanks." The older man stood up and looked around at the quiet desert landscape between Magnificiti and the palace, taking in the long shadows from now-low Phobos and the spires and pinnacles at either end of the road. "If you remember me, and what I taught you, then I think maybe my life was not thrown away." Then he laughed and slapped his thigh. "Weehu, a man gets morbid when he crosses into his third century. Come on, puppy, we've had a good walk, and that was a lot of wine back at the tavern. I need to mark my territory behind that boulder."

"Let's make it a social occasion," Jak said, recognizing the peace overture and happy just to be with his good old uncle, who had often been wrong, but always sought what was best for Jak and the family. "Praise Nakasen for a warm night and a dark shadow where we need it."

Having nothing to do, Jak slept most of the next day. He had just finished a long workout and a longer bath, and was contemplating early bed, when his purse said, "Sorry, urgent call from Clarbo Waynong."

Jak groaned and said, "All right, put him on."

You really had to give Waynong credit for perfect grooming, because there wasn't much else that you could give him credit for.

"Hello, Jak, listen, I've been talking to some of the old pizos up in Hive Intel and they've decided—well, we've decided—well, I said it and they didn't say anything I understood in reply—well, anyway, we decided."

"Decided what?" Jak hated himself for asking.

"Oh, that. Yes. We decided that all this has gone on more than long enough. Cyxy is a charming old tove, and Princess Shyf is very beautiful, and the golf here has been flawless, but I do have a career to get on with, and this is simply taking too long, masen? So the time has come to take more direct action. That was exactly the words I used with the station chief from Deimos and I think that's what he didn't disagree with, anyway, so it's time for more direct action. You know what I mean by more direct action?"

"Something you should not discuss over a communications link in the middle of a foreign capital?"

"It's funny, you know, several people have said that to me, masen? Anyway, see you at the meeting."

"What meeting?"

"Oh, that was what I called about. I reserved a room in the pavilion for it. Downstairs."

"Is it a highly secure matter?"

"Well, yes, I suppose it is." Clarbo had apparently not thought about the question till then, but now he looked excited to be involved with something highly secure. "Um, actually—well, toktru," he said, his voice now firmly commanding, "it's a top secret matter."

"Then let's have your purse download a set of security routines from mine, and have it clear the room where you're holding the meeting. I have some really good software you should use for that."

"Why, thank you. Yes. Of course. Purse, did you hear that?"

Jak heard Waynong's purse say that it had, and that it was already doing the downloads.

"That was awfully nice of you, Jak."

"Part of my job. What time is the meeting?"

"Oh, in about forty minutes. If it's not too much trouble, I suppose. Or I guess one shouldn't say that about an important meeting. It was awfully nice of you to provide some help, Jak. I do find a lot of this difficult because it is awfully complicated and there's so much to remember, masen? And it is nice to have the help. If you think of things, I wouldn't mind getting a little discreet advice now and then."

"If I think of things," Jak agreed. "All right, then. I'll see you at the meeting."

When they had all gathered in the meeting room, Clarbo began by saying, "I imagine you're wondering why I've called you all here."

"Especially since Jak is the commanding officer," Pikia said.

"Er, um, yes, but everyone knows that . . . well, I suppose

everyone doesn't know it because this is a secret mission . . . or do you all know it?"

"I'm finding it hard to think of a question I could ask," Dujuv said.

"Well, exactly, so let's proceed. Now, since it's clear that negotiations have broken down—"

"It is?" Sib asked.

"Um, I was supposed to say that." Waynong looked at the palm of his left hand and asked his purse, "What does it say in that little speech?" After reading for a moment, he said, "Yes, I was right. It *is* clear that negotiations have broken down. Anything else I should check?"

Sib appeared to be trying to push his eyes up onto his forehead. He gestured for Waynong to go on.

"Now, therefore, we're going to attempt to recover that lifelog for the Hive by physical means. Uh, that means we're going to try to steal it—"

The door opened and Princess Shyf walked in, Kawib at her heels. The door constricted and Shyf said, "Sorry we're late. What's the plan for stealing the lifelog?"

"Er," Jak said, "security has been compromised on this operation and so we'd better call it off until we reestablish full security."

"Oh, that's not a problem," Clarbo assured him. "I just happened to be chatting with the Princess here, and she mentioned she hasn't had a real adventure in quite a long while, so I offered her the chance to come along on this one, and she jumped at it. And I'm sure Kawib is here because she brought him. That would be why they came in together."

"Your deductive abilities seem to be as sharp as ever," Shadow said.

Jak felt a tingle in his left hand. He glanced down at the

palm display and saw a flashing red dot—urgent, highest priority, something was up. He put his left hand over his ear and pressed the code with his thumb.

A voice quietly said, "This is Mejitarian, Hive Intel, Jinnaka. You seem to have a problem here. Let me clarify the situation. Your orders to bring back the lifelog ASAP and to bring in a personal success for Clarbo Waynong supersede all others. This includes making sure it's a real personal victory, so just doing it and giving him the credit is not an option.

"Therefore whatever silly plan Waynong may have, no matter how foolish—make it work." The signal cut off.

Jak needed a great idea, right now, and all he had was a fair-to-middling one. He stood up and said, "That was a message from a high level of the home government, and I'm not allowed to say more than that. Security is pretty badly compromised on this operation, so they insist that we go right now, before word can get around any more. Clarbo, I'm sure you had a very complex plan waiting to go—"

"It's something I put together with some devices that Hive Intel had available—had them all shipped in today, you know, on my personal account since headquarters—"

"And those came through regular delivery?" Dujuv asked. "Not through any secure channel?"

"It seemed important to get the things here quickly, and going through the secure channel takes much longer—"

"So Red Amber Magenta Green postal inspectors have almost certainly seen what's in the box," Jak said.

"Oh, of course, they opened it—there's a note right where they resealed the box."

Jak glanced down at Dujuv's left hand and saw his oldest, best tove send two quick signals: first, *I'll back you,* and second, *I have no hope.*

Jak looked down for a moment, looked up, and said, "Well, then, we have an operation that has already leaked so badly that agents of a foreign power know all about it and came to the meeting, and sometime this afternoon local security discovered that one of our party was importing spy gear, burglary tools, maybe weapons."

"Well, of course, it seemed like you'd need those," Waynong said, crossly, clearly eager to get on with explaining his plan.

"So at any moment our party can expect a rupture of diplomatic relations, and just possibly our arrest on espionage, sedition, conspiracy—well, quite a list. We could drop everything and run for it—"

"—but I just bought all this equipment!"

"—or we can follow our most recent orders, try for the lifelog right away, and hope Red Amber Magenta Green is still specking things out. I'd rather not just run back home with our tails between our legs. And I'm assuming our Greenworld friends feel the same way?"

"Absolutely," Shyf said. "We came to the meeting and didn't tell Witerio or Cyx about it—we're up to our necks in it too. Let's get going."

"All right," Jak said. "Clarbo, what's your plan? The short version of course—"

"Oh, of course. Time is of the essence, masen? I always wanted to do something where time was of the essence, and get to say that." The handsome young man opened the shipping container and began pulling out boxes. "I tried to keep it very simple so I restricted myself to just three pieces of hardware, two because they looked very useful and one because I thought, that's so interesting, I just have to include *that!*"

Jak's palm tingled, and he looked down; his purse was signaling him to hold it to his ear. When he did, Mejitarian's voice said, "Yes, we are aware of the quality of Mister Waynong's planning. All the other considerations still apply. Make it work. How is up to you." A harsh little click, and silence.

"The, um, high level source has just confirmed that they want us to proceed," Jak told everyone. "Well, let's see what you have for us, Clarbo. Try to keep it brief because we'll need to start soon."

"Certainly, certainly, toktru masen. Well, now, this first thing is a spy-scout." Waynong shook the box, which was a cube about half a meter on a side. Three small black spheres, about the size of golf balls and completely featureless, rolled out. "As anyone can see, I've got three little balls, one for each team in my plan.

"This can connect direct to your purse, and you can use the purse screen or a pair of goggles that plug into the purse. Either way, it lets you see in any direction from any surface of the rolling ball. Though I don't know why anyone would want to look at the floor. But you can see in all the other directions too, and there will be guards and things in those directions. So the plan is, we put our balls in first, and see how things are going. Then team one comes in using these." Clarbo Waynong shook out a second, larger box, and what looked like half a dozen slippers fell out. "These are ceiling sticking shoes; team one will be way up on the ceiling with their faces about level with the guards' faces. Totally disorienting. Toktru it's my favorite part of it all.

"Now, we're not supposed to hurt the guards if we can

help it, so the last special weapon here is a nonlethal control weapon. It's a net gun—the slug expands into a big, spinning net that grabs and holds everything in its path and won't let go till we give it the code. Which we'll message to the local police as soon as we've made our getaway.

"So the plan, once the balls have given us a picture of the room, is that team one will come in on the ceiling as a diversion, team two will run in on the ground and shoot the guards from behind with the net gun while they're staring at team one, and then team three will run in, and grab the—um, what was it?"

"The lifelog?" Pikia asked.

"Just so."

"How is all this coordinated?" Gweshira asked, looking down at the floor.

"Oh, we just agree on a time, of course," Waynong said. "Our purses are more than accurate enough to synchronize the three teams."

"Er, what if there's a change in plan or a hitch with one team?"

"There won't be. We have perfect intelligence."

"We do?"

"In our little balls." Clarbo Waynong looked around the room emphatically, seeming to pose for a camera that wasn't there. "So given that we have perfect intelligence, we won't need to change plans, and therefore we can just set our clocks and go. Much more secure than talking back and forth all the time. Now here are my team assignments. I will lead team three, and Sibroillo and Jak will be members of it as well. Team one, which gets to walk on the ceiling—that seems like so much fun I almost wanted to do it myself but they told me *very* sternly, excessively sternly if you ask me, that I had to be the one who grabbed the—um—"

"The lifelog?" Pikia asked. Her expression was so innocent that if Jak had been her great-great-grandfather he'd have grounded her for a year on suspicion alone.

"Yes, yes, exactly. I'm glad someone remembers it."

"It's what I'm here for," Pikia assured him.

"All right, now where was I? Team assignments! Well, then. Team one, the diversion team, the ceiling walkers, call them what you will"—he gestured grandly—"team commander will be Dujuv, with Pikia and Shadow dividing command backup responsibility. And since we also have our guests from Greenworld, and one spare pair of these walking upside-down shoes—toktru they seem like so much fun but I can't figure out any way for me to wear them and be the actual person who grabs—"

"The lifelog!" Pikia's smile was wide but her eyes were sparkling strangely.

"—the lifelog, thank you, Pikia, then the last pair of shoes might as well go to Kawib, mightn't they? And therefore he will be the fourth member of team one.

"Now for team two, we have these." He set two very oversized pistols onto the table in front of him. "As long as all three guards stick together, one shot should make them all, um, stick together. The net spreads out to a three-meter-by-three-meter square you see, and flies across the room, and tangles them all up very much like a spiderweb. So team two, you will fire the first net gun at the guards, and that should be enough to take care of them."

"And who's in team two?" Gweshira asked.

"Well, it's not quite as light a team as the other two, is it, masen? No really light equipment and doesn't get the glory of actually grabbing the lifelog. On the other hand it doesn't take much physical strength or mental ability to pull that trigger, so I suppose we could give it to anyone. I had selected"—he checked his notes in his purse—"you for the main shooter and Xlini Copermisr for the backup."

The corner of Gweshira's mouth twitched. Jak knew that twitch; he had sparred in the Disciplines with Gweshira many, many times. Usually it preceded a good wanging. "But if I miss my shot, and Xlini misses hers, then won't the whole plan come apart?"

"I do not create the sort of plans that 'come apart.' And you really ought to have more confidence in yourself. You won't miss that shot. But since you're worried about it—"

"I was about to ask for a few minutes to practice with the weapon. I've never used a weapon in combat without having practiced first."

"Out of the question. I only ordered two and it's a single-shot disposable weapon."

Gweshira's mouth opened to speak, but before she made a sound, she jumped as if bitten or shocked. She turned her left hand palm upward to look down at her purse, then clapped her purse to her left ear; she looked as if poison were being poured into her ear. After a long breath, she muttered "Understood" and let her hand drop to her side, where it hung like a dead snake over a fence rail.

Meanwhile, the situation had been aggravated: Clarbo Waynong had been thinking. "You know," he said, "I think the thing to do is autoprogram those net guns; I can set them up so that they fire as soon as you pop out of the corridor into the room with the lifelog. I hate to do it but if people are going to be second-guessing the plan all the time . . . well, we'd better get on with it." He looked around and said, "So for team three, the ones who will actually grab the lifelog, we have myself, of course, plus Sibroillo and Jak Jinnaka will divide backup command responsibility, and of course—"

Princess Shyf looked at him coolly. "And of course Her Utmost Grace, me, will do something she's valuable at, rather than hanging about in a hallway, and will cause Prince Cyx, who is supposed to be in charge in the event of emergencies tonight (while his father gets a badly needed good night's sleep), to hang out an array of fearsome DO NOT DISTURB signs, real and virtual, on his door, thereby ensuring that any possible response to the theft of the lifelog will be feeble and delayed, due to everyone's being very cautious about disturbing the Prince. Not to mention that given that this is apt to be a very stressful evening for Cyx, this will help him to maintain a sense of proportion and a feeling that life isn't actually so bad after all, which will be of some importance in the subsequent negotiations to soothe Red Amber Magenta Green's official diplomatic feelings. As soon as I know at exactly what time the Prince should be most occupied, I shall get to work on looking and smelling good, which happens to be one of my major talents. (And let me add that if you attempt to designate me as 'team four,' I shall ignore you, possibly forever.) So thank you for my assignment and please do proceed with your meeting so I can get on with it."

"Er, just so, yes," Waynong said.

As he waited in the dark hallway, Jak woefully ticked off the long list of what was wrong with all this, and the short list of what was right. He was standing elbow to elbow with Uncle Sib, dividing the command backup—an easy division of zero by two, since there was nothing for a second in command to command, and nothing for either second in command to do. Probably Clarbo had thought that Jak and Sib were the two people most likely to assume command in a crisis, and therefore he had put them where they couldn't.

Glumly Jak watched the little square screen on his palm as it showed a rat's-eye view of the floor of the private viewing room in the Royal Splendiferous Museum where Nakasen's lifelog was being kept. The spy-scouts were built like compound eyes, covered with microscopic fish-eye lenses. A picture assembler in the purse software assembled the thousands of images so that the view did not tumble rapidly, but moved with the ball, staying in a given orientation until pointed elsewhere, like a single tiny camera creeping across the floor.

Just then, the camera from Dujuv and Shadow's team was sitting quietly in the corner of the room, providing a wide angle view of the three bored, elderly guards: two men and a woman, decked out in big coats and sashes, practically asleep on their feet. It occurred to Jak that any of the three teams could simply rush in, knock the old people down, and run with the lifelog, and get away with it. He would have placed his own odds of succeeding at that, all by himself, at about three to two, and Dujuv or Shadow, with much greater strength and speed, at about ten to one.

But orders were orders . . . and he wanted his real posting to a real Hive Intel job, and to be allowed complete deconditioning, and he didn't want the consequences of disobeying Mejitarian.

The thought of deconditioning reminded Jak of Shyf, who was with Cyx right now. That caused him to need to do some Disciplines breathing, just as Sibroillo had taught him to do ever since he could remember. At least the conditioned jealous rage Jak felt was helping him to stay awake.

Team two's spy-scout was rolled up against the pedestal on which the lifelog sat, and was slowly creeping around it, scanning up and down, giving a complete view of the room every couple of minutes.

The third spy-scout, operated by Clarbo Waynong, was wandering around randomly, its selected view straight down. It showed a dark spot at the center and a distorted gray smear of floor in other directions. Occasionally it would pass in view of spy-scout one or spy-scout two. Despite his admonitions to everyone else to be very quiet, Waynong was muttering and swearing to himself as he tried to get control of his spy-scout.

At last a momentary red flash from their purses alerted them. Waynong jumped; he had been so engrossed in trying to get the little black ball to work properly that he had lost track of the time. Jak saw the spy-scout imaging career wildly on the main screen of his purse, but he was mostly watching the countdown—seventeen seconds till time to run forward.

On the tiny screen in the palm of his left hand, the image of a boot toe burst into a black blur as the ball hit the guard's foot. The view spun in a great vertical arc, periodically revealing three puzzled guards staring down at the ball.

Jak and Sib dashed down the corridor together, Clarbo's cry of "Wait, it's too soon—" ringing behind them. They reached the display room just in time to see team one—Dujuv, Shadow on the Frost, Pikia, and Kawib—coming in at a slow walk on the ceiling. The guards did not—they were all bent over the small black ball, heads together, trying to figure out what it was.

Jak had just an instant to think how badly this was working before Xlini and Gweshira burst in from the main entry corridor. Activated automatically on entering the room, both their net guns went off, firing at the most prominent moving objects above the floor—which were not the three bent-over guards, but the team on the ceiling.

A long time afterward, when he thought about it more calmly, Jak had to admit that whoever had designed those net guns had done a bang-up job. The two nets, a fine transparent mesh just thick enough not to cut skin, with a "smart surface" that stuck to anything it touched except the net itself, seemed to pour into the air from the muzzles of the net guns and billow across the room like two raging translucent jellyfish. In less than a heartbeat they had flown around all four people, contracting very slowly but with tremendous force, hesitating wherever resistance was too great so that no bones were broken. The nets merged and crept inward, tightening, finding holds to draw tighter, freeing sections to flow to other looser spots on the struggling mass, so that in just a few seconds, one 130-kg Rubahy, one furious panth, and two unmodified humans were quite unhurt but being held tightly in a white spider-bag on the ceiling.

This, of course, had gotten the guards' attention. They were old and they were slow and sleepy, but they had once been police or soldiers, to judge by how quickly they drew their slug pistols and covered the bewildered party of would-be thieves.

CHAPTER 9

A Double-Sided Snipe Hunt

At the holding jail, Kawib was separated from the rest of them; perhaps because he was not a Hive citizen? But then, neither was Shadow . . . and of course the situation was so unusual that very possibly they were just making up procedure as they went. Jak resolved not to worry about it.

There wasn't much time to worry about anything, actually, because it was less than an hour before they were all brought before King Witerio. They stood, hands bound behind their backs, facing the King's official business throne; behind them stood a row of serious, trained, effective guards, from RAMG's small-but-not-hopeless army. Beside the prisoners the three elderly minor nobles, who had been the guards for the lifelog, looked so proud that Jak couldn't help feeling better—*someone* was having a good day.

Jak's "command" was in predictably sad shape; he summarized his report to himself as *three banged up, four exhausted, and one still a ninny.* Shadow looked worse than anyone else; the net had taken so many feathers that he looked like a half-plucked chicken. Jak knew that when the Rubahy had a single feather pulled out it hurt, so he imagined that his friend was probably in real pain, and the Rubahy's head hung and his shoulders slumped as they did when he was exhausted. Dujuv was bruised from his struggle to get out of the net and from the stunning they had given him to make him stop. Pikia would have looked all right if they hadn't had to cut off much of the hair on one side of her head to get the net detached; its "release" feature had apparently been somewhat oversold.

Xlini, Gweshira, and Sib merely looked very tired. Jak suspected the same would be true of himself.

Clarbo Waynong was bouncing with energy. As the King nodded to the bailiff, Waynong whooped, "Cyxy!"

Cyx entered and strode to his friend, almost shaking his hand before he saw that it was cuffed behind his back. This gave the Prince time to remember that they were "very nearly at war, old tove, toktru I'm sorry but I don't speck I should be too friendly, wouldn't do to have the Prince consorting with traitors—oh, but you're not a citizen so you can't be a traitor to us—well, anyway—"

"Sit over there and don't say anything," the King explained. Prince Cyx seemed to teleport into the chair. "Now," King Witerio said, turning to his prisoners, "it seems to me that since I have already remanded this case to myself and I know all the evidence I care to know, there's really very little point in hearing anyone's arguments. It so happens that I know everything about the matter—"

Jak tried. "Your Splendor, I will have to agree that we are guilty of very serious offenses, but there are a few things that you—"

"If they are things Princess Shyf could tell me, then I am reasonably certain I've already been told," Witerio said, smiling for the first time, not pleasantly.

Jak was about to think of a response—he could feel it forming—when Shyf walked in with Kawib at her side.

They were unguarded, unescorted, and obviously *not* prisoners.

"Your Splendor," she said, "I trust we have proven the friendship of Greenworld's people toward yours, and the strength of our bond of royal friendship, by assisting the invincible guards of the Splendor"—(here the old gwonts to Jak's left puffed out their chests)—"in preserving the lifelog where it rightfully belongs, in your hands. Let me offer you an alliance and a treaty, in which Greenworld will guarantee the security of the lifelog and you will retain it here; Greenworld will pay all necessary expenses for its security and preservation, hire all the appropriate scientists and scholars, and create and fund the Karrinynya Center for the Study of the Nakasen Lifelog right here in Magnificiti."

"That is a very generous offer and one I am very inclined to accept," Witerio said.

Sibroillo cleared his throat and said, "Your Splendor, I know that we can be in no favor at all with you right now, and that you will not believe that I am any sort of friend, and yet I feel that it is my duty to point out that if you consider the heartless and calculated way in which this young woman betrayed old close friends, and an important ally, then surely you must realize—"

"That she is apt to betray me?" Witerio asked. His mouth folded into a sardonic smile. "Of course. But she has betrayed you more recently than me, and she stands to profit more by being loyal to us. Besides, she betrayed you only because she was already working for us."

"But—" Waynong sputtered, "but, er, she said—I mean, I thought that—Shyf, can't you explain—"

Shyf smiled deeply at Clarbo Waynong, and approached him with that warm, seductive grin that always made Jak's heart hammer. "Mister Waynong," she said, "the fact that I smile and pretend to be fascinated with you really should not be taken to mean anything. In fact, since you are wealthy and of a good family, and rather easily deceived, you should be very wary when women smile like I'm smiling now. More so when it's a princess. I would advise you to take the smile, the gaze, and the attention coming from a princess no more seriously than you do when they are coming from any good-looking little clerk from a nobody family, or from this ragamuffin child here."

Within the time of a heartbeat, a small drama happened to Jak's right; Pikia seemed to speck whether she could move fast enough to kick Shyf before being restrained, and sadly dak she couldn't.

The Crown Princess of Greenworld stood close to Waynong and whispered tenderly, "By the way, you are easily the dullest man I have ever listened to for that length of time, and frankly, if I had it to do over again, I wouldn't." She had been standing with her hands folded in front of her; faster than the eye could see, her top hand snapped out and slapped Waynong in the crotch, hard enough to double him and make him groan. *For the first time,* Jak thought, *since I've known him, he doesn't look happy. And once again Shyf is reserving all the really enjoyable parts of the evening for herself.*

"Now," Shyf said to King Witerio, "do we have a deal?"

Jak stammered, "But . . . Greenworld and the Hive have been allies for two hundred years . . . you can't—"

Shyf shrugged. "Of course we can. Didn't you learn in your fancy PSA classes that the more essential ally gets away with whatever it wants? Well, who's the most essential to whom? The Hive needs us to prevent the unification of the Aerie, which is vital, and you have no one but us for it. *We* only need a powerful backer from outside the Aerie, and aside from the Hive, we can turn to the Jovian League, or to Titan, or to any of the great monopolies—most especially Uranium—or even to the Rubahy. You won't be happy, but even after this, you'll beg for the chance to do us more favors, just to keep us as allies."

"But you personally are under the guns of Deimos," Dujuv pointed out, "and there are fifty thousand troops up there—"

She laughed. "And our battlesphere is co-orbiting with Deimos. Every ship you have would have to come out of launch bays covered by our guns and move onto a loop that we could knock apart with a single shot. Right here, at the moment, you have the crew of one warshuttle, currently confined to Red Amber Magenta Green's prisons. I suppose you could blow up the lifelog by hitting Magnificiti from Deimos (violating so many treaties that I doubt we could count them all), or even open fire on *Rufus Karrinynya* with Deimos's heavy artillery . . . if it's worth starting a major war. Or you could gracefully accept that you've lost."

"It doesn't really matter whether they are graceful about it or not," Witerio said. "Lock them up."

The holding cell for Red Amber Magenta Green's prison was familiar by now. They were no sooner locked up in it than Clarbo Waynong said, "Now, here's my plan. First we escape—"

"Did you have a method in mind for that?" Jak asked, mildly, hoping to avoid Dujuv's actually killing the young patrician.

"Oh, probably through the ventilator shafts, that's what it usually is in the viv games—"

"Would that be those ventilators?" Jak pointed to the dozen openings in the ceiling, none of them any bigger in diameter than his own thumb, each covered with a grate with no visible means of attachment; the ceiling itself was just over a meter above their heads.

"Well, now I didn't say it was going to be easy, but if people are going to take a negative attitude—"

Jak glanced around and gestured for Dujuv to press himself against the wall to the left of the main door; before he could signal Shadow on the Frost, the Rubahy had taken up a position to the right of the door. Sibroillo joined Dujuv and Gweshira joined Shadow.

"What's all this—" Clarbo began, but Jak said, "Now, explain to me one more time about the ventilator shafts because I'm sure you had a plan—"

"Well, in one of my favorite vivs, *No Truce with Terriers!*— er, no offense, of course, Shadow—"

"None that won't eventually be avenged."

"Thank you, you're very understanding—anyway, in the middle part it turns out that even though there are only little vents like those in the ceiling, behind the vents there are big wide—"

Jak had been glancing around; as far as he could tell the main camera on the room was the one right over the door, probably a fish-eye lens, so this ought to work. "What if someone were screaming like she was being killed?" Jak asked. "Could they hear that through the ventilator shafts?"

"That's completely irrelevant—"

Pikia shrieked in agony. Jak turned to face her, guiding

her back against the wall, covering the camera's view of her with his body. He whispered, "Lots of drama."

She always did tend to do more and better than he asked. He only wished he had earplugs. As he slammed his hand into the wall beside her head, over and over, Pikia emitted screams and wails that would have summoned pity from a block of ice, loud enough to hear over a warshuttle taking off. Anyone would have thought that at least a dozen Pikias were being killed.

The two guards who had just locked them up were back within seconds. The door whooshed to its full dilation and they rushed in. Dujuv grabbed the guard on his side from behind, yanking his elbows back; Sib drove a thrust-kick into the man's solar plexus. As the guard doubled in Dujuv's grip, Sib followed up with a brutal uppercut that made the guard's head fly back and cracked his teeth together with a sound like a hammer breaking a castanet. Dujuv let the guard drop to the floor.

Meanwhile, Shadow on the Frost snaked an arm behind his guard's head, took a grip on the man's long hair, and whipped him over in a circular motion—possible due to Rubahy strength, Martian gravity, and Shadow's imagination. The guard flopped over with a scream that stopped when Gweshira administered a hard stomp to his belly; as the man clutched his gut and sat up, she spread her hands around the back of his head and yanked his face against her rising knee. The man sagged and lay still.

"Are you people actually—" Waynong began as the rest of the party charged out the door.

They raced through the hall to the pile of their purses on the front desk; the guards had not had time to lock them away before they had been drawn by Pikia's screams. As they tugged their purses on, Jak noted regretfully that Clarbo Waynong had been quick enough not to be trapped in the cell when the door reconstricted—possibly the first time anyone had ever had cause to complain that Waynong was too quick.

Shadow was studying the map of emergency evacuation routes; he raised a hand to indicate he had found the right one, and pointed down a corridor.

Waynong started to say "What?" but it came out as a cough due to Pikia's swift, accurate elbow. They all rushed after Shadow on the Frost, who ran up to the emergency box on the door and shouted into it, "Password Splendor! Ambulance for two men right away! Soft lockdown! Evacuate this corridor only!"

The door swung open and they rushed through en masse into a broad parking area, devoid of vehicles. Phobos had risen not long before, so there was plenty of light.

"Now that we can talk," Jak said, "Shadow, exactly what did you just do?"

"Created a diversion that I hope will give us at least an hour's head start. The security system in that lockup is of Rubahy manufacture, and in fact a distant cousin—someone I am connected to mostly through my uncle-group for honor, but also through my mother's commanding officer's sex-partner, in a way that is rather complicated—was the chief designer. Like most things here in the Harmless Zone, it's designed to be cheap and simple. So when I gave it that sequence of commands, it didn't have a camera to look with or an AI to evaluate. It has now closed off the corridor we came through from the rest of the area, and flooded everywhere else with knockout gas. Now they'll have to bring in troops in respirators to search the area, looking for us and the guards."

"And was calling the ambulance part of the diversion?" Sibroillo asked.

"We knocked two men unconscious. They probably have concussions, perhaps more serious injuries. It did not occur to me that they ought to die to cover our escape." It always amazed Jak that a creature with no facial expressions could so vividly express what he thought.

Uncle Sib muttered something about never understanding Rubahy honor, and Shadow on the Frost quietly said, "This is not a matter of honor, but of ordinary pity. Like your Principle 8: 'Do not do things to others that would seem spiteful, petty, vicious, or shameless if they were done to you.' Is that a bad Principle?"

"Of course not," Sibroillo said, "and your point is made."

"One more question," Dujuv asked. "How did you know the password?"

"Well, it was the one I would have guessed. But no need to guess when they have it taped to the emergency evacuation box."

"Well, anyway," Clarbo Waynong said, "if you people are done with all the chitchat, I think we have any number of things to get on with. But I'm afraid I really don't think I should go with you, wherever you're going."

"You don't?" Jak asked, because he couldn't think of anything else to say, and that was the most obvious way to find out what (or if) Waynong was thinking.

"No, I don't think I can continue to give you the benefits of my leadership without much more cooperation than you have all shown up till now," Waynong said. "In any case, there are procedures to be followed, which I should look up—"

"If you try to use your purse here," Jak said, "you will be spotted right away. At least wait to use it till you're out in open country and it can call through multiple routings."

Waynong's purse spoke up, "From a security standpoint, Mister Jinnaka is right."

"Oh, very well." Waynong stamped away like a petulant small child, talking to his purse. After about fifty meters he seemed to straighten up and pick a destination, somewhere on the opposite side of the prison complex, for he headed along the fence as if looking for a way around.

"I'm afraid we've ruined his trip," Sibroillo said.

"I can't say that makes me unhappy," Dujuv said.

"I didn't say I was unhappy. I said I was afraid. A powerful idiot is still powerful."

"And an idiot."

"Stipulated."

They decided that the simplest procedure, since it was likely that their escape would not be detected for some hours (unless Waynong made some fresh mess, in which case with any luck he would draw off the pursuit toward himself), would be to walk across the desert to the nearest Pertrans line and simply take a long-range taxi (expensive, but they were all on expense accounts after all) to Freehold, the capital of Magenta Yellow Amber Cyan, about forty kilometers away. But after they had walked no more than two hundred meters, Shadow on the Frost said, "I am struck by a thought."

He stood still in the bright Phobos-light, his silhouette like a scraggly feathered monument to an extraordinarily ugly philosopher.

"What is it?" Dujuv asked, after a long pause.

"Should we not proceed at once to resteal the lifelog? It would wipe out every blot on all our honor, accomplish the mission's main objective, incidentally prevent a positive outcome for Clarbo Waynong—"

"There's a lot to like about the idea," Jak admitted.

Sibroillo said, "And since we have to keep our purses silent, we can always claim we could get no orders and just misjudged what their priorities were. Shadow, you are utterly right. Shame on me for not having thought of it myself. It's quite possible that nobody even knows we've escaped yet. There will never be another chance as good as this one—it's almost as good as the one we threw away earlier tonight."

"Precisely," Shadow said. "Surprise. Probably our last chance for it. A great human thinker once said that the first punch is worth fifteen kilos. An unexpected kick in the head from behind is beyond price."

Dujuv clapped his hands together softly, and clicked his tongue with approval. "Toktru masen! How soon can we hit them? And do we know where they're keeping the lifelog?"

"On the Princess's yacht," Gweshira said.

"How do you know that?" Jak asked.

His uncle's demmy shrugged. "Where would *she* most prefer it to be? And did you see the way the King and the Prince were looking at her? Allow another hour for her to work on them, since, and where does the Nakasen lifelog *have* to be?"

Jak winced as he nodded. It made painful sense. "The landing field is an hour's walk, going around Magnificiti. None of us dares use a purse or our credit. Is there any way to steal transportation or spoof a taxi?"

No one had any ideas, so they started walking. Phobos, which circles Mars faster than the planet rotates, hurtled across the sky above them, waning as it went. It was halfway down toward the east, and they were most of the way to the landing field, when Sibroillo drifted back to walk beside Jak. For a while he said nothing, just walking beside his nephew as if they were out for a companionable stroll together. It made Jak think how constantly he had been with Sib when he was younger, and how much of what he thought was things his uncle had told him. It felt strange to be on his own, an adult, in command, and yet have the gaunt, goateed old man striding along beside him, as vigorous as ever and yet as if returned from a time trip to the ancient world.

Finally Sib spoke. "I imagine you are wondering how I feel about following the sword, when the sword follows an idiot."

"Well, toktru, you silly old gwont. Especially when the purpose seems to be for the sword to help the idiot take power, and to preserve the fool from the consequences of his folly."

Their boots crunched on the crusty, broken soil, and Sib was quiet. "Sometimes the right action is to show deference to a fool."

"Um, sir," Dujuv said, "I've learned a lot from you over the years, and I have a lot of respect for things you say, um . . ."

"Well, Dujuv," he said, his voice soft, a little raspy with his two hundred years, but calm and confident as if it were his voice that called the dark hills in the distance into being. After a few steps, he began again. "Well, then, let me try to explain it. I know that it seems as if the world would be a much more reasonable place if we didn't have to look after the arbitrary privileges of well-born fools. I felt that way myself for, oh, I don't know, about a week. When I was about twenty. But look at every time human beings have tried being 'reasonable'—the periods when people were trying to be equal and make sure everyone got taken care of.

"There were some whole centuries like that in Late Medieval times. And the result was invariable—malaise, ennui, art that petered out into experiments in meaninglessness, religion that demanded nothing of people but vague good intentions, wages so high that anyone could get into the best places, wars that dragged on forever, politics like one vast rug market, and a population so demoralized that you couldn't get it to *do* much of anything *about* much of anything. One disaster after another as the human soul rotted away.

"I know your hobby is reading ancient languages. Look up 'leisure class,' 'welfare state,' or 'consumer society.' You can see what the absence of real leadership does to people."

"Well, I notice what the absence of Waynong's leadership is doing to us," Jak ventured.

Sib laughed. "All right. Very fair, very fair." He chuckled again. "Very nearly the perfect retort. Yet you know as well as I do that if—as you suggested to your superiors, Jak—we had just sent Dujuv (with perhaps Xlini Copermisr) to acquire the lifelog, it would all be done by now, there would be no noise of any kind about it, and in consequence there would be no glory, no achievement, nothing to say other than 'that's taken care of.' The biggest religious event of the last few hundred years, marked by a procedure as ordinary as checking a thumbprint for a visa."

"What's wrong with that?" Dujuv asked.

"Shouldn't history arrive with a little more . . . fanfare?"

"I'd like it to arrive gently," Dujuv said.

"No glory, no struggle, no challenge? Everything run smoothly and neatly by nice gray people in simple gray buildings? You'd really prefer that to all the color and glory of life?"

Shadow on the Frost coughed; he had been walking beside Jak for some time, listening intently, his silhouette in Phobos's light rather like a basketball player wearing a bunny suit. "We Rubahy would say that one of the best things in life is going on a stupid, wrongheaded, needless mission, especially one plagued with bad leadership and worse luck. To succeed in the circumstances—oh, now, *that* is honor. Futility and having nothing at stake means you don't have recourse to the sort of courage that derives from the trivial circumstance that things are deeply important or that a lot is depending on you. One of our Rubahy arms masters taught: 'Anyone can be brave, standing and dying for the honor of his kin-groups and the reputation of his affinity-groups; a hero will risk his life to defend a single feather on a disliked stranger.'"

"Beautiful," Sib said.

"Toktru insane," Dujuv said.

They trudged on over the Martian desert in silence, toward the landing field.

"I am having some thoughts about this operation," Shadow said. "Let's do it right this time. That will be the last thing they are expecting of us."

Everyone laughed, and after a moment the Rubahy began to make a noise like bubbles rising in a metal bucket. "It is good to be with friends who appreciate a joke. But this was what I believe your species calls a truth spoken in jest. We really should try to do this well. What I had in mind was a real, genuine, big diversion, followed by grabbing the lifelog and running like bunnies."

Sib grunted. "Elementary—which is why it will be so embarrassing if we don't get it right."

Jak said, "All right, so . . . what's the simplest thing we can do? Send most of the party somewhere to make a lot of noise and cause a lot of excitement, while a couple of us go in and grab."

"Me and Shadow for going in and grabbing," Dujuv said. "Strength, speed, and skill, you know. And if it's in the Princess's yacht, it will be in her safe, in her bedroom. That means it's right where they're best prepared to defend it. So you need a *big* diversion that will pull off the whole launch crew."

"How big?" Pikia asked.

"Big as possible," Dujuv said. "The kind of thing that would make someone not notice a brass band in gorilla suits and tutus. Why? Do you have an idea?"

"Well, in the first place, isn't that the Princess's yacht sitting in that launch cradle? And you can just bet she has some good reason to have it all fueled up and ready to go, masen? Which means if she takes it into her mind to just take that lifelog and run—"

"That has to be their main worry," Jak said. "I think I see where you're going. So figure Shyf and Witerio don't trust each other at all; the ship's on the cradle, so it could take off any instant, but on the other hand Witerio could probably wreck it, fairly harmlessly, just by having the cradle drop suddenly—and then his troops would be more than enough to take the lifelog back. So both sides are sitting there watching each other, fingers on the buttons, all set to hit or run or both. Anything could start right now."

"Exactly what I was thinking," Pikia said. "Have you ever seen a double-sided snipe hunt? . . . you tell one group that snipe are attracted by whistling and you can hear them coming when they thump the ground; you tell the other group that they are attracted by thumping the ground, and they whistle as they approach. Then you just put the two groups near each other." She shrugged, a lopsided-looking gesture because of what had happened to her hair. "So by analogy . . ."

CHAPTER 10

A Panty Raid Is Not Standard Procedure

They were behind the ridgeline of an anchored dune that looked down on Red Amber Magenta Green's landing field, across the landing linducer and toward the cradles. Their purses were on again, but under strict orders to stay silent, both acoustically and electronically, so that each purse functioned solely as a notepad and a watch.

Phobos was now well down the sky toward the east, waning as it approached the sun that would rise in just under two hours. Pikia's plan, as modified by Shadow, Sib, and Gweshira, would take just about an hour to execute, leaving them an hour of darkness to help their escape. With luck, it would be just enough.

Always assuming that we are trying to steal the lifelog from the right place, Jak added to himself. *But no question, Cyx had that look about him, and Shyf looked like she'd set the hook pretty firmly. And if there's anyplace she'd want it, it would be on her personal launch.*

Three hundred meters to the southeast, the local Pertrans service crossed the landing track, passing through an underpass. To the left of the underpass was the quai where they had come in and where Shyf had arrived. Beyond the quai, the landing track bent around to become an ordinary heavy-duty linducer track, curving around to deliver spacecraft, suburbs, and aircraft to the hangar, the marshaling loop, and the cradles.

Directly behind the quai, the main hangar rose 350 meters above the field, and stretched almost a half kilometer long. It hid most of the field from them; they were relying on everyone's memory, afraid to call in satellite pictures or to look up maps, lest their purses' transmissions give them away. Studded with warning lights and lighted windows, the top of the tower, eight hundred meters above the desert below, reached far above the hangar. The hangar itself was dark and quiet, all its big doors closed.

Aside from the control tower and the hangar, two other features were visible. Just to the right of the control tower, looking much shorter because it was only about half as high and because it was much farther away, the monitor tower— the spaceport's central firefighting facility—stood like a castle turret from some medieval adventure viv, the kind of place you expected to see standing off an assault by armored knights in Helicopters. Under 15X magnification, the monitors themselves—the giant waterguns on the rooftop—were clearly visible.

The last feature was their goal. Cradles One and Three must be in down position, for they were not visible over the hangar or the ridgelines, but just to the right of the hangar, peeking over the ridge, was the raised tip of Cradle Two, in the up position. And since the next commercial flight out of the spaceport was more than a day away, the logical guess was that the reason Cradle Two was up was because it contained the Princess's yacht; as Gweshira had pointed out, Shyf could not trust her new ally any more than Witerio could trust her, so undoubtedly she had insisted on being poised and fueled for takeoff, he had insisted that the cradle be down and the tanks empty, and the bluest eyes had won.

A launch cradle was not an absolute necessity, but when one was available it could save as much as a third of the on-board fuel for takeoffs from a planetary surface. Physically, the cradle was a broad trough, rounded at one end and open on the other, about two hundred meters long by sixty wide and sixty deep, with linducer track running down its center and all the way up the curving back. When the cradle was tilted to vertical, a ship moving on linducers could climb into the back of the cradle; lowering the cradle to horizontal made it easy to bring the ship forward for maintenance and outfitting. To be ready for launch, the cradle was again tipped up and rotated to point into the correct trajectory; at the moment of launch, a surge through the linducers would hurl the ship forward and out the open end, taking the place of a booster stage.

Cradle Two was motionless and pointed upward at about a sixty-degree angle, turned slightly away from them—the position for a fast launch into equatorial orbit, exactly what would be needed for a quick getaway and rendezvous with *Rufus Karrinynya*.

It was impossible to see through the hangar, but "If I remember right," Jak said, "the fuel tanks are on the far side of the cradles, from where we're sitting."

"That's what I remember too," Dujuv said. "If not, I guess we'll have to make something up. My team is the only one that will be affected if they're on this side of the cradles."

"Anyone else remember anything about the lay of the land?" Jak asked. Xlini Copermisr shrugged slightly. "Usually *Splendor One*, which is a really ancient warshuttle (four hundred years if it's a day) and also happens to be the entire Spatial of Red Amber Magenta Green, is on the marshaling loop for Cradle One. Sometimes it's on the main marshaling loop, but since that's where they've got *John Carter* bottled up, I don't imagine they're doing that right now."

"If it's there," Pikia said, "then I know what I'm going to do for my part of the op." She sketched it quickly for them, and they all nodded vigorously. Jak, Sibroillo, and Pikia had the most improvisational parts of the plan; each of them was supposed to run to a particular location and, at the right time, make the sort of noise and chaos that would cause the Princess's yacht to unbutton and give Dujuv and Shadow a chance to get into it in the confusion.

"That's a first-rate bit of confusion you have in mind," Sibroillo said when she had explained. "And as Jak has probably quoted my saying, many times, always sow as much confusion as possible." Actually Jak seldom quoted Sib at all, and never on that point, because every time he had taken the advice himself, it had led to disaster. But Pikia had the good sense to nod eagerly, as if she'd heard it many times. Her gift for deceiving the old gwont was nearly equal to Jak's own; he was glad for the thousandth time to have her along.

"Well," she said, "so there's at least a tentative scheme for causing confusion . . . everyone else has an assignment . . . and somewhere to be once it's completed . . . everyone have the notes they need?" Everyone nodded. "Are we at the point—"

"Mmmph," Jak said. "I'm going to be obsessively cautious and just recheck the basic things that can go wrong. One, the lifelog's not on the launch. In that case, everyone just runs for it, right? Split up and go any way that seems good to you. Two, the Princess's beanies and crew might decide they're safer buttoned up than bringing the thing down. So if you get a chance, anyone, at any point, hit the cradle machinery, because it safeties to the down position, and once it does that they at least aren't going anywhere, and it might help them to think they want to sortie. Three, we're all tired, easily confused, easily fixated. Resist that. We've got practically no intelligence and no time to reconnoiter. So be alert and keep making it up, because any idea that's more than a few minutes old might already be past its expiration date, masen?"

"Toktru," Dujuv said.

"Any other issues I haven't covered?"

Shadow ahemed and said, "Just to make sure that I understand your customs . . . there is good reason to avoid lethal force when we can, perhaps to damage only property, and to surrender if trapped or wounded?"

Xlini Copermisr said, "Exactly right. If you're captured they'll just put you in jail till the Hive can transmit the ransom for your release. You don't want your captors to have any reason to be mad at you if you can help it. So try to keep it all on the level of a major act of vandalism, not war."

Shadow made a low, ululating whistle, very softly—the equivalent of a human tongue click, a noise of slight frustration and exasperation. "All right, but this is severely limiting the chances for any real gain in honor."

"It's a sacrifice I am forced to ask of my oath-friend," Jak said. Shadow bowed his head gravely, accepting the request in that context.

"All right, has anyone else thought of any other problem?"

"You're sure you can keep up?" Dujuv asked Pikia.

"I ran cross-country in the All-Martian Gen School Meet last year. Make sure *you* can keep up with *me*."

"All right, you will be running with a panth and Rubahy, you know. Not everyone can."

"I'm not everyone."

"Toktru masen. That was my last worry, Jak."

"Best to get it rolling," Gweshira said. "We'll want as much as we can get of that last hour of darkness for fleeing, no matter how this comes out."

"All right," Jak said. "Then tee will equal zero in . . . two minutes?"

"Five," Sib said, "I need to go around the back of a dune for a second. I swear to Nakasen and every Principle there is, when they're doling out my organs, I pity whoever gets my bladder. If it weren't for the alternative, nobody would ever want to live to be two hundred."

As Jak and Sib trotted over the ridgeline of the third and last anchored dune, Jak glanced to his right; far off, something flickered for just an instant, crossing the ridgeline perhaps half a kilometer farther west. *Probably Dujuv, Shadow and Pikia—at least they go that far.*

Jak turned to look at the broad expanse of the Red Amber Magenta Green landing field in front of him. At least, from this much better vantage point, he could see that collectively they had been right in what they remembered: the sixty-meter spheres that were tanks of hot-jet fuel were south of the cradles they served, the main marshaling loop where *John Carter* was trapped between suburbs was indeed south of the main hangar and east of the tower, and as Xlini had said it would be, *Splendor One* sat on the smaller marshaling loop beside Cradle One. As soon as they were safely back in the shadows and off the ridgeline, Jak pointed that out to Sib.

"Good, Pikia will do something with that," Sib said. "Weehu. I can still run a few kilometers, but it's a bigger deal than it used to be. Where to now?"

"I'd say we run for that underpass where the Pertrans dives under the heavy-linducer line that comes out of the main hangar. We'll have to pop over the landing linducer, but we'd have to no matter what, and they're probably not on alert. We can squat under the underpass and check out the ground, and then it's a short dash for you to the control tower and me to the warshuttle. I don't see any other good hiding place that close."

"Toktru." The older man bent for a minute and sucked in a deep lungful of the good Martian night air; the Chryse Bay, sixty kilometers away, tended to send warm moist air flowing into this part of the Harmless Zone after midnight every night. Sibroillo coughed twice and added, "Well, I'll have to remember not to do anything like this on my *three* hundredth birthday trip."

It was easy running down the side of the old dune. They blazed across the flat ground, and went up the embankment of the landing linducer in one swift, smooth, silent rush. They leapt onto the half-meter high concrete track that housed the linducers, across the shiny metallic slot, and down the other side, neatly and cleanly. They ran onto the main operations area, toward now-setting Phobos, a narrow, lumpy crescent bowed toward the eastern horizon as it rushed on to meet the sun.

In less than two minutes since they had looked from the top of the dune, Jak and his uncle were squatting in the Pertrans underpass. Low gravity and a very high oxygen content worked their customary miracles; both men were recovered in a very short time. "Well," Sib said, "I see the main door to the control tower, and when you don't know how to get in—"

" 'Always barge in through the front door.' I could never forget that one, Uncle Sib. I'll be muttering it on my deathbed. Don't embarrass me with your part of the mission, you silly old gwont."

"Don't screw up as much as I expect you to, you insolent puppy."

They shook hands.

Jak trotted along the base of the embankment of the heavy-load linducer line, letting it lead him into the main marshaling loop. Sib would be in the control tower in no time, and the more noise Jak could make at the warshuttle, the safer his uncle would be at the tower.

Dujuv squatted on his heels beside Shadow on the Frost, who stood perfectly still. They were in the dark, west-reaching shadow behind the big fuel sphere for Cradle Two, and for the moment they were about as out of the action as it was possible to be.

Shadow's feathered, two-thumbed hand dropped onto Dujuv's shoulder to get his attention; one long articulated finger pointed toward the stretched silvery ellipsoid of *Splendor One,* just south of them, where it rested behind Cradle One. A lighted square had appeared on the side; in it stood a human figure, talking to another one, half in darkness. Then there was a flurry of movement, the guard tumbled down the ramp, and the square of light winked out. Pikia had gotten in.

*   *   *

When the door opened on the side of *Splendor One,* Pikia had her best "I'm a helpless little girl and I need a nice man to help me" smile glued on tight. She was slightly out of practice because it didn't work on Dujuv or Jak and she wouldn't have given it to Clarbo Waynong in any circumstances, but the guard seemed to respond the way most male teachers and pokheets did; he tried to appear gruff and in fact his eyes twinkled as he said, "What can I do for you, miss?"

"I must have gotten off at the wrong Pertrans station, and I thought this was where the Pertrans line would be for me to get back to Magnificiti, and I've been walking just toktru forever, and now that I'm here I don't see any Pertrans station—"

"Oh, you can always just get back on anyplace you got off, and tell the Pertrans car where you want to go, and it will figure everything out for you," the guard said. He looked to be about fifty, his face unlined and his body firm and strong, but self-assured; he might have been an advertisement for longevity drugs, especially with that beaming, stupid, confident smile.

"You can *do* that?" Pikia tried to sound amazed; she didn't think much of her act, but the guard seemed to be less of a critic.

"Toktru masen. That's how it works. Now, there's a Pertrans station right over there—"

"Over where?" She turned her back to him, staring wildly everywhere except where he had pointed, clasping her hands in front of herself like a medieval movie actor portraying confusion and helplessness.

"See that low building? That's the bunker for Cradle

One. Now, next to it—" He pointed over her shoulder. She tensed her clasped hands against each other.

"Next to the big curvy thing?"

He took a half step and extended his arm more emphatically. "Right, toktru, right there where—"

She let her tensed hands fly apart and dropped into a deep knee bend. Her right fist flew away, curving low and back, to hammer the guard's scrotum against his pubic bone; she kept contact as she opened her hand and turned her wrist, taking a deep forceful grip. As the guard pitched forward with a gasp of pain, his jaw met the fast-rising heel of Pikia's left hand, and his head flew back, putting him into an awkward position—bending over while standing on his toes with his head up. She caught his extended wrist in front of her, stood on one leg while thrusting back with the other, and whipped her hands in a big forward circle. He went whirling over her hip, led by the wrist and pulled by the balls, sailing high into the air in the light Martian gravity, then falling to the base of the ramp in disorderly thrashing agony.

Pikia did not see that rough landing; she had already slipped in through the open door and pushed the emergency close. She checked the guard's display; it showed that there was no one else aboard tonight. She had the flagship of Red Amber Magenta Green's Spatial entirely to herself. Taking a few good guesses, and using the skills that were the reason her school records held high scores in several courses she had never taken, she made a few changes, locking out the rest of the world and opening the cockpit.

By the time that muffled thuds and shouted threats and insults were coming through the sealed door, Pikia was comfortably seated in the captain's chair in the worryball, gobbling a ration pack and a bulb of coffee, watching Fuel Tank One through the monitors.

Not bad for my first time in action, she thought, *and I'm starting even younger than Jak did. Now if Jak does his part soon, and Sib is as ready as I am, there will have been some point to it besides beating up one poor guard.* She plugged her purse into the console through the universal jack. Her up-to-date purse cut through the centuries-old security system like a red-hot wire through snow; in a few seconds she would be able to do anything she wanted. She found Red Amber Magenta Green's standard Spatial terminology guide, and the voiceprints for the crew, and knew that now she had struck pure gold.

The guard was bored stiff; if it weren't for the honor of being here, he'd rather have been home, getting drunk and working through what he thought was the finest collection of viv pornography, certainly in Magnificiti, probably in the Harmless Zone, possibly in the solar system. (He was wrong; it was in fact a mediocre collection, though perfectly aimed at his peculiar and limited tastes.) As a second son of minor *noblesse de robe,* he had to hang about the court of the Splendor, which meant he had to have this job. If his father or either of his aunts had been just slightly higher in rank, he would at least not have to have a night shift, or could be excused the next day from morning court functions, but there was no such luck in his life.

Many of the nobility, faced with performing minor jobs as guards, ceremonial unit officers, factotums, ministers for nonexistent affairs, and so forth, made a show of making the job as real as possible, behaving as if it mattered and could only be done by a well-qualified live human being.

This guard was not one of those people. He was eighty years old but looked like a badly preserved 140, not having kept up with enough exercise for his doctors to be able to give him the stronger rejuvenation drugs, which were dangerous to the sedentary. His kitchen automatically supplemented his diet with the usual array of necessary trace chemicals, but nothing could overcome his love of sweet and gooey food, or his tendency, once he started a bottle, to finish three more. He did not greatly care; he was bored with life, but having nothing to do with the life he had been given, he had donated it, grudgingly, to family affairs, and though he would rather not have been here standing about uselessly while robots did his job, there was also nowhere else he had any real desire to be.

It was thus particularly unfair that no robot had been provided to do the actual fighting, shouting, warning, or improvising that a real guard might have done, and that when a few seconds of real work turned up, the guard was bored, sleepy, and dyspeptic. The door covering the entrance to the control tower dilated with a grinding *tchunk!* indicating that repairs were in the hands of people every bit as concerned about their duties as this guard was about his.

Since there had been no alert or bell, the guard looked up in some surprise and irritation and said "Can I help—" before Sibroillo Jinnaka's sharp rising punch knocked him out. He didn't know it then, but aside from launching him backward off the floor and into a corner, it would launch him as a dinner guest for the next few months as well.

Meanwhile, Sibroillo helped himself to the guard's slug-pistol and put his purse to the job of hacking the elevator to the top, silently if possible, but within three minutes no matter what. He was on schedule but only just.

* * *

As Jak dashed toward the landing field's main marshaling loop, where *John Carter* was parked, he raised his purse to his mouth and said, "Please check purely local, no data access calls. Do we have copies of universal access codes that will get us onto *John Carter*?"

"We do; Hive Intel gave us a full set of universals. You can access nuclear weapons if *Carter* is carrying them."

"Thank you. Please have all relevant codes available for instant use." and Jak put his head down and ran harder; there was really nowhere to hide out here, especially since if anyone was watching, and Jak had no way of knowing from what direction or angle. Best to just get through the vulnerable zone as quickly as possible.

The purse supplied the right code at a rear access door. Though Red Amber Magenta Green had put a prize crew on board, they had not bothered to change the locks, and Jak's purse had no trouble overriding the simple software-based alarm. In less than a minute more, the purse had cleared and recaptured the system, a tribute more to the ineptitude and low budget of a Harmless Zone army than to Jak's special skill or the purse's capability.

Now that *John Carter* was working for the Hive again, it took only a moment for Jak to determine that there were three guards on board—one in the cockpit and the other two sacked out on bunks in the VIP suite. He slipped down the corridor, silent and ready, his way shown by the glowing blue outlines in the goggles he had plugged into his purse, as he passed through the utterly dark corridors as confidently as if it had been in daylight. He waited outside the door until he was sure he knew what he would find on the other side; according to the only active computer in the worryball, the guard was playing with a flight simulator program, and if he or she was facing the screen, would be facing away from this door. Jak cued his purse to go in two seconds, and stepped close to the door.

It dilated abruptly. In one-third g, Jak reached the training pilot's chair in a single leap and his left hand had locked on to the guard's viv helmet before the guard reacted. He drove the guard's head forward and to the side, then slammed three quick, brutal punches into the side of the neck.

Jak felt him spasm, choke, gasp, and go limp. He yanked the guard's laser pistol free from its holster (a laser pistol in the Harmless Zone? Interesting . . . the man was a war criminal), and tore the guard's slug-rifle from his shoulder, letting the limp guard fall to the floor in a barely struggling heap, well on his way to unconsciousness—*no, her way, it's a small woman,* Jak realized.

Well, whatever. He jerked her viv helmet off, probably guaranteeing the woman a sore neck, and kicked her once in the head to make certain. She fell over, hands and feet twitching, probably concussed. It probably hurt, but anyway the ambulance would be here in less than an hour, and Uncle Sib had always said the leading cause of injuries was being in the wrong place at the wrong time.

Jak used the captain's override to open the worryball's small weapons locker. He got out three stunners; intended for riot control, and not much good for any other purpose, each stunner was a single-shot device and they had to be in contact with the skin above the neck to work as intended.

Jak killed lights all over the ship and turned on sound suppression. He waited till he was sure that the other two guards were still asleep. Then he slipped into the VIP suites, clapped the stunner to the forehead of each sleeping guard in turn, and sent them under with the maximum dose.

Back at the cockpit, when he turned on the lights, he found the first guard had rolled over and gotten her hands under her, and was trying to push up from the deck, without much success. He squatted down in front of her. Her eyes widened in fear. "Look," Jak said quietly, "you're hurt pretty bad and you can't do a thing for yourself or your nation right now, masen?"

The woman was probably only a year or so older than Pikia. Bruises were already coming up on her face and neck. Tears of pain ran down her cheeks to join the snot below her nose. "I guess I can't," she admitted.

"Well, I can't parole you. I can tie you up, which will be uncomfortable, or give you a light stun, which wouldn't be good for you with the concussion I already gave you. Or I guess I could kick you in the head again, but I'd hate it, and you'd hate it more."

She seemed to be thinking as hard as she could, but it just wasn't coming fast. After a second she asked, "Can you lock me in the brig? After you release the prisoner that's in there?"

Jak checked his purse and discovered that there was a prisoner in the brig, right enough; probably some crewman left behind for one reason or another, or maybe it was the captain being held separately from his officers. In any case, an extra hand would be welcome, and locking the guard in the brig seemed much more reasonable than hurting her further, so Jak helped her to her feet and guided her down the corridor, supporting her with one arm while keeping his hand on the pistol in case all this was a trick.

He put her in brig cell number two and made sure she lay

facedown so that she wouldn't choke if she vomited; he hooked her to a medical monitor so that if anything went suddenly, seriously wrong, he and the ambulances would know at once. Then he locked her in and unlocked brig unit number one, where the prisoner was.

When the door dilated, Jak was looking into the mildly startled face of Clarbo Waynong. "This is odd. My purse told me that they had suppressed it, and it couldn't call Hive Intel for help."

"This is purely an accident," Jak said grimly. "Follow me and try not to say or do anything else. I've got a mission to accomplish." He turned and left Clarbo Waynong sputtering something about needing to use the lavatory and the difficulty of getting organized on such short notice.

"Is your short-range patch into the worryball good from outside the warshuttle?" Jak asked his purse.

"Probably. A test will be necessary to be sure."

"Open the weapons locker nearest me." Jak pulled out charge blocks, three slug rifles, and half a dozen hand weapons, plus a sling-bag. The equipment was truly primitive stuff—the firearms weren't even equipped to identify the user and would work for the enemy as easily as for your own side—but it was a treaty violation to carry anything any better into the Harmless Zone. He packed them into the sling-bag and hung it over his shoulder. If he could rejoin his party, at least they would all be adequately armed.

He was two steps from the exit when he heard footsteps, and glanced back to see Clarbo Waynong catching up with him, that perfect hair still somehow not the least bit mussed, the resolute jaw still set, and to all appearances, not tired in the least. "So, whatever your plan is, it seems to be working, so just let me know what my part is and I'll be happy to—"

Jak kept walking down the boarding ramp. "Still in contact over the short range?" he asked his purse.

"Perfectly."

"All right, then, when I say 'Mark,' patch me through to the highest officer of the Red Amber Magenta Green military that you can find. Preferably one we can wake up on his home com. Override whatever his alert protocols are and sound a siren on maximum volume. Send in clear. Make sure there's some echo noise coming out of *John Carter* so that anyone with any equipment at all can confirm the origin.

"When I say 'Next message,' switch over to any contact you can find on *Splendor One,* same procedures and protocol. When I say 'Next message' after that, call up the main room of the control tower, same procedures and protocol. Then when I say 'Next message' after *that,* get me the highest-ranking person you can on the Princess of Greenworld's personal launch. Is that coherent?"

"Got it."

"Can you control any of the warshuttle's guns or lasers?"

"Yes, but none of them is loaded and they're all blocked from reload or recharge."

"All right, then, When I say 'Mark,' we'll start the procedure."

Waynong looked as if he wanted to say something but could not quite imagine what.

Jak stared at him, hoping to make his gaze intimidating. "The plan needs you to stay absolutely silent for the next couple of minutes, while I make these calls and do some shooting. Then when I run, follow me."

"All right." Was it possible that the young patrician even sounded a tiny bit chastened?

Jak looked out from the boarding ramp to the rest of the landscape. To the southwest, Cradle Two aimed up at the sky, and somewhere in it, presumably, was the Princess's yacht. Next to the cradle sat the big sphere of the fuel tank; somewhere behind that, Dujuv and Shadow would be crouching right now. Far beyond that, almost a third of a kilometer, lay Cradle One and its fuel tank, with the low round bulk of *Splendor One* just showing on the small marshaling loop above; he hoped that Pikia was safely inside *Splendor One*. Then he shrugged and lifted his purse to his face. "Mark."

Half a second later, a panicked voice, just yanked from sleep into blurry alertness, shouted "What?"

"This is Captain Tror Adlongongu of *John Carter*. Per your orders, we are proceeding to recapture the lifelog from the Greenworld delegation, and we have brought the Princess's yacht under fire." Jak pointed with his laser pistol and put several bright spots on Cradle Two. "We are proceeding as you ordered and we will also polish the sled dog with bathtub wax as soon as the wrenches have been cooked in baby oil. I've never liked you but I like having sex with your family. Sorry, you're breaking up—Next message."

"Was that siren necessary?" Pikia's voice had all the fury of someone who had been startled into dropping a third of a milk shake onto her pants.

"Sorry. All right, this is the Sixth Hive Rangers. We're preparing to storm that launch on Cradle Two. Please lay down covering fire."

The side of *Splendor One* erupted with spattering sparks; it took Jak a moment to realize that those were the riot-protection guns, hurling heavy soft bean-bag rounds at moderate speeds but a very high rate of fire. As always, Pikia had tinkered a bit and improved things from the original plan; the bag rounds would probably not cause anyone any serious injury, but they would sound like cracks of doom on the fuselage of the Princess's yacht.

"Use default ring on this next one," Jak told his purse. "Next message."

"Control tower," Sib's voice said.

"This is *Splendor One*. We are under attack by beanies from the Princess of Greenworld's launch. We're taking heavy casualties, and we're completely unable to—never mind, just send over a clean shirt and six pizzas! Everything is on fire, do you hear me, everything is on fire! Naked! Completely naked! Next message."

"Identify yourself—" It was Shyf's voice, and she didn't sound happy. That siren effect must be impressive.

Jak felt his gut sink and roll over; deliberately annoying her was almost out of his emotional reach, as the conditioning was still very strong. "I saw that dress you wore tonight. It makes you look fat." He hung up and stepped to the side. He sighted on the fuel tank for Cradle One and gave it a max-duration, max-power shot from his laser pistol.

Flames burst from the tank and soared upward. Hot-jet fuel was not explosive; its knotted and balled molecules required catalysis to unlock and expand them in the reaction that drove rockets. But though more inclined to smolder than to flare, it was combustible in high-oxygen Martian air, and at least as dangerous as burning salad oil.

"What was that for?" Waynong asked.

Jak held up a hand for silence and said to his purse, "All right, patch into general communications traffic via the cockpit center, and make sure anything you send or receive looks like it's passing through there."

"Done."

"Scan for anything of interest, switch every ten seconds."

Pikia's voice came through, ordering nonexistent units of the Red Amber Magenta Green army to seize the Princess's yacht, the control tower, the main marshaling loop, the Royal Palace in Magnificiti, and a party of thieves escaping to the west with the lifelog. Sib's voice came on, clearing *Splendor One* for launch, ordering Cradle Two lowered, and announcing that five Hive warshuttles were landing on the field, in opposed-combat mode, and had opened fire on the fuel tanks. Then there was more of Pikia, screaming for the monitor tower to get water on Fuel Tank Three at once (it was One that was burning).

Jak clicked his communications on and hailed the nonexistent warshuttles, bounced over to demand of the monitor tower why they hadn't put out the fire on Tank Three yet, and gave orders to a platoon of Hive beanies to seize *Splendor One* and then proceed to the Royal Palace. He switched his laser pistol to stutter-burst and swung it back and forth across the supports and operating machinery for Cradle Two, producing a gratifying burst of flares, sparks, and shrieks of breaking metal. The cradle slumped slightly to the side, and then the emergency systems cut in and lowered it. The Princess wouldn't be going anywhere tonight.

"Use your purse to call up Prince Cyx," Jak said to Waynong.

Waynong told his purse to get Cyx. "He's on maximum privacy."

"Tell your purse to use its override software. Then repeat after me," Jak said.

Waynong did and looked up expectantly. Faintly, Jak heard the slurred voice of Prince Cyx demanding to know what this was about. Jak nodded and said, "Oh, hello, Cyxy—"

" 'Oh, hello, Cyxy—' "

"Just wanted to call you up to say that I fucked her first, and now I've got a nasty dose of clap."

In a state of utter bewilderment, Waynong repeated.

"Better wipe it down good. By the way, we're taking that old lifelog thing with us, launching in two minutes," Jak added.

Waynong looked confused, but after he had repeated Jak's words the slow spread of comprehension on Waynong's face seemed to release Jak from any need for an explanation. Cyx's voice was still shouting, faintly, through Waynong's purse.

"Now hang up."

Waynong did.

Jak clicked back over to general communications and found Pikia shouting that she was trapped in the burning *Splendor One* surrounded by Greenworld beanies and couldn't hold out much longer, and Sib calling the Royal Palace to demand to know whether or not the King was still alive, and if so, what they were going to do about it. On another channel, Princess Shyf was shouting that she had been insulted and that the sudden lowering of the cradle had spilled her bath all over her private quarters. He fought back the irrational desire to call her up and comfort her, and instead told her that a crew of men with mops and buckets would be coming in right away.

"I'm not dressed yet," she said. "Tell them to wait two minutes—"

"It's all right, they don't care how fat you are," Jak said, and clicked over to another channel, ordering Pikia to surrender the lifelog and evacuate *Splendor One* before it was blown up. Then he called the monitor tower and asked them what was wrong with them, putting water on Cradle Three when it was Fuel Tank Two that was burning.

His purse said, "Endpoint One reached," and Jak, motioning Waynong to follow, ran toward the monitor tower. Endpoint One meant that the first part of the operation was over: the Princess's yacht was opening its doors.

The monitor tower was only about two hundred meters high, much lower than the control tower; it had fire monitors all up its length, and a large sealed turret at the top studded with more monitors. Jak ran straight for its single entrance, the sling-bag of weapons clattering on his back. Not trying for any subtlety or deception—time was far too important—he used his laser pistol to cut a large circular hole in the door, and lunged through.

The guard inside was unarmed; it had probably never occurred to anyone that anybody would ever want to seize a monitor tower. Jak stepped through, blocked the guard's tentatively reaching right hand, turned his wrist in a monkey paw around the guard's forearm, yanked him off balance, clapped his hand to the back of the man's neck, and slammed his elbow forward into the startled man's face. He swept the stunned guard's feet from under him, stepped over him, and jumped into the elevator, telling his purse, "Hack this thing and get me to the top, *now*. And I want full control of all building functions by the time I get there."

Sadly, Clarbo Waynong at least had enough presence of mind to follow Jak into the elevator.

"That wasn't exactly . . . sportsmanlike, was it?"

"That's why it worked," Jak said.

"Oh."

"Not everything unsportsmanlike works," Jak hastened to add, visions of what Clarbo might do (if he raised that to a general rule) suddenly alarming him. "But for example—"

The elevator door popped open at the top. Jak had to give the technician some points for courage and presence of mind—he came through the door already jabbing with the broom handle. Jak's Disciplines-trained reflexes took over; he thrust downward with crossed forearms, pushing the broom handle to the side. The tech whipped the handle downward and brought the broom end over toward Jak's face; Jak caught the broom at the midpoint where the technician gripped it, yanked hard to the side, and leg-swept; the man staggered and lost his grip on the broom. Jak spun it to rap his opponent smartly on the forehead, let the tip slide down over the mouth and nose (that must have hurt), and poked the man hard in the solar plexus; he fell backward with a groan, into a sitting position, and Jak snap-kicked him in the forehead, thudding the back of his head against the wall. The tech lay crumpled as Jak turned to see two more techs, both clearly just waking from a doze in their chairs. Their eyes widened, and it took Jak half a second to realize that they were seeing a man carrying a personal arsenal on his back holding them at broom point.

"Pick that heet up and carry him into the elevator," Jak barked at them.

They grabbed their unconscious comrade and went into the elevator. "Take 'em to the bottom," Jak told his purse. There was a loud whoosh. "Highest safe speed."

"You should have told me that before I started," the purse complained.

"Are they hurt?"

"No, but they are not happy."

Jak turned back to the control and observation panels; none of it made any sense to him, so he asked his purse, "Can you give me an enlarged display of the area around the Princess's yacht?"

"From two to five power. Up to one hundred power if you're willing to lose some area."

"Five power, then."

One of the turret windows suddenly cleared and revealed an infrared display of the area. Jak watched for a long moment and then said, "There they go."

"There who go?" Waynong asked, still sounding as if he had only recently awakened from sleep.

"Dujuv and Shadow. Running for the door of the Princess's lander. Nothing else on feet moves as fast as those two and of course Shadow is seven feet tall and at a different body temperature." The two figures climbed the access ladders on the side of the cradle, bounded over the edges, and slid down on their bottoms as if on a giant playground slide. "All right," Jak said to his purse. "Do you have control of the monitors?"

"Yes."

"Leave the two that are watering down the Fuel Tank One fire in place—we don't want that to get out of control—but use every other monitor that will bear to wash out the space between Cradle Two and *Splendor One.* Including every side of the fuel tank you can see. Try to knock down as many running men as you can."

The thunder in the tower was about as loud as doom cracking at a motorcycle race, accompanied by an amplified million-piece brass band. The whole tower shook and the floor of the top turret glided perceptibly back and forth under their feet. Jak had to key into his purse—it could not hear him—and so it took some extra seconds to shut the water off. "How many monitors at full force was that?" Jak asked his purse.

"Not counting the two fighting the fuel tank fire, one hundred eleven."

"If you leave the two on the fire, how many can you put on the command deck of the control tower and on the nose of the Princess's yacht, combined? And how does that break out?"

"We can have forty-one on the Princess's yacht, one hundred six on the control tower, and another fifty-three that could hit either."

"All right, assemble a command to be called, um—'Hose 'em down.' On that command, allocate monitors as: Fifty on the Princess's yacht with thirty right on the nose and the rest scattered evenly over whatever fuselage you can hit. Fifty on the command deck of the control tower. Five monitors on each control tower door that you can hit. The rest of the monitors to play up and down the control tower at random. All at full on. Once you activate it, put in antitampering in the software to make it difficult or impossible for anyone but me to turn it off."

"All set up," the purse said, cheerfully.

The elevator door opened, and Jak turned to cover it. Sib stepped in with a merry salute. "You must have softened up that guard down there quite a bit. He was staggering around and tried to demand my identity, so I just gave him a quick kick and punch and he went down."

"I'm surprised he even got up. Duj and Shadow are inside the launch right now. I don't see much other diverting we can do until we know how it's going for them, so I'm just watching the launch with five-power magnification, since I also don't know what door they're going to come out of. Pikia's due here in another few minutes but she's such an overachiever I'm sure she'll be early. And it's just about half an hour till pickup."

"If you're reporting," the familiar patrician voice said, "I think I should be included in the report."

"Oh, yeah, Uncle Sib, I also accidentally rescued a prisoner."

Clarbo Waynong's presence registered on Sibroillo for the first time. To his credit, the old diplomat barely blinked. "Well, glad we got you out."

"No one is telling me what's going on," Waynong said, sounding like a man who really hopes he isn't whining.

Pikia had had time to grab a sling of slug throwers (since beam weapons were prohibited in the Harmless Zone, that was what there was to grab), a few thousand rounds of ammunition (it was good that ammo was about the size of a grain of rice), a fresh chocolate shake, and most of a large cup of coffee, when she decided that the sortie from the Princess's yacht was definitely coming this way. "Activate plan 'Bugger all' as soon as we leave the ship," she told her purse as she trotted toward the emergency hatch on the fuel tank side near the nose. "Open emergency hatch Front Right Four now."

"It's locked manually," the purse reported. "So are all other emergency ports."

"Nakasen's bleeding bung," she muttered, "I could've checked that, couldn't I?"

"You had about nine minutes in which to do so," her purse said, helpfully.

"Take your helpfulness level down by about—no, forget

it, keep helpfulness where it is." She sighed. It was hardly her purse's fault that she had assumed an emergency exit would not be locked. "How close are they?"

"Forty meters from the gangplank—"

"Activate 'Bugger all,' now. And find me a door you can open on this side of the ship."

She turned and ran down the passage; faintly, she could hear the outside loudspeakers demanding that the Greenworld guards throw down their weapons, telling them that they were covered by the combined arms of the Hive and the Splendor. The riot-protection guns opened up, not hurting anyone since all the guards were in armor, but undoubtedly making their helmets ring like gongs. Sure enough, there was the hiss and crackle of fighting lasers lashing into the old warshuttle's skin, and now the control room was anxiously calling for help from the Splendor's forces, identifying its attackers as being from Greenworld.

Each of the emergency hatches she passed was manually locked, and she didn't know the combination—a thought struck her. "Hey, purse, find out who's authorized to open each hatch, right now."

"Right now no one is on duty, so no one is."

"Sorry, modify command." She rounded a corner and found herself face-to-face with Kawib Presgano, who stared at her for a second, then leveled his slug thrower at her, laughing uproariously.

"Oh, Nakasen's hairy bag," he said, "now it all makes sense." He raised his purse to his face, keeping the pistol leveled at her. "All units. Everything connected with *Splendor One* is a diversion. Return to the Princess's yacht at once. Repeat, emphasized: break off all action and return to the Princess's yacht at once." He lowered his left hand and shook his head, seemingly in admiration. "I have to admit, that was a pretty good try, but it didn't work out, so come on along. We're very civilized about POWs and we might as well get you over to the launch early, so you can get one of the nicer brig cells. And really, don't worry, we'll have you released and on your way home in a couple of days." He waited a moment for her to comply. "Now, come on, set down that arsenal and come along."

"Kawib," she said, "(I hope it's all right to call you Kawib, even in the present circumstances) um . . . would you actually *shoot* me if I tried to get away, considering how little is at stake? I mean, would you blow a big hole in me when my getting away would make no difference?"

"Well," Kawib said, "of course not." He holstered his pistol.

"Good." She ducked and ran, made more awkward by the sling-bag she still wore and her purse clapped to her ear. "Find me a way out of this ship *now*," she whispered.

"I was able to construct your probable intent from your last question and from the correction you began to make at that point," the purse said quietly into her ear, with a certain smugness that she would normally have reprimanded it for. "Turn left."

She did; a slug rang off the ceiling behind her, so either Kawib had been lying or he had some nonlethal rounds with him and had reloaded. Since nonlethals had effects like being whacked with a long-handled rubber mallet wielded by a large man, she kept running.

"Up the ladder in front of you."

She was leaving the safety of the lower deck, but she really had no choice but to follow her purse's instructions. In the light gravity, she jumped more than climbed to the next level. "One more level," her left hand said faintly.

She went on up and planted her feet on the deck. "Straight down this corridor, turn left at the tee," her purse said. She could hear shouting below, but her pursuers did not seem to know exactly where she was; perhaps her hacking of *Splendor One*'s information systems was still holding. Her feet threw her down the short corridor, and she had to kick out against the wall to keep her footing as she made the turn.

"Exit to your right," the purse said. She turned and found an emergency crash-evac door—not usually a feature on a warship, but then *Splendor One* hadn't been shot at, before now, since retiring from the Hive Spatial centuries before, and it had rather often hauled passengers. "Code follows," the purse said. "Push the red button. Now push four, seven, six, nine. Now the green button. Now two, seven. Now the red button—"

With a deafening *kerfoom!* the emergency hatch blew off, revealing the warm Martian desert night and the light of the still-burning Fuel Tank One. A moment later the evacuation slide deployed, rolling out like an old-fashioned carpet, stiffening and reshaping until it was simply a large version of a playground slide. Pikia leapt up, grabbed the overhead bar, pulled her feet up, and swung out into the night, dropping onto the slide and whooshing down it like any otter or small child. The slide took her all the way down the side of the embankment that supported the linducer track.

She came up in a neat roll at the end of the slide and ran toward the blazing Fuel Tank One. "I set off all the internal fire alarms when the exit deployed," her purse said, more smugly than ever. "And about half of the sprinklers. And two of the foam-smother systems. They'll be busy for a little while."

Pikia dashed toward the blazing tank, as tall as a seven-story building. She specked that getting a fire that big, even a relatively cool and controlled one, behind her would be a pretty good way to shake off any pursuers, and anyway, it was only a slightly longer way to the monitor tower.

She was running more slowly than usual, with her hands clasped in front of her, holding down the reward spot on her purse, so hard and for so long that its happy cheebles blurred into a trill. She could do something about the smugness some other time.

Jak and Sib had begun to reassure each other frequently (in a way that meant, to anyone who knew them, they were both nervous) when they saw the abnormally tall, oddly jointed figure break from one side of the Princess's yacht, followed by the smaller, more muscular one; both leapt over the end of the lowered cradle in one long bound, and raced for the monitor tower. Jak specked that pursuit had to be white-hot. He raised his purse to his mouth to give an order—

"Let 'em get clear," Sibroillo said, "but if there's any sign of pursuit—"

A nose gun on the Princess's yacht fired, but it didn't depress quite enough; the hypersonic round left a bright streak of artificial lightning in the thick air, and Dujuv and Shadow went sprawling from its sonic boom, but a moment later they had rolled back up to their feet and they were running again.

Jak couldn't let that gun fire again—especially because as Dujuv and Shadow got farther away from it, it would be able to bear on them—so he just had to hope that Dujuv and Shadow on the Frost were far enough away. "Hose 'em down," he said to his purse.

The monitor tower thundered and boomed like the end of the world, but the Princess's yacht vanished in a great swirl of rolling and curling white water that flooded the cradle and piled in mountains of foam over the edges. If they'd left any doors open, they were probably regretting (and trying to correct) it, right now. Jak hoped to Nakasen that no one was trapped between the yacht and the cradle wall—anyone in that situation had surely been battered unconscious and then drowned.

"Weehu," Uncle Sib hollered into Jak's ear, "*that* did more than you planned on. I'm glad I forced everyone out of the tower before I left."

Jak turned to see the control tower bending, dancing, wobbling, like a drunken dancer who is trying to get the engineer's attention in a slec space (the kind of drunken dancer no slec engineer will ever point a camera at). "Long lever arm," he said, cupping his hands around Sib's ear. "The command deck is at the top, and it's wide, and the whole tower is almost a kilometer tall. It's like a man trying to hold up a snow shovel against a fire hose. Where did you send the tower crew?"

"Over to the main hangar. If they didn't turn back—and these were technicians, not soldiers, they wouldn't turn back, I don't speck they would—well, anyway, they should have gotten there before now."

With a bass twang that they felt through the soles of their feet, the control tower went over backward.

"If that just landed on the main hangar," Jak shouted, "I think those technicians are feeling very unlucky right now."

He told his purse to switch the water jets that had been on the control tower over to the Pertrans and main linducer tracks.

The elevator doors opened, and Dujuv bellowed, above the din, "That was the most inept guard I've ever seen. He just walked up to Shadow, completely unfocused, and said, 'Papers?' Shadow threw him against the wall."

"It seemed like the minimum necessary. Is Pikia here yet?"

"No, but we still have fifteen minutes till pickup."

"Then she will be. She has considerable skill and she is a person of honor."

"Did you get the lifelog?"

Shadow on the Frost shouted, "Thanks to your clever friend Dujuv, yes. Without his intuition we would have been lost."

Dujuv unfastened his tunic and pulled out a scorched, soggy, multicolored ball of lacy fabric. "I was running with it in my hands till that gun went off and you wet them down. Which I'm glad you did, because that flash had set my shirt to smoldering, too. Anyway, I scooped it up, and if all these provided enough protection—"

Jak began to laugh, and then Sib joined in.

Shadow explained. "We got into the Princess's yacht and liberated weapons; smashed into her boudoir and sealed the door to the room where she was bathing; blasted her safe, and found . . . nothing. It was about to be for nothing. And then Dujuv whacked his forehead and said, 'Where do women put something valuable?'"

"And it was in her underwear drawer, right enough," the panth finished. "Which also gave me something to wrap it in." Nakasen's lifelog lay on the plotting desk, among a large heap of soggy, shredded, and scorched lace panties, but the layers nearest it seemed to be dry and undamaged. "By the way, sir," he shouted to Sibroillo, over the roar of the monitors, "you're right about historic events needing something to frame them! The biggest religious revelation in centuries didn't arrive through normal diplomacy and bureaucratic procedure. It arrived in a panty raid!"

Pikia stared in dismay at the artificial river now pouring past her; the water washing from Cradle Two had created a torrent that she was guessing was at least as deep as she was tall. She couldn't very well swim that, let alone wade it.

Well, it would have to fan out sooner or later. She trotted beside it for a half kilometer before she came to a place where she judged it safe enough to try for a crossing. She was almost right; she only went down into potholes twice, going over her head each time but immediately washing up onto the soft sand on the downstream side, spitting mud and using language that might have surprised her friends.

As she climbed out onto the far bank, she considered her mauled hair from earlier in the evening, the drenching she had just taken, and her exhaustion, and decided that she wanted to see Clarbo Waynong again soon, and she wanted him to say something about her appearance, so that she could rip off his genitals and force-feed them to him.

Once she was on the right side of the water, it was a relatively short dash to the monitor tower, and the prospect of having all of this be someone else's decisions to make and problems to solve seemed very promising indeed. As she approached the tower, she lost all ability to hear, for outside the din of the big monitors was even louder than inside. It was like standing close to a large waterfall.

As she rushed in through the door, she thought she might have to fight the guard, but something about her seemed to make him cower in the corner and say, "Don't hurt me." The elevator doors opened, and the rest of the party stood there, staring at her—soaking wet, missing hair from half her head, covered with mud, grinning like a maniac, and clutching a sling-bag of weapons. "Hey," she said, "can you boys come out and play?"

CHAPTER 11

The Third Purpose of a Rubahy Dagger

Outside it was far too noisy to hear the two ground-effect buses, and Gweshira and Xlini were driving with the lights off, so they were almost on top of the party when they braked by the monitor tower. "Looks like you had success at the motor pool. One hour of dark remaining," Jak said. "That should just cover our run to Freehold."

"Will someone, somewhere, sometime, tell me what is going on?" Waynong asked, and got no answer. Everyone climbed in as quickly as possible, and the hovercars shot off into the night.

The hovercars were capable of about 250 kph on flat ground or calm water, and in this part of the Chryse Desert, the anchored dunes rolled gently and low. Freehold was only about twenty minutes away, and figuring that it would take at least ten minutes for the other side to organize a pursuit—which could not be coming by anything much faster than a hovercar—it seemed certain that they would reach Freehold, and assured political asylum, well before anything could close in on them.

Freehold was the capital of Magenta Yellow Amber Cyan, a Harmless Zone nation devoted to a kind of passionately mad capitalism in which every odd thing the market did was taken to be a parable of moral instruction. A sudden rise in the price of plums might be read as instruction on chastity; a brief shortfall of soap powder, as a lesson on the vanity of earthly greatness. Whatever happened in the city's markets—a decline in rents in one neighborhood, an increase in durable goods orders, a brief blip in the consumer interest rate—was interpreted by an academy of priest-economists for the archive that Freehold maintained "for whenever the solar system is ready for it." One popular tour guide described Freehold as "Emerald City if it had been designed by Ayn Rand specifically to produce self-help books." But peculiar as Freehold was, it had a tradition of giving asylum to all who asked, and it was close.

The hovercars were self-piloting and built to seat eight, so four people in each had some room to stretch out as they whizzed across the desert. Shortly there was no conversation, just snoring.

Jak's purse buzzed and rattled to wake him. He sat up and reflexively checked the time—they should be in Freehold in eight minutes—

"Emergency," his purse said. "Massive communications and information penetration is under way. It appears to be an attempt to take control of—"

The hoverjets shut off abruptly and the car dropped the ten centimeters onto the desert floor in less than two seconds as the overpressure leaked out from under the flexible skirt that surrounded its base. The normal soft-landing safeties were shut off, so the hovercar was still moving at over 200 kph when its bottom struck the rock-strewn gravel hillside. In a sudden, mad, four-g whirl, the car flipped over twice before coming to rest on its side.

"Sorry," the purse said.

"What happened?" Jak looked around; everyone had been belted in and the crash prediction system had worked as advertised, so Sib, Pikia, and Gweshira, at least, were all right.

Before his purse could answer, Jak got a call from Dujuv. "Jak, are you all right?"

"We just crashed. Probably a software attack. Can you get the lifelog to Freehold?"

"We just crashed too. We're about eighty meters behind you. Nobody's hurt here. At least we stayed upright."

"Must've been your skill and daring, old pizo. All of us are all right here, too. But I think we may have a battle at any moment. And it's possible our purses have been penetrated and turned." He thought only for a moment; the situation was clear enough—the hovercars had simultaneously crashed during a hostile infopenetration, hardly likely to be a coincidence. Besides, toktru Jak didn't want to hear Sib's six standard pieces of advice right now. "All right, then, we have to figure we're about to have to fight. Be careful what you send over your purse and run all your defensive software *now*. Everyone out and meet between the hovercars."

When Jak's group joined Dujuv's, in a little depression between the two wrecked hovercars, the first streaks of dawn were beginning to appear in the eastern sky; another effect of the very large-scale height and the dense gas mix on terraformed Mars was that light scattered far before and behind the sun, so that sunsets and sunrises lingered for hours. In the dim glow, he saw Dujuv concentrating on his left palm and muttering.

Jak knew Dujuv too well to worry about security; if Dujuv was using the purse, it was secure to his satisfaction, and that was more than good enough for Jak. "Getting anything, Duj?"

"Looks like nine heets riding strap-on flyers. Speed and altitude are more than Harmless Zone legal for military—so I bet payload and weapons are too, and that those are off the Princess's yacht. Or in short, big, mean, and really open for business."

"If it's the Royal Palace Guards, we're outnumbered but not badly, but if it's B&Es, we're dead," Sibroillo observed.

"That would be my assessment, also," Shadow on the Frost said, quietly hefting two of the weapons from the sling-bags. "Was there a B&E contingent on the Princess's yacht? I didn't see any evidence of one, and I don't recall hearing anything about it."

"Me either," Jak said, and the headshakes around him made it unanimous. "But it wouldn't be hard for them to have concealed nine beanies, and if that's what is coming after us, Sib is toktru singing-on right."

Dujuv grunted. "Well, whatever they are, they'll be overhead in four minutes. We can't outrun them and we won't stay hidden for long. That leaves fighting or giving up. And fighting has a lot of uncertainties, all of them between bad and worse. I'd say we're on the bad side of entropy, old pizo, and maybe we ought to just admit it."

"Not fight?" Clarbo Waynong asked, sounding shocked.

"I wasn't calling for a vote," Jak said. "But since you mention the issue, I'm thinking compromise. Let's take their first assault or hear their first offer, and then I'll decide."

Everyone except Dujuv was nodding slowly. Jak said, "Duj, I want to hear what you're thinking."

"I'd hate to have any of us get killed—or even any of

them—just so you won't have to give up without a fight, or to give you a basis for making up your mind."

Jak swallowed hard; it was an irritating point, but Dujuv was telling him the toktru truth, just as Jak had asked. Nonetheless . . . "Duj, it's a good point, but . . . this is a high-stakes mission. I can't quite bring myself to give up when we're so close to Freehold and to attaining all the mission objectives. Not when there's a chance, and I think there is."

"Besides," Waynong said, "this is the mission that's essential to my career."

In the gray, gradually rising light, Jak could see Dujuv's eyebrow go up, so hard and fast that he could practically hear it crunch to a stop on his friend's forehead.

"So—with reservations noted—" Jak said, "we're going to fight, but I want everyone to stay alert and ready to roll over fast if we have to." Dujuv nodded deeply, once, almost bowing. Jak nodded back. "All right, what's the axis of approach?" Jak asked.

"About nine degrees south of true west."

"All right, then," Jak said. "Box guard, by the numbers, just like in gen school Citizen Basic. Set the square at three hundred meters. Northwest—Sib. Southwest—Shadow. Northeast—Gweshira. Southeast—Dujuv." Jak was playing this very much like Citizen Basic, the year of military training that all Hive citizen-candidates underwent in gen school at the age of sixteen. In a solar system where war had been endemic for a thousand years, every citizen of a large, powerful republic had to have some understanding of basic military procedures, and of what it was to command and to follow.

Box guard was a way for a small armed group to defend

itself against an oncoming airborne attack; it was neither the best nor the most effective way, but it was easy to learn, and not severely flawed, and therefore everyone in gen school basic had practiced leading and following through a box guard deployment.

Sibroillo, Dujuv, Gweshira, and Shadow on the Frost were the best trained and the best shots in the group; the orthodox way was to put the best shots at the outer corners. Jak added, "Sib, you're the closest thing to an expert we have with the laser pistol—you take that." His uncle accepted it gravely, checking the charge and swapping in a fresh block.

Next, within that square, Jak set up the interior diamond, seventy-five meters on the side: "West—me. South—Pikia. East—Xlini. North—Clarbo. Fire on the first shot from either side, except Gweshira—Gweshira, take the first shot, on your initiative. It's your call, but if you can make your first shot at their rearmost, we'll have a pretty much classical ambush, as you no doubt know."

Clarbo raised a hand as if to speak and Pikia turned and handed him a slug rifle; he appeared to start at it, then to stare at it as if he had never seen one, but it clearly made him forget whatever he was about to say.

Jak was hoping to have some good luck, for once, just for variety; if it was possible for Gweshira to hold fire until she could hit the enemy rear, since she was the one farthest from them, it should put the foremost enemy at point-blank range for Jak's front shooters, and ensure that their whole party was attacked at once; whatever surprise was possible (probably none) it would be maximized (probably to zero). "Now, places, people, and get under cover. Good luck."

At least there was an abundance of broken terrain to take

cover in. The area they had crashed in was a little spandrel, less than half a kilometer on a side, between three very-weathered Bombardment craters. The thrice-smashed soil had collapsed and bulged in so many different directions that there were dozens of small peaks and pits to hide in.

Jak found a position between two head-high boulders, with a good natural firing slit pointing in the right direction between them, and an overhang to stay under until the enemy aircraft grounded. His purse told him that he was less than three meters from the map coordinates of his assigned spot in the inner diamond. He checked and readied his slug rifle; it was Hive manufacture and had been Hive Spatial maintained, so it was in fine shape.

Light from the gray-blue sky overhead was now bright enough to read by, though the sun itself would not rise for another half hour. Jak laid out mag reloads even though the battle would probably not last two hundred shots or five minutes.

With the spare magazines at hand, Jak put on his goggles and sat watching his sector of the sky. "Purse, comcheck everyone."

"All other purses in the party are set to your general channel."

"Good. Do I have back channels to Gweshira and Dujuv?"

"You do now. I've set them up and their purses have acknowledged."

"Good." Jak pressed the reward spot and his purse cheebled softly, happy to have pleased him. "Now put a situation map up on my goggles, transparent, overlaid on a five-power real-time view."

A ghostly map faded into existence before Jak's eyes; the

surrounding landscape seemed to leap closer. The approaching green wedges of the enemy would have cleared the horizon within two minutes, had they continued flying at that
speed and altitude. But even as Jak made that estimate, the
oncoming flyers began a quick descent to cover just over the
horizon. So far, whoever their pursuers were, their tactics
were just as by-the-book as Jak's were.

Jak's forces as yet had no way to engage the enemy: their
one laser pistol could only fire in a straight line, and the slug
throwers were treaty-limited for the Harmless Zone, and
reached only about two kilometers at best, not even to the
horizon. Jak regretted that very much because right now
would have been the perfect time to hit the enemy, before
they were down and into cover. At least the other side
seemed to be at a complementary disadvantage; though they
apparently had non-Harmless Zone-legal tech, they weren't
firing, which meant, probably, that they hadn't specked the
positions of Jak's team closely enough to use their far superior firepower.

As soon as the other side had gotten off their flyers, they
sent them on robot pilot at Jak's forces, the tiny craft coming over the horizon zigging and zagging close to the surface as if scouting or doing close air support. The buzzing
wing-and-rotor craft were supposed to draw fire and cause
Jak's force to give away positions, but they were backlit by
the bright predawn. Everyone could easily see that they carried no weapons and that their trapeze seats were empty.

Jak kept his attention on the now-flickering green
wedges on the map. Now that the nine fighters from the
other side were on the ground, the purse was having a hard
time assembling enough information from overhead satellites, stray radar, and all the myriad other clues out on the

net. Consequently the green wedges flickered in and out of existence and instead of an identifying number often bore only a yellow x, indicating that there was definitely one of them there but the purse was unconfident about which, or even a yellow question mark, indicating the purse only thought that it was more likely than not that one was there.

But the flickering green wedges, when they existed, were drawing ever closer, and as they came closer, some of the party's own instruments began to pick up the enemy forces, so that the green wedges flickered less, and bore black numbers more often.

The terrain was just as broken for the attackers as it was for Jak's team; their cover was as good, and they darted and zigzagged their way toward his position. Eventually he had a clear fix on all nine of them on his map, and had settled on following the guide dots in his goggles to find Enemy Number Five, the one at the center of the formation who might possibly be the commander. (Though Enemy Number Three or Enemy Number Eight might also be.)

Almost, it might have been a fight between the beanies in a friendly game of Maniples, except that through the map, in the real image with its steadily improving light, he caught glimpses of the tiny black stick-figure of his target, crossing between two rocks or coming over a low ridge. Jak waited for the moment and hoped the figure would be in his sights when it was time to pull the trigger.

Enemy Number Nine, the rearmost green wedge, crossed the faint, blue line on the map overlay that indicated the outermost accurate range of Gweshira's slug rifle. For a long breath nothing happened, and then Enemy Number Nine must have exposed himself, for a single shot cracked from her rifle. The green wedge with the black 9 on it stopped moving on the faintly glowing map; he had taken cover or been hit.

Jak spared that no thought. The side of Enemy Number Five's head was just emerging beside a big rock, and Jak fired at it less than a heartbeat after Gweshira's shot. The figure fell forward into the open and lay still. Jak tracked with his rifle, looking for another target.

To his right, a laser drew a white line between Sib and Enemy Number Three; there was a flurry of activity around that green wedge and Jak saw the indicator for a grenade launch flicker next to the green wedge with the black 3. Then the wedge turned white—shortwave IR had come from it—Sib had scored a hit with the laser, and a puff of superheated steam had emerged from the body.

But then the grenade landed. Sib's position, the cluster of rocks ahead and to Jak's right, lit in a blue-white glow, an instantaneous five-meter dome the color and brightness of a welding arc.

When Jak's goggles had cleared, two seconds later, dust billowed up from that point, the center of the cloud glowing dull red from the furious heat within. Gravel and small rocks spattered down around Jak.

The thunder of that explosion fell to tolerable levels and Jak's headphones let it in. Momentarily Sib's laser pistol swung its white cutting beam crazily about the sky, like a wobbling column of light lashing out from the dust cloud. The charge ran out, and now there was only the black plume against the gray-pink sky.

"Truce." The voice crackled in Jak's ears. "We have three men down and need to retrieve them. Invoking Harmless Zone war protocols."

"Truce accepted," Jak said, cuing it through his purse to his whole team. "We have a man down ourselves."

As he ran to where the grenade had gone off—to where Uncle Sib had been—his heart in his throat and unable to breathe, a far distant corner of his mind was grateful that Dujuv was not the sort to say "I told you so."

Clarbo had actually gotten there slightly ahead of him— he wondered for an instant if the fool had broken cover before getting the truce notice. The grenade had been one of the standard military issue used all over the solar system, just a blob of hot-jet fuel blasted into a little flask of liquid oxygen by a pinhead-sized bit of explosive, so that they mixed at high temperature and energy release was complete. The base of the dust plume was already cooling and the last gravel was pattering down from above. In the clearing space between the rocks, Jak could see the crumpled, burned body, flames still flickering from parts of it.

The flash of high-temperature gas expands so rapidly that it flows in a nearly straight line out from the grenade; the parts of Sib that had been pointed toward the grenade had been burned deeply, through clothes and skin and into the internal organs, at the same time that the shadowed parts had barely been touched. One elegant eyebrow still arched over one unseeing, dead eye, but the other side of Sib's head was charred and mostly gone.

Pikia raced past him, holding a fire extinguisher she must have grabbed from one of the wrecked hovercars, and sprayed foam on the evil green dancing flames that sprang along the rib cage and washed the separated arm; when she stopped, a moment later, most of the corpse was mercifully swathed in thick gray-brown goo.

Jak continued to stare, his eyes fixing on where Sib's unburned left hand stuck from under the foam, at the thick raised veins that ran under the soft skin, between the hard bulges of the bones; *a hand that worked hard and well for a long time,* Jak thought, *that's how they get to be so developed and yet so coarse—*

Another blur shot by Jak, and Gweshira was kneeling beside the body, on the ground, pressing that hand to her face the way a child holds a crumbling, aged teddy bear, and it seemed to Jak that he really only began to be able to hear again when she opened her mouth and wailed, a long, gasping shriek that ended in gut-punching sobs.

"Who's in command here?" a voice said. Jak turned to see the tear-streaked face of a seventeen- or eighteen-year-old wearing the field uniform of the Greenworld Royal Palace Guards, the preposterous drum-major-in-a-gay-porn-movie, too-tight and too-gaudy, good-only-for-dancing-and-posing outfit that Jak himself had worn during his time in Shyf's service.

Jak didn't dak, didn't even speck, the question. Then he felt a hand tighten on his shoulder—when had Dujuv arrived? How long had his toktru tove's hand been resting there?

"This is him but things are pretty bad right now," Dujuv said. "I guess I'm the second."

"I'm the third myself," the young man said. "Brimiyan Presgano. I hate to ask but . . . well, most of our 'force' wasn't trained people like you have and a lot of them are just sitting down and crying—and they won't listen to me, they know I was only an officer because I was the captain's cousin—"

A sinking feeling hit Jak even as he felt Dujuv's hand tighten on his shoulder, but it seemed to help clear Jak's head—leaving him horribly conscious and functional in the middle of this grim little battlefield, with the sun just coming up and everyone standing around as if at the scene of an air crash. "Kawib Presgano was your captain, wasn't he?" Jak asked.

"He was . . . he's dead now, over there . . ." Brimiyan seemed about to break down.

Kawib Presgano and Sibroillo Jinnaka had killed each other. Kawib lay flat on his back, and two young men holding each other's hands wept beside him. Brimiyan whispered, "I know you were in the Royal Palace Guards so you know what it is and what it's all about. Well, I never knew Xabo, but people always said he and Kawib were like mom and dad to all of us, and we *needed* somebody. You know why—"

"We do," Dujuv said, "so you don't have to speak of it unless you want to."

"He wasn't really the same after he lost Seubla, and then after he lost Xabo they said he was just drifting through the motions." Brimiyan's eyes were filling with tears and he was wiping them furiously from his eyes with his sleeve. "But just the same, after Xabo was killed and Vifu took over, Kawib and Vifu still took care of us and made sure we were adjusting and kept our spirits up and they were always there to help—"

Jak had a sick feeling, realizing that there was about a fifty percent chance that he had shot Vifu, whom he knew. But then Sib and Kawib were dead too . . . it was all too much. He put an arm around Brimiyan, and the man—released now to be a miserable boy—clutched Jak and sobbed.

Jak looked at Dujuv, making a slight *what can I do?* face at his toktru tove, but Dujuv was not looking at him; the panth was staring at Kawib's head. Jak followed his friend's gaze.

Kawib had apparently popped his head out just after firing his grenade in Sib's direction, and Sib in turn had caught him with the classic most-effective laser shot, across the face through the eyes, leaving Kawib with a black carbon mask with two deep black holes in it, and a strange swelling in the head where his brain had exploded into steam.

"Nakasen's balls," Dujuv muttered to Jak. "Oh, Nakasen's bleeding balls. Just like Seubla."

Seubla had been Kawib's only demmy, ever. He had loved her deeply, and the two had been devoted, but because their bloodlines were a threat to the Karrinynya, Princess Shyf had kept them in a frustrating together-and-apart relationship, with Kawib in the RPG and Seubla a lady in waiting, always seeing each other but never able to be alone or to court each other. Though Shyf had liked Seubla and trusted her as a friend (as much as any princess could do any such thing), eventually Seubla's ancestry, tracing back to more than one possible pretender to the Karrinynya throne, had led Shyf to decide to end the problem forever. Jak and Dujuv had been there at the party when Seubla had been assassinated; Dujuv had killed the assassin with his bare hands, scant seconds too late.

Seubla too had died with a laser cut across the eyes—the way Hive Intel taught you to make it. The professional way, whether "assisting a friendly monarch" or "preserving the consistency of the Wager."

Nakasen had taught nothing of the afterlife, holding that it was unknowable and irrelevant to right action in the present besides. But seven hundred years had not yet eradicated the idea from human consciousness; "Wherever he is, I hope he's with her," Jak murmured, and Dujuv whispered back, "Toktru, old tove."

Shadow arrived then, and knelt beside the body. He drew his family dagger from the short leather skirt that the Rubahy wore into battle; it was used for just three purposes. The first as a last-ditch weapon—Rubahy honor required it was always to be the last one drawn, and to draw it in a fight effectively made a binding vow to kill or die; hence their expression about "fighting till daggers are drawn." The second was in order to kill an oath-sworn enemy, to administer the coup de grace to an enemy of great prestige and power whose killing would win honor for the whole family.

And the third purpose was this one: Shadow on the Frost knelt, raised the knife in both hands above his face, and brought it down to form a gash on his left shoulder, where the mourning scars for friends were traditionally administered. Blue-green blood flowed out and stained the white feathers; Shadow leaned forward and let a little drip onto Kawib's lip, where it lay like a sapphire on a ruby in the now-bright early morning sunlight.

He stood and said, "Dujuv, my oath-friend, you and I together are strong enough to move the bodies. Perhaps we should get them together, and then consider calling for help? We are not within the limits of Freehold but I think they would come out as a compassionate mission."

Dujuv nodded. "It seems like—"

"Attention parties from Greenworld and the Hive." The voice was loud, and it came through all their purses at once, as an override. *"You are ordered not to fight and not to move from your present location. We will be arriving in less than one minute. Be careful to avoid all weapons discharges as our automated systems will home on the source and fire."*

"Send a reply," Jak told his purse.

"Can't identify the source."

"Then broadcast, general hailing. And copy to all our team."

"Ready."

"Complying. All Hive forces, lock down."

Brimiyan lifted his purse to his face, and gave the same order to the Greenworld forces. Both sides were in the open, scattered, hopelessly intermingled with an enemy, and already stood down; whoever the new players in the game might be, they were the ones who had the drop.

"It's Paxhaven," Gweshira said, coming up beside Jak, her face still drenched, looking down at the ground and clearly keeping her voice level and even only by considerable force of will. "They're finally here."

"Finally?" Jak asked. "Should we have been expecting them?" As far as he knew, Paxhaven was usually inconsiderable, a quaint little island on the other side of the pole, a few thousand kilometers away.

"Oh, yes," she said, nodding, and then her breath caught. "So stupid," she added. "I almost said, 'Sib will be so disappointed . . .'"

CHAPTER 12

A Reasonable Assessment of
My Performance Is Total Failure

The Paxhaven forces arrived: four big statisaucers, donut-shaped aircraft lifted by counterrotating, electrostatically driven central rotors. They were silent, graceful, and elegant, but did not move quickly; Jak would eventually realize that this nicely summarized why Paxhavians preferred them.

At the time he was mostly awed by the silence of the approach and the swift grace of the descent. The troops that emerged did not act like peacekeepers or like commandos, but walked out of the ship as if walking was the only thing on their minds. Jak wasn't sure whether they were in uniform or just dressed alike; they wore what everyone in Paxhaven wore, something that looked rather like an ancient-style martial arts gi, with press-fastenings to close the lapels and soft, brightly colored undershirts beneath the uwagi. There were no badges of rank visible but clearly some were giving, and some were following, orders.

The woman in the center of the group said a few things in a pleasant, conversational tone, the people around her turned and said things to the people around them, and they all walked off in several directions, to perform their various duties. It all seemed very civilized and very calm.

She approached Jak and said, "Jak Jinnaka, my name is Petol Porizeux. I am here from Paxhaven because we know that your two forces were fighting over the lifelog of Paj Nakasen. We hold mandates from the League of Polities that we could reasonably construe to mean that we have title to that object. Unlike anyone who has touched it so far, we intend to submit a case to the League of Polities and to abide by their decision. I should add that we also are well aware that the only other polity that might sustain a claim on the lifelog is yours, the Hive. Will you allow us to take possession of the lifelog?"

"With all my heart," Jak said. "You can't imagine how sick of the stupid thing I am."

She smiled slightly. "Given that Nakasen's lifelog is the most sacred relic now existing in the human part of the solar system—and the quite likely source of a great era of religious revelation that may run for centuries hence—and that you are referring to it as 'the stupid thing,' I believe I *have* imagined how sick of it you must be. I am sorry it has been such a burden. No doubt when you picked it up, your reasons seemed good, and now they seem very foolish."

Jak's eyes stung with tears; Petol Porizeux took a step toward him, put a hand gently on his shoulder, and looked into his eyes. He felt curiously calm, as if all the evil and tragedy of the last few hours were temporarily lifted off him. She said, so softly that probably only Jak heard, "We all carry such burdens; be grateful you have set one down."

"How did you know my name?" Jak asked.

"It was in our files, along with many identifiers for you," she said. "You have been of great interest to us, because of your uncle. We had just been contemplating what invitations to issue to him, and to Gweshira, when this tragedy struck.

If you will let us, we can give him a loving and respectful
burial. We think he might have liked to come back to Paxhaven."

On the Hive, bodies were powdered into fine dust and
then dropped into the central black hole, warming and nour-
ishing the whole space colony; for reasons he could feel but
not name, Jak knew Sib would have preferred Petol's offer.

"Then we are decided," she said. "We will take you and
your party, the Greenworld RPGs, and the lifelog back to
Paxhaven with us, and sort out everything there." Again she
leaned in to whisper something to him, as if they were members of the same zybot or shared a family history. "You'll
see. This is the best thing." Then she took a step back from
him, and without raising her voice, gave orders that were
obeyed instantly by everyone. Only Clarbo, very briefly,
tried to raise some objection, and at her glance, he fell silent
and got into the statisaucer where he was supposed to go.

With four corpses in the holds, and thirteen passengers in
the visitor seats, the statisaucers rose from the face of Mars,
as silently as they had arrived, high into the bright morning
sky. Jak glanced down for the last time at the black scorch
between the rocks that marked the place of Uncle Sib's
death, and began to cry, harder and harder, holding on to
Dujuv's hand as if it were a life preserver. Below them, it
was a beautiful, clear early summer day in the northern
desert, broken by with the occasional brilliant blue river and
lake surrounded rich green blotches of foliage, heat shim-
mering off the flat rocky places and the sun sometimes
glancing at them from the little circular Bombardment-
crater lakes, like a pupil recurring in a thousand eyes.

It was the first time Jak had flown in an aircraft in Mars,
and he remembered how Uncle Sib had always wanted him

to be aware of the scenery (and he never really had) wherever he went, and even as he wept, he tried to wipe his face so that he could see and remember. After a while, he fell into exhausted, often-waking sleep.

When Jak awoke, Gweshira was sitting next to him. "We need to talk a little, Jak. You're going to learn things here—things that Sib and I weren't sure you'd ever need to know, things that maybe we'd have been better off if you'd never had to learn them, but you're going to learn them now and I suppose it would be better to have you prepared. Paxhaven is where Sibroillo studied to become the fighter and agent that he was, and it's where Circle Four had much of its leadership for a while. Sibroillo and I both studied there, though I arrived about a decade after he left. And it's also where Bex Riveroma had his training."

Jak felt, as he always did, a cold surge in his liver at the mention of his mortal enemy.

"Paxhaven," she went on, "though it isn't mentioned much, because they like to keep this quiet, is the home of many important social innovations. It's not an accident that many zybots have been headquartered there or had a presence there, even though it's a little place with barely two million people scattered around the islands in the ring. And among their social innovations, they were the mother school of all the Disciplines training—it was to Paxhaven that all the great martial arts masters fled at the end of the Old Empire, and it was at Paxhaven that Paj Nakasen converted the Great Mother Dojo, en masse, to the Wager, and the Disciplines came out of the integration of the ancient arts with the Wager. Paxhaven was also where Maniples was first played . . . and many other things. So for the warrior-to-be, it was—and for that matter it is—*the* place to go to train.

"Sibroillo, you see, had very mixed feelings about how he himself had turned out . . . and he felt that for every more-or-less decent individual such as himself, the place had bred a dozen Bex Riveromas. True, the program under which they trained had been redone . . . but you were his last living blood kin, and he felt that the Jinnaka line would have a better chance at the fine destiny he thought it deserved, with you growing up as you did, fostered by him, than in the narrow, rigid world that would have been school at Pax-haven. I suppose someday, when you know Paxhaven well and you know the world well, you might form an opinion about how right, or not, his decision was."

"So that's where he became enemies with Bex Riveroma. He must have been about my age at the time—" Jak said.

"About your age when he was at Paxhaven, yes. While they were there, the two of them were mostly friends, and for a long time very close friends. By the time they left they were fierce rivals. Enmity didn't come for a while after that, but it came. Now that Sibroillo is dead, you'll be free to learn something of your family and your origins, and you will find that that's a pattern with Jinnaka men; intense friendship and intense enmity and nothing between."

They sat quietly for a while, before Jak said, "And was Sib happy while he was at Paxhaven?"

"I can't say for sure—I didn't meet him till we were both past fifty—but he always said that the years at Paxhaven were the happiest in his life, and to judge by the way his eyes would light up when he talked of it, I think that was true."

Jak stared out the window at the sun-washed blue-green

sea below, and said, "Well, then, if Sib liked it there, it will be a good place for him to have his funeral." He sighed and added, "He and Kawib had sat and talked at dinner, not two days before. And now they've killed each other, in a quarrel over something that I don't think either of them gave a fart in a windstorm about. I don't know which one I feel sorrier for, Aunt Gweshira."

He had only rarely called her that since he had turned ten and understood that she wasn't really his aunt; nowadays it was only when he felt close and wanted to remind her how important she was to him. The older woman leaned her head on his shoulder and let tears flow slowly into his tunic. "Everybody remembers that Principle 136 is one of the warrior's principles," she said. " 'It is useless to feel sorry for the dead but some things that are useless are good.' But nobody ever seems to remember why it's in there. Maybe it's too painful to remember that." She sighed and pressed her face harder against his arm; Jak held her hand, thought about how much he missed Sib, and thought about how much more she must be missing him. It was a long while before she spoke again.

"It's funny," she said. "Social engineering is a violent art, and it's what zybots are about, and I've seen many people die violently—caused it more than once, myself—and yet . . . this just seems like such a violation of the rules, Jak. The aristos kill each other, low-level grunts of all kinds die all the time, but the middle class is protected—that's the basic rule of civilization, as Sib used to explain," Gweshira said. "God I miss the fact that I'll never hear him pointlessly explain that (or anything else) to people who already know it, again."

"I'd like to be told some obvious things myself," Jak

said, smiling a little at the memory. "And hear a lecture that goes on past my 'okay' ten or twelve times . . . he was the best, you know. Might as well have been my mother *and* my father."

"Do you remember them?"

"My mother died in childbirth. You think of that as archaic, you know? As if she'd been eaten by a dinosaur. But childbirth is a big shock to the system, no matter how advanced medicine gets, and some people just don't make it through . . . My dad was away as a merc for some Rubahy honor-group, fighting on the surface of Charon, and before I was one year old he had collected a bunch of medals, and before I was two there was white nitrogen frost on his dark grave, out where the sun is only the brightest star . . . that was what the Rubahy honor-verse about him said."

"You were quite the bigot against the Rubahy when you were younger—"

"Another great thing about Sib. He never let me forget that my dad's name was inscribed in Rubahy rolls of honor. And he made it obvious to me that he looked on the prejudices I picked up, from living in the Hive, as being something like picking my nose. Unappetizing, not permitted around him, something he hoped I'd outgrow, something he would always find obnoxious if I didn't. So of course I clung to it while I was a teenager and then dropped it as soon as I really wanted to be an adult."

"He did worry that you wouldn't outgrow it."

"That's what I mean, that he was the best. He worried about the right stuff." Jak looked out the window at the Boreal Ocean; a lovely crystal blue, absolutely transparent, and even from a few kilometers up, they could see down through the water to the pods of whales and the great schools of fish feasting. "It's so beautiful," Jak said, "that was something else Uncle Sib tried to teach me, to have my eyes open. And maybe he did a little. I learned more from him than he intended."

"He was a natural teacher—in fact his biggest problem was that he knew that and he'd teach when there wasn't any reason to."

Jak laughed. It was only a little sighing of breath, a small squeeze in the chest, but it seemed to come from far down inside him, from more than twenty years of memories, and then he felt something break, like the face of a mighty dam giving way around a crack you could have bridged with your hand, and he was laughing and crying all at once, grateful for the old man's having graced his life, miserable for the loss, and when he really thought about Sibroillo Jinnaka, unable to stop laughing. "You know," he said, "one thing toktru I loved about Sib was how he could be so dignified and defensive about it, the way he wanted his respect, one millisecond, and the next *micro*second, he'd be realizing that he had made a fool of himself and he'd just roar with laughter. Like a geyser under an ice pond, you know? Always forming a new crust and always blasting it apart."

"And then muttering to me about that silly kid, afterward," Gweshira said, smearing the back of her hand across her eyes.

"Toktru. I speck he was mad at me three-quarters of the time but still he just always seemed glad I was around; every so often his hand was on my shoulder when I really needed it, and I'll never forget that." Jak drifted off into the memory of the sharp glint in Sib's eye—as if he were expecting a good punch line or a fierce battle—whenever Jak showed any evidence of brains or ambition (that one probably hadn't happened as much as it should have). He was trying to get an exact picture of that expression in his head when Gweshira said, "If you don't mind my saying it, he was always very patient with you." She seemed to be trying to draw things out of him; perhaps she thought Jak needed to talk, or perhaps she wanted confirmation of her own memory.

"Oh, toktru masen! He needed to be. It was either be patient with me or drop me out an airlock. But that was Sib. He didn't just teach patiently, he taught patience," Jak said. "I remember when I was about ten, I got it into my head that I was going to be a Maniples genius, that I had the talent to be a Master or a Great Master and a child prodigy at it, so I entered a tournament at a level that was toktru far beyond me. Triple elimination, so I had to go through three successive stompings, and seeded-on-the-fly so each stomping got worse than the last. I came home feeling like the biggest loser and fool in the world. And Sib never said a word, even though I knew he'd been watching the tournament in real time and knew exactly what had happened. Instead, he told me to suit up for Disciplines practice. I thought it was going to be a punishment session, one of those times when he just took me into the practice room and beat the snot out of me (which he only did when I had a real excess of snot, which happens in young kids). Because toktru I knew I'd puffed myself up with pride and gotten arrogant and disgraced myself.

"So I went in there scared out of my mind, and he asked me to show him all the training forms, all the *kihons* that they start little kids on, and he kept asking me to remember how hard they had been for me and how bad I had been at them when I started. And I thought I was getting his point . . . so he started knocking me down and dumping me on my butt, and I thought this was my punishment . . . but every time he knocked me down, he'd make me stop, practice my breathing, focus, try to do better, and then he'd do it again. It was all afternoon, but finally I dakked it all singing-on.

"He didn't care whether I'd won or lost. I was a kid, I was supposed to lose. He didn't even care if I was good at it yet, I was just learning, just starting to learn, how could good-or-not matter yet? What he wanted me to see was that the whole job was getting knocked down and getting back up again, always seeing if you can make it work this time, until one time it works, then until sometimes it works, then until it works more often than not, then until it works every time. You just look and say, I won, I lost, I screwed up, I did well, and you draw a breath and draw a lesson and go on and try again. You don't throw a party when you get it right and you don't hold a funeral when you screw up."

He felt what he had said, and Gweshira smiled and squeezed his arm. "But sometimes you do hold a funeral when you screw up. You know Sib would have told you that he took a classic example of a bad position, just that one time. No covered escape. Couldn't just shoot and scoot. And then he fired at a bad target, three times, before he got a clear shot. Those bad shots gave his position away and that's why he got hit with the grenade." She sighed. "That happens. You follow your sword through life, and one day you aren't quick enough or you lose your grip or you're just unlucky, and you have followed your sword all the way to your death. It's the way we live, Jak." Her hand tightened on his arm. "And it's the way he chose to live, and maybe even the way he chose to die. I don't think he wanted to spend his last fifteen years hooked up to life support, visiting his friends through the viv and wandering around in a waking dream, waiting for something out in the physical world to cave in faster than they could patch up, so that he'd just go out like a song when you switch it off." Her eyes flooded and her cheeks were drenched, but both her hands were clenched on Jak's forearm, squeezing the muscles painfully hard.

With his free hand, Jak gently drew his handkerchief and wiped Gweshira's face. "You knew him better than I did," he said, "even though I knew him all my life. And you're right. I'm sure it hurt and I'm sure the instant when the grenade landed, before it blew, and Sib dakked that he'd screwed up, was bad . . . but that was the death his whole life was pointing to, masen?"

"Toktru." Gweshira curled around to put her hand on Jak's shoulder, still keeping her grip; she was so still and quiet that Jak only knew when she had gone to sleep by the sudden release of pressure on his arm. They crossed the North Pole, where a few rafts of ice, left over from winter, still shone in the polar sunlight, and on down into the wedge of night, the sea growing black beneath them. After a long time, in which Jak just sat and breathed and remembered, the statisaucer, still utterly silent and smooth in its flight, began a descent, and ahead of him he could see the sharp spires and rocky rim of Korolev Atoll, a wide crater rim that stuck up above the polar sea, forming a circle of curving mountainous islands, each honeycombed with the excavated dwellings of the Paxhavians, and gloriously spattered with the lights of their pavilions, terraces, and plazas. Sib would have loved this sight—had loved it, apparently. Jak tried to settle his mind to let it move him, as it had moved Sib, as Sib would have wanted.

*   *   *

They had kept Jak under, using a mild medical version of the stunner, until his body worked its way around to the cycle for local time. By the clock he had slept more than twenty hours, by his brain wave function map he had slept deeply and well, and by the way his gritty eyes ached and his sore throat craved water, he had barely slept at all. He got that drink of water from the dispenser and consumed it in restful quiet. He had barely glanced at this room last night and now he realized he had seen everything then; it might have been any hotel room since a thousand years before the Wager.

He pulled on his purse and turned it on.

"Do you want to be awake?" it asked.

"I guess so."

"I have a message for you, but it is supposed to wait until after you have had a shower and something to eat."

"Those both sound kind of good."

"Take a long shower; there is a food order already, and I shall activate it and have it here when you are dry."

The shower seemed to help, and the meal was his favorite, traditional-style Lunar Greek baked hamster and glutles, warm and comforting. After he had wiped up and dressed, his purse asked, "Shall I give you the message I've been holding for you?"

"Yes, please."

It was simple text message: please notify two representatives of the Paxhaven Fighting Academy whenever he felt up to talking, as they would need some hours of his time to prepare for Sib's memorial service. Jak told his purse to send a reply, poured himself another glass of water, and deopaqued the windows.

The outside was as spectacular as the inside was bland.

Korolev was not a Bombardment crater—it was far too large for that—but it had something of the same shape for some of the same reasons, an impact by something relatively small moving at unusually high velocity. Whatever had formed Crater Korolev had come in almost at right angles to the orbits of the planets, and socked into Mars up close to the North Pole and nearly perpendicular to its surface, at a velocity that was high even for a meteor. The crater was almost perfectly round and its sharp-sloping wall stuck far up above the surrounding plain. When, after a few years of the Bombardment, the polar ice cap had melted and the water had flowed north from the mud-ocean underlying Chryse, the rising water of the resurrected Boreal Ocean had first surrounded Korolev, and then lapped over the low spots in the wall, forming a deep, beautiful lagoon, surrounded by a circular string of mountainous islands.

If there were a spot of level ground anywhere that wasn't man-made, Jak couldn't see where it would be. Each of the knife-blade narrow, curving islands reared up out of the sea as if it were lunging to grab the stars; their jagged tops bore ice, even this far into summer, and between the twisted and battered trees that clung to their red-rock sides, innumerable strands of waterfalls poured down over them, little lines and bows of silver in the sun. The islands farther away seemed to sink into the sea, and from Jak's high window, looking out over the deep blue lagoon, he could just see little snowcaps, barely peeking out of the water, framing the horizon.

The lagoon itself was filled with sailboats; some must be for pleasure, some perhaps for fishing or cargo, but everywhere within the lagoon the white and silver sails moved silently and majestically. Jak wondered if any of them took passengers.

Leaning out the window to see, Jak discovered that his hotel—if he was in a hotel—was built into the side of one of the great craggy islands. When he looked right and left, the smooth walls ended in ridges of what appeared to be natural stone.

Below him there were red tile rooftops and narrow alleys between buildings, and then the deep blue lagoon: the shadow of this island reached a quarter of the way to the horizon, darkening and smoothing the waters and letting Jak see down into them a little way, to where a school of fish, each twice the length of divers hanging onto their fins, was swimming slowly in toward the island.

He could see why Sib had liked it here.

There was a soft ping from his purse and it said, "The representatives of the Paxhaven Fighting Academy are here."

"Dilate the door." Jak turned. The two men who came in were in their late teens or early twenties, younger than Jak but not much younger, and dressed in what Jak thought of as the "Paxhaven uniform": a soft shirt in a bright color (both wore a vivid deep blue), the jacket, pants, and belt of an ancient martial arts gi (on both of these men it was in pastel blue), and a long cloak (black) over it. The smaller of the two men said, "Hello, I'm Rej Waramez, and this is my partner Maruk Sebaskawa. We are here on orders of our teachers, partly as a matter of compassion and pity, but also as trainees, to acquire the story of a fallen warrior of our school."

"It is the belief of our teachers that you need to and we need to tell the story of your uncle and we need to listen to it," Maruk added.

Jak nodded. "Well, I need to talk, and I suppose students

always need to listen. Shall we sit down? May I offer you anything?"

"We were going to suggest that it's a beautiful day," Maruk said, "and you've been in this room for a long time. Perhaps it would help to get out and walk a bit?"

When they had told him they thought they might walk around a farm for a while, he had had visions of something like the farms he had visited in Africa, on Earth, or that perhaps this would be one of those dreary countries where they want you to look at the sewage-to-hydroponics plant. He had not expected that it would be a tremendous array of brick planters, wedged against the natural rock into every possible crevice, and linked by catwalks, all over the seaward side of the island. It was a calm day, and the big, slow, low-gravity swells came in from the southeast as if their procession might grind to a halt at any moment. The sunward side of the island was if anything steeper than the lagoon side, and the catwalks were narrow, but since his companions seemed comfortable, Jak resolved to let himself get used to the height . . . though looking twenty meters straight down into the heaving, chopping, foaming water, this was easier resolved than done.

The many planters were crowded with broccoli, tomatoes, endive, and many plants that Jak was sure he had eaten but wouldn't happen to recognize. After a time they came around to a wider ledge with benches, where brightly colored flowers bounced in the sea breeze. "Nasturtiums," Maruk said. "They're edible, but I prefer to think we overproduce them just because they're pretty. That would explain why we're always getting a couple on the plate at every meal at every restaurant, and why now and then I find that some bartender has dropped one into my martini."

Jak chuckled. "That seems strange. Somehow the clothing, and the setting, and so forth, made me think this place would be ascetic."

"Only to the extent that it brings us pleasure," Rej said, grinning.

"I speck I dak some of what Sib loved about this place."

"That's very flattering," Maruk said. "Well. We won't be interrupted here (we've reserved this platform for an important official duty) so I suppose we should get started, if you're ready."

"I'll never be ready, but we can start." Jak looked out at the far horizon, where the blues of the sea and the sky joined, and up at the high cliff above him, where dozens of people wandered about the catwalks, one by one or in chattering groups, and then at the sun on the great banks of nasturtiums, and said, "So what is it, exactly, that we're doing?"

Rej nodded and said, "Well, part of our training is to know the stories of those who went before us. Our school is now a few centuries old and we think it's good to have legends about our successful graduates in oral memory. The way we do that is that each of us who is training to become an advanced master must learn, in precise words, the stories of ten fallen warriors of our school, and at least one of those stories must be one that we collected and composed ourselves. So we are here to collect the story of Sibroillo Jinnaka, and your testimony will be one important source for us. Then at his memorial service, each of us will recite our composition of his history."

Jak nodded. "Did Sib have to do this?"

"The requirement was imposed almost a century after his time," Maruk explained. "We evolve, develop, and change."

"And we make a distinction between those three," Rej

added, "which is why we try to have plenty of stories to tell and examine. Now, just talk about your uncle . . . we'll ask you questions . . . and don't worry about trying to get everything, as we will be talking to many others."

For four days, one or the other of them walked with Jak along the catwalks of the farm, or through the narrow alleys between the natural stone buildings, and Jak looked out at water and talked about Sibroillo, and Maruk and Rej asked questions, gently, almost shyly. The last day, Rej joined Maruk and Jak for the last couple of hours, and mostly they asked, "Would it be fair to say that . . . ?"

Then they told him that the funeral service would be in four days, and that after that there would be a small ceremony for Kawib, and the day following Jak and his party would be presented to the King.

At the end of that day, when Jak returned to his room sad and drained, there was a message from Dujuv: if Jak was ready, would he have dinner with Dujuv, Pikia, Shadow, and "another friend"? Jak had his purse send an immediate affirmative. He showered and changed and went to see them, if not happy, at least feeling better.

When Jak arrived, everyone was already seated, and a lively conversation was already under way. He started to say hello to his trusted toves when he realized who else was at the table. "Myx!"

Myxenna Bonxiao was one of Jak's oldest and closest friends, in addition to being a fast-rising star at Hive Intel. He had known she was coming to Mars, and would be catching up with his party, of course, but in the chaos and misery of the last few days, he had lost track of it; now he was delighted to see her. She jumped up to hug him, spilling the pitcher of beer on the table, and somehow it was the funniest thing that ever happened for everyone there.

When they had gotten a clean table, more beer, and an order in for food, Jak sat down and said, "Well, I've been going through the interviews with the warrior-trainees or whatever they're called."

"So have we," Dujuv said, "but it didn't take up as much of our time. A lot of my time has been spent being a presence at the Royal Archive. That's where they put the Nakasen lifelog. So I sit there, or Xlini does, and we keep asserting that it's ours. And they keep politely pointing out that that remains to be settled and that anyway, whoever's it may be, they've got it. It's a pleasant little ritual that doesn't take ten minutes a day. Once that's completed, we do the fun part."

"Which is . . . ?"

"I read the Paxhaven histories and look at their documents. Jak, do you know what an amazing place this is? First of all, there was a major town here within a hundred years of the first landings on Mars, way back in the Middle Ages—if you can believe it, this town was founded by people from Europe, back before the glaciers buried it. It was the northern summer home for the Old Emperors before the First Rubahy War, and the ruins of the resort town are under the lagoon—apparently there's a great scuba tour of it. When the Boreal Ocean re-formed during the Bombardment, they moved up here onto the crater rim and rebuilt—but basically this is one of the three or four oldest towns still occupied on Mars.

"And you know how people say that the King of Paxhaven would be the closest thing to an heir to the Old Emperors? Well, he's a lot more than *close*. The King really is the heir to the Old Empire. DNA-authenticated and the whole whacking djeste! He's actually a lineal descendant, always at least at the level of a prince, of the last Old Martian Emperor, and he has a separate line of descent from both dynasties of the Second Empire, too. Not to mention that also he's probably descended from a Chicagoan Catholic Papal Concubine, a Grand Mufti of Luna City, a Japanese Emperor, and two Presidents of the United States.

"Going so far back that one of those was even elected," Pikia put in. "I've been sort of watching over Dujuv's shoulder. *And* King Dexorth is a distant cousin of Paj Nakasen, a fairly close one of Ralph Smith, and the great-grandson of Elora Qanaganser. I don't think there's room for him to have a more distinguished bloodline; everybody in his ancestry is somebody."

Dujuv nodded. "It really looks like Paxhaven went out of its way to combine all sorts of interesting bloodlines, over and over, so they would always have that claim available. Oh, and one other detail—his mother was Scaboron of Greenworld's older sister. Dexorth is Shyf's first cousin."

"Well," Jak said, letting his stomach roll over for a moment, but enjoying it, "at least we know his bloodline isn't *perfect.*"

"Seriously, though," Dujuv said, "why have we never heard much about Paxhaven? This is also the place where they invented the Disciplines, and Maniples, and half a dozen other major things. A tiny little place where that much brains and talent make that much happen? It ought to be as famous as Athens, Florence, Weimar, Santa Clara, or Tycho City."

Shadow bobbed his head emphatically. "We Rubahy study your people and your customs very carefully (it is a matter of survival for us), and while we do not have an exact equivalent to your universities, you could probably fairly say that I hold a scholarly distinction something like your masters degree, in a field that would translate as 'human studies.' And I had not realized until this week that Pax-haven was of any particular importance whatever. I shall be careful in revealing what I have learned about this, for we have a conspiratist faction that would argue, from the fact that you have hidden it so well, that this entire city must be the home of a human secret weapon—and I would be loath to have a place so beautiful become a target, even hypothet-ically."

Dinner ran long; it was the sort of occasion when old friends need to visit and reminisce, and new friends need to be welcomed into the circle, and Myxenna seemed to take to Pikia as much as Shadow on the Frost and Dujuv already had. Jak noted after a while that Myx and Duj hardly spoke to each other, though they occasionally filled in a detail in an old story for each other. The had been lovers once, bitter with each other, friends again . . . and now, apparently, just slightly sore spots in each other's lives.

It was late but the sun was still out; there would be no true dark tonight, here at nearly seventy-eight degrees north. At last everyone split up to walk back to their quarters. Myxenna seemed to be going the same way as Jak—or, he suspected, to have Hive Intel matters to discuss with him. If so, she was taking her time about it; they went up to his room, and she gave him a bath and a backrub (without sug-gesting they renew their off-again on-again affair), and fi-nally she said, "Jak, my bosses have no idea what to do with you or about you. I am supposed to exercise my judgment and understanding, which, I suppose, is a way for them to say that I'm supposed to decide, and if it works out they'll take credit for giving me my head, and if not, they'll be able to pin the failure on me."

He rolled over on his back and looked up at her; when had she undressed? She was sitting cross-legged, looking back down at him, so that from his viewpoint her face was upside down. He thought for a moment and said, "I don't know what to say, Myx. I've failed at pretty nearly everything I've tried, and I've hurt a lot of innocent people. I had four assignments Hive Intel gave me—get the lifelog for the Hive, make sure Clarbo Waynong gets credit, preserve my cover in PASC, and keep their channel open to Shyf. A reasonable assessment of my performance is total failure at all four. Paxhaven has the lifelog. Waynong is the only person on this mission who looks like a bigger idiot than me (and as idiots go he's a talented professional to my gifted amateur). *Everybody* knows I work for Hive Intel. And Shyf might have finally lost interest in me, which is a good thing but does mean I don't even make a good *passive* spy."

Myxenna nodded. Her dark, wavy hair fell around her face in curtains. Jak couldn't read her expression. "That's not a bad assessment at a first whack, old tove, but you're overlooking how close you've come and how bad your circumstances have been. It is the opinion of Caccitepe—"

"Him."

"Yes, him. He's on your side, believe it or not."

Jak made a face. "Let's go with 'or not.' " Caccitepe had nominally been the Dean of Students at the Public Service Academy when he, Myxenna, and Dujuv had been there, and had actually been the recruiter/organizer for Hive Intel, cherrypicking the talented students into deep-cover placements in other agencies. Jak owed his present position to

Caccitepe, which was reason enough to hate him; but there had been a couple of peculiarly nasty, creepy meetings with Caccitepe as well—meetings in which the Dean of Students had seemed determined to rub Jak's nose in just what sort of a human being he was, and why an agency that specialized in assassination and corruption would want Jak. During his senior year, Jak had made a ritual of showering after every meeting with the Dean; it hadn't helped.

Myxenna rested her hand lightly on Jak's cheek. "Jak, I can't let you say anything more than that. It will make a mess of a lot of things if I do."

"All right, I don't like Caccitepe, but what does he have to say?"

Myxenna leaned down, very close, as if she were going to kiss Jak, but turned her head to barely breathe in his ear, "Well, to me, he usually says, 'Take off your clothes,' and I do." She sat back and looked into Jak's eyes. His heart crumbled inside him. He knew Myxenna was from a nobody family, ordinary middle-class people on the mid decks of the Hive, and he'd always known she'd do whatever it took to succeed. He just hadn't thought much about what it would take. He nodded, though, to show her he understood. Anything her purse picked up might be relayed to Caccitepe, who was spiteful and a monster of ego; she could be blamed for not objecting to what Jak said.

He wanted to ask if she was all right, but even here, naked together on his bed, the two of them—old friends, toktru toves, trusted pizos, and the best kind of open lovers though they were—dared not speak of any such thing. He could guess that one reason why Caccitepe had not simply sacked him, or had him killed, was that Myxenna had promised that she could "fix" him, and that she had made the promise to save him. Now for her sake he needed to get fixed . . . or at least ensure that whatever went wrong next was plainly not her fault. He had to help Myx to salvage him, and thereby both their asses. "Well," he said, "I'm blown with PASC, no question. No fixing that."

"We'd come to the same conclusion."

"This place is the solar system's center for martial arts. No elderly ceremonial guards. My chances of stealing the lifelog again are pretty slim. If I do find a way, I guess I can try to make Clarbo get the credit. Though that poor gweetz could probably get stuck with the blame for a rainstorm. And as for Shyf . . . well, that one's a no, Myx, I just can't. I'll rob my hosts, I'll give the credit to a fool, but . . . you don't know what she does to me or how nasty she is about it."

"I have an idea," she said. "I knew Seubla too, Jak. And Xabo. And two or three of her other victims who weren't as close friends to me. And to judge by what she's putting together for Kawib's memorial, I can make too many guesses about what she does to you. But you're in luck. Caccitepe says if you can win free of her, he won't stand in your way. He just won't help, and he's expecting full reports until you do win free. You see, he *does* know you. He knew which thing he couldn't ask for. That's one of his secrets. He always knows that . . ." She got off the bed and began to dress. "I don't think we should do anything until your feelings are more settled, Jak, is that all right? I want to do the right thing by my friend."

"You are," he said, and rolled sideways to kiss the middle of her back. Her skin was as soft and tender as ever.

Myxenna got up off the bed with swift grace, not hurrying, but not wasting a moment, dressed, and went out. The door constricted after her. Jak lay back to stare into space.

When it was time for Sib's memorial service, Rej and Maruk came for him, and he walked between them to the funeral-launch facility. It was a beautiful day—most days in Paxhaven were beautiful—and as Jak took his seat on the bench between his Paxhavian "keepers," he thought that 180 years ago, this place must have seemed, to the young Sibroillo, as if it had just reached out and hugged him.

Dujuv, Shadow, Pikia, and Myxenna were already there, seated on a bench together, behind Gweshira, who kept leaning back to talk to them, anxiously, about something. Clarbo Waynong and Xlini Copermisr sat on a bench in the back, probably more hoping not to be noticed than anything else.

Jak whispered to Maruk, "The dignified, older man over there, sitting by himself—"

"That's King Dexorth. He teaches at the Paxhaven Fighting Academy and he was a student there, once, with your uncle."

Jak glanced up to see King Witerio and Prince Cyx enter and take seats as well, and his heart leapt up to see Princess Shyf join the crowd. Sib would have been so utterly pleased to have kings and princes at his funeral. Devotion to the aristos had been the cornerstone of his life, and it seemed only fitting that they return some small measure of that devotion now.

It was almost time to begin, and the sun was just beginning to be a little too warm, when Jak almost jumped out of his skin. Bex Riveroma had walked in.

Jak could not have missed the big shoulders, shaved head, or hawklike mask of an expression anywhere at any time, and his most-feared enemy was doing nothing to conceal who he was.

Jak felt Rej's hand on his arm. "You are here under the strongest of peace bonds. *He* is here to pay respects to a worthy, honored opponent, and to someone who was once his closest friend. That is a fine and honorable courtesy in Riveroma. See that yours is no less. Do you dak?"

"I dak. Toktru masen. I was just startled."

Bex Riveroma bowed deeply to Jak Jinnaka, and Jak stood and returned the bow. Then, with what even Jak had to admit was perfect courtesy, Riveroma bowed successively to Gweshira, to Dujuv, and to Shadow, presumably his salute to worthy opponents. He saluted each of the aristos present as well; apparently if an extremely wanted criminal was going to appear at a public function, he would need to mind his manners.

The Paxhavian funeral ceremony is simple, direct, and aimed at what matters—Jak Jinnaka was later to realize that in this, it was like everything else about Paxhaven. In ascending order of closeness to the deceased, each person in the room stood and uttered a remembrance, touching either on something good and fine about Sibroillo Jinnaka that the speaker had personally witnessed, or on some lesson in life learned by having known Sibroillo, or finally about how his or her life had been shaped by knowing Sib. Jak was glad this was being recorded; he knew he would want to look at it many times.

When there were only three people left to speak, Bex Riveroma told his story of two bright, ambitious boys, always in competition and always inseparable, so warmly and well that Jak seemed to see the two of them scrambling down a cliff face together on some long-ago summer day, and thought of himself and Dujuv, and felt so warm and happy for Sib that he completely forgot, for the moment, that the man speaking was a war criminal, a would-be tyrant, and one of the most dangerous killers in the solar system.

Then it was Gweshira's turn, and she talked of the world of adventure and of the understanding of Nakasen's Principles that Sib had opened up for her (carefully, for she could not safely mention that it was the Circle Four interpretation of Nakasen's Principles that he had brought her into and encouraged her in). And now it was Jak's turn . . . he had prepared carefully, but he found when he stood in front of everyone that all he could do was talk about Sib's kindness and tenderness to him when he was very small; he meant to mention so many things on a carefully prepared list, but all the things he talked about had happened before he was seven years old, moments when his uncle had seemed to be all the love and justice and mercy that there needed to be in the universe, and he blubbered his way through the entire thing. He felt like he was making a fool of himself, but he saw that his friends were weeping with him, and took comfort in that.

At last Rej and Maruk got up to recite their new hero tales about Sib. Jak listened attentively, learning much that he had never known, and linking many things together for the first time. Truly, he thought, his uncle had followed his sword, lived at the service of the aristos, and every crowned head in the solar system was a little safer, every throne a little more stable, because of the love and the care Sib had lavished on preserving the established order. There were battles and raids, political intrigues and matters of honor, affairs and duels, times when the futures of nations had been car-

ried in Sib's cupped hands, times when Sib had risked life
and honor itself because he had given his word to one in-
significant person and he would not break it. The tales were
complex and rich, and if there was much overlap, the different takes were interesting too, Rej concentrating on Sib's
technique and cleverness, Maruk on his strategy and wisdom.

And now all the speaking was done, and the small rocket
stood gleaming in the sunlight, waiting for the laser to kick
it away from the island. They all filed by it, touching the
rocket for the last time, and retreated to a safe distance. It
rose in a cloud of fire on its laser propulsion; they watched
it until there was nothing left but the steam trail leading up
into the sunlit sky. Somewhere up there, Jak knew, the
rocket would activate the breakup commands, and turn itself
into a cloud of metal dust; Sib's body would fall naked back
into the atmosphere, to burn up and spread itself across the
Boreal Ocean. And forever after, so finely divided are
atoms, that everywhere on Mars, but especially in Paxhaven,
you would always be somewhere near a little bit of Sibroillo
Jinnaka.

Later that day, as everyone had predicted, Shyf's memorial for Kawib Presgano was a ghastly affair. She wailed and
keened all the way through a vast photo montage of still-
shots and moving pictures of her commander of guards;
many of them featured him with Seubla, which was almost
more than Jak could bear. It was very much her way; she
held her potential enemies close to her, loved them and cherished them and depended on them emotionally (which they
cooperated with mainly due to conditioning, but also because it was the only way to stay alive for any length of
time). At last she would tire of them, or become perma-

nently afraid of them, or any of a thousand reactions that were unfortunate for them . . . and they would die in some arranged accident, or because she continually exposed them to grave risks, or at the hands of her paid killers.

And then she would miss them and grieve for them endlessly. She knew that the hundred or so people she always had in her stable of conditioned slaves would all be overwhelmed with sympathy for her—sympathy that lay like a thick coat of sweet cream frosting on a cake made up of solid dogshit. She liked that best of all—the way she could break your heart while making you want to throw up.

Jak went home, worked through the Disciplines twice (once to honor Sib, once to honor Kawib), did his deconditioning, and was sound asleep well before dinnertime. There were times, nowadays, when he thought he might like to sleep forever.

CHAPTER 13

In the Hall of the Martian King

Jak and Dujuv had both been presented at the courts of Uranium and of Greenworld, two of the more affluent and famed courts of the solar system. Dujuv had been presented at dozens of courts in the Harmless Zone, all of them small, of course, but all very theatrical in a comic opera kind of way. And Jak had seen the opening of the Chamber of Deputies on Venus—not real royalty, of course, but still an awe-inspiring ceremony.

Yet afterward, talking with each other, both Jak and Dujuv agreed: their presentation to the King of Paxhaven was the most beautiful either of them had ever seen. (More than a hundred years later, they would still agree.)

It would have been in the King's right for the event to be gaudy; with his ancestry and with Paxhaven's history, he could have chosen to bedeck his great hall like a carnival midway, and few would have begrudged him that. After all, that was what kings, princes, and dukes with a tenth of Dexorth's credentials did.

But instead Paxhaven's Great Hall was merely a human-scale empty space, perfect in its form and shape, an endless iteration of golden sections joined to spheres like a geometric proof, all in steel and glass that reflected the bright afternoon polar sunlight pouring in from the many high elliptical windows. The transparent and reflective surfaces scattered a vivid amber shadowless indirect light everywhere and filled the upper parts of the room with countless curved and distorted images of the scene below intermingled with views of the sky outside. The alternating clear and mirrored columns and balls led the eye to the domed ceiling by one path and returned it by another, so that Jak felt that if he gave in to the impulse to follow his eyes, he would circle his head as if trying to limber his neck.

King Dexorth of Paxhaven and his court stood on a curved dais at the end of the central aisle between the rows of columns. His throne had been brought from Earth, and on Earth it had been very old before the first rocket reached toward the sky; old before Columbus had sailed, in fact. Dexorth wore a very old and very plain silver crown, a simple, unadorned set of battle fatigues, and black low-topped sneakers; the clothing of someone who meant to work. The nobles around him wore equally plain battle fatigues, white gis, or plain blue floor-length robes with academic hoods and stoles.

All stood in perfect quiet and silence; every other court that Jak had ever seen had been buzzing with whispering people leaning in to each other, and bustling quietly as people checked notes, discreetly spoke into their purses, and forgot where they were and scratched where it itched. These men and women were as silent and as still as any Disciplines master; Jak was shortly to learn that that was what they all were. Their posture was a perfect shizen-tai, the shoulder-width neutral stance of strong, patient defense, which expects nothing but can react to anything.

As Jak and the party from the Hive followed Shyf and the Greenworld party up the aisle through the glorious light toward the peaceful warriors on the dais, Jak's peripheral vision caught a subtle movement; from behind the pillars, as the party passed, guards with a bo-ken and a beam pistol would step out, facing the guests, assuming a neutral posture, staff held vertical in the left hand, right elbow cocked tightly against the body, pistol in the right hand pointed at the ceiling. As the party passed, the guards would bow, holster the pistol, hold the bo-ken vertical in both hands in front of them in the ancient Warrior Salute, and vanish back behind the pillar. It was simple and elegant like everything here, but it also kept the arriving party constantly surrounded by fighters at the ready.

They arrived before the dais, and at a whispered word from Gweshira, they knelt. The floor beneath their knees at once formed soft, cushiony spots. They bowed their heads.

"Look up," King Dexorth said. "Be among friends." He stepped off the dais and advanced to them, his balance still perfect and his body still neutral. "You have come a great way through terrible difficulties. We keep peace here. We may be able to find some of it that you can take with you when you go. Here in Paxhaven, we say to a friend, when arriving or departing, 'Find your way,' and they answer, 'Know where you are.' You may consider that your first lesson."

"We didn't exactly come here for lessons oomp," Clarbo Waynong said. Jak noted with satisfaction that Pikia had speared his solar plexus, striking behind her with extended fingers, without looking back. Her Disciplines work was coming along marvelously.

"Then perhaps you won't exactly learn anything, Clarbo Vaynong. But that would be a sad thing, and we won't speak of such possibilities. Your project will be developed between you and your trainer.

"Now, let me talk to all of you, Hive and Greenworld alike. Through your party, we have recovered an object of extremely disputable ownership. We believe our own claim to it is strong, as is that of the Hive, as is that of the Splendor of the Splendiferous Chrysetic People. Our diplomats on the Hive and in Magnificiti, and at the League of Polities headquarters in the Aerie, will be talking to everyone, exchanging ideas, to see if perhaps a consensus solution can be devised. Meanwhile the lifelog is safe here with us, and should we decide to send it to the Hive, we have a party authorized to carry it, right here, on hand. This seems very convenient for us. We shall try to make it convenient for you, by offering to do our best to make your stay with us worthwhile. Princess, your guards and men at arms will find we can sharpen their skills, no matter how good they already are, and we offer them this training at no cost to you or them. Now . . . we must find a project for each of you."

He looked from face to face in the group and said, "Jak Jinnaka, I believe? The nephew of Sibroillo Jinnaka?"

"Yes, sir."

"You hold your body like a man in pain, and I do not think it is your recent grief, for I can see that clearly as well, and this is something different."

"Yes, your—er—"

"The correct title is Your Perception. I'm afraid our protocol is not well known."

"Yes, Your Perception."

"Now, I think that you have been subjected to some crude and brutal form of mind control—you have several of the traces of it about you—am I right?"

"You are right, Your Perception." Jak's eyes filled with tears and he didn't know why; he wanted to throw his arms around the King's legs and beg for something, he didn't know what.

Dexorth's smile was kindly. "Well, then, that gives you a project to do here. No one stays in Paxhaven without a project, you see, and not just any project will do. We know a great deal about treating such things, and about recovery from them . . . so your project will be to be free of the crude control, and at least of its grosser damage, before you leave."

"Er, Your Perception, I have been told it will take many months—"

"Whoever told you that lied," the King said. Jak heard a hint of anger. "But like most lies, there was an admixture of truth in it—in this case, that in the outside world it would take a long time. We'll have you over it in a couple of weeks. We know more than they do, you see."

The King turned his attention to the others, and one by one set them to projects; Pikia to advancing quickly in the Disciplines, Shadow on the Frost to learning the true place of Paxhaven among the human nations, Myxenna to finding a sense of peace with her ambition and her own ruthlessness. He hesitated a moment and said, "Teacher Xlini Copermisr, and Dujuv Gonzawara . . . I know you are both scholars of ancient languages, one of you professionally, one of you as a hobby. Now, since the lifelog will be read while you are here, you are welcome to participate in the process of translation, though I think we will make sure that someone else sees everything first, before you see it, and we may be selective in what you are allowed to see from the lifelog. For you, Teacher Copermisr, I think this will be a suitable enough project; you seem to know your place in the world, and to be happy with the way on which you have set your feet, and it is time for you to understand more of Nakasen, certainly. And for you, Dujuv . . . you have been, I believe, harassed and humiliated all your life by the assumption that a panth is stupid?"

"I have been, Your Perception," Dujuv said, looking at the floor, his voice barely more than a whisper.

"We have reviewed your correspondence with your friend Phrysaba Fears-the-Stars, which we took the liberty of finding in your purse. You have the scholar's touch, if you want to use it . . . so perhaps while you are here, you will let us guide and develop that gift for you."

"I would like that very much, Your Perception."

"Your project will be to learn to appreciate your gift. It is relatively easy for others to know that you are bright; it seems to be difficult for you to know. We will change you so that you cannot forget it."

"Thank you, Your Perception." Dujuv seemed to be choking up.

"Now, Gweshira. Your return here at this time in your life is fortunate for us all. You have a chance to look for your way, again; we are at your disposal to help. At this sad time in your life, this may be a comfort and a source of strength to you; it also brings, to us, the valuable perception of someone who has been out in the world recently."

Gweshira pressed her face to the floor; the King nodded and turned to Shyf. "It must be difficult to be you, cousin."

"I've always thought so," she said, looking him boldly in the eye.

"You are witty. Would you like to contemplate the possibility of being happier?"

"You mean, would I like to be happier? Who wouldn't?"

"I asked you if you would like to contemplate it."

"You can't just . . ." She seemed to feel the air in front of her, as if searching through a floating cloud of invisible objects. "You can't just make me happier?"

"Not unless you want to be, and you don't."

Shyf stared at him and scratched her head in a completely unprincessly way. "You're right. I don't. Why don't I?"

"Perhaps you'd like to contemplate that, and find out?"

"I—yes. I think I would like that."

"Good. A meditation master will call on you tomorrow morning." The King looked around at the assembled visitors and said, "Now you all have your projects. Perhaps a little history will clarify who we are and what we are, here. When Paj Nakasen set up the Wager and began its propagation, he planned to have five pillars to sustain and uphold it. I myself do not know what three of them were, but one was the Hive, and one was Paxhaven. The Hive was to supply force, collective spirit, and orthodoxy; Paxhaven was to supply insight, individuality, and change. So the Hive supplies the guidebooks, the preachers, the missionaries . . . we let whoever wishes, come here, and we give them a project.

"Thank you for supplying us with a reason to exist. The audience is over. It's a nice day. Would anyone like to go outside and play?"

The next morning a very rude middle-aged panth named Borcles tumbled Jak out of bed two hours before he had expected his alarm to go off. The man was clearly a Disciplines master, and he combined that with panth speed and grace; Jak was helpless as a kitten in sparring with him. After three strenuous hours, Borcles suddenly gave Jak a hard push on the chest and let him land on his ass on the mat. "Your problem," Borcles said, very calmly, "is that you are a worthless piece of shit, and therefore you will never be worthy of the Princess."

Jak came up in a tight roll, sprang forward, and went right into Borcles's fist, nose first. His head exploded in pain. The panth smiled broadly at him and said, "Your problem is that the only worthwhile thing you have ever done in your life is fuck that woman, and now that she doesn't want that, there's no reason for you to keep existing."

Jak swung again; his hand was hooked out of the way and the heel of Borcles's other hand snapped against Jak's jaw, staggering him.

"Your problem is that you don't know anything except that you're hot for the Princess."

Jak came to guard but did not strike.

"Your problem is that you don't care about yourself or anyone else and the Princess is the only excuse you have not to die."

"You're right—" Jak started to say, when Borcles kicked him in the belly and knocked him flat on the mat. Jak curled in a protective position, trying to get his feet pointed at the master, beginning to feel real fear.

"Your problem, pizo, is that you don't know shit," Borcles said, and walked away.

"You need to think about these experiences," a soft, feminine voice said, beside Jak. He rolled over to see a tiny blond woman with skin of pure white and pink eyes. "Don't be startled," she said. "Oh, too late, you already are. Anyway, it's a normal genetic variation and you will get used to it. I'm Blireana. I'm your meditation master. Get into the lotus position, get your breathing under control, and we'll see what we can do for you next."

The meditation was demanding and lengthy, but Blireana seemed kind and patient enough. Then Jak was finally allowed a light meal, followed by a nap under hypnosis (it gave him nightmares, which the doctors assured him were normal), followed by working through the Disciplines katas, and then off to "your head doctor," as the happy, smiling Novita, his Disciplines trainer, explained to him.

"Uh, the doctor in charge, or the doctor for my head?" Jak asked, rubbing his face down with the warm wet towel she had handed him.

"We'll let you decide. He's the heet you see next, masen?"

"Toktru masen." Jak was tired and he knew he'd be sore the next day, but it was the kind of healthy tired and sore that promised he'd be better eventually. "Uh, is this my daily routine?"

"Well, it will always start with Borcles, and you're on my schedule for at least the next week." She stretched, practicing a couple of the moves forward-into-a-grip. "So your routine will be pretty close to this. A lot depends on how things go with your head doctor. Right through there—"

"Are you—um, do you train a lot of people at Disciplines katas?"

"Just four a day. You're the new one."

"And—may I ask—do you get perfect scores all the time, the way you just did?"

"Oh, Nakasen, no, not more than eighty percent."

"Supposedly the official record is sixty-six percent. Achieved by a heet who works through the full katas seven times a day and does nothing else. He's about eighty years old."

"That would explain it. He's overtraining. And if he keeps it up, in twenty years, he'll be a hundred. Right through that door—second one on the right on that third cat-walk up above—Doctor Falimoraza is expecting you."

Falimoraza was a simi—the ape genes in that breed's ancestry were very apparent, and he looked more like an orangutan or a gorilla than like a human, at first glance, though he could stand erect, his head had a big brain dome, he spoke better Standard than Jak, and the clear intelligence looking out of his eyes would have been apparent to anyone. He asked Jak many questions, drew him out gently on many sensitive subjects, took a series of neural scans and measurements, and finally downloaded a bedtime routine into Jak's purse. "Get to bed before twenty-one o'clock, or Borcles will be dragging you out tired and grumpy again," he added.

That night, Jak had bad dreams, but not impossibly bad ones, and the next day Borcles woke him, and it started again. Four days went by and Jak mostly worked out, went to his treatments, and went to bed early. The dreams did not fade, but neither did they become worse.

The message on his purse said, "Matter of importance to the mission," and it was from Dujuv and Xlini Copermisr. Since they had to meet on a particular platform at a particular farm, clearly they didn't want the conversation overheard.

Dujuv arrived first, dressed like a Paxhavian, in gi, cloak, and high-tops, with a low hat that concealed his bald head. Jak was about to tease him about his "disguise" when he realized that that was just what Dujuv intended, and that probably someone who was not Dujuv's best friend would not have recognized him. "This is serious," Jak said.

"It is, old pizo. They don't come any more serious."

When Copermisr arrived with her hair in a scarf and wearing something that could easily be mistaken for a medical uniform, Jak considered that she was one of the most practical and one of the least romantic of the group, and said, "All right, now I'm intrigued. What have you learned that's so important?"

Dujuv started to speak, then turned to Copermisr for help. She shrugged and said, "Nothing that will come as that much of a surprise to scholars of the period, except that it's really indisputable evidence of something that we've all whispered to each other. There were always a number of things you didn't publish if you were smart, things anyone could read in any library almost anywhere that nonetheless were just ignored. If you had a smart grad student get interested in it, you steered the student away. If you had somebody like, oh, let's call him Clarbo, and you wanted to bury his career forever, you encouraged his interest in it."

"What is 'it'?" Jak asked, exasperated.

"The thing that I'm afraid to say in public, even now. The strangeness about Nakasen that was always easy enough to detect, the oddity of some of the things that went into founding the Wager. The invisible ten-ton elephant in the living room of our philosophy, or the crazy uncle rattling his chains in the attic of our religion. That which we don't talk about even though all of us know it. 'It.'

"Now, there were always known to be certain touchy and iffy things about Nakasen's record. The man lived more than two hundred years and wrote prolifically; the Principles, the

Teachings, and the Suggestions weren't even five percent of his known output, and they were *far* from characteristic. He wrote a few notes and letters per day for a hundred ninety years, and yet the edition of the Collected Letters most of us read in school has only about a hundred letters in it . . . in all that voluminous material, you see, there's something hiding in plain sight.

"Finding the lifelog has about tripled the amount of his writings we have . . . and if it were like all the other material, that would make it harder to see the problem. But Dujuv got curious about why the lifelog held so much correspondence with the Nontakers, looked into it, and found something that will go straight up everybody's nose—a brilliant piece of work, and your tove really ought to consider life as a scholar, just as the King said, by the way, and you should be proud of him."

Dujuv seemed very uncomfortable and embarrassed, which, Jak knew, was the way he usually reacted to anyone's saying anything that made him happy and proud.

"Uh, before we discuss any further," Jak said, "I should remind you that my purse might as well be a Hive Intel bug—"

"That's one reason for discussing it with you," Dujuv said. "This is urgent. The right people have to know that this stuff is about to break on the solar system, and they need to know it earlier than when it happens. It's a lot more than just 'the biggest religious revelation in centuries,' Jak. This is something . . . I don't even know how to start."

Copermisr made an impatient little flutter of her hands. "Dujuv, doubt does you credit, but you've found overwhelming evidence. Jak, do you know who the Nontakers were?"

"People who rejected the wager. A lot of them became rebels and led some of the anti-Wager organizations. The way the history books go, they're sort of the bad guys, but not really, because usually it's said that they just didn't understand—"

"Almost all the early Nontakers—the leaders, later— were close friends of Bob Patterson, later known as Paj Nakasen. They were the people who knew him best, the ones he worked with, at his old job. And what did he do for a living before founding the Wager?"

"Um, some kind of writer?"

"Head writer for one of the most popular comedy vid series in history. He was a funny man. He made up jokes."

"Yeah, they're always pointing that out in school, how witty he was—"

"Oh, he was witty. But what Dujuv discovered was his best joke ever."

The panth hunched his shoulders and said, "Most of the Nontakers were his old friends, his fellow comedy writers . . . and he wrote some letters to them while he was working on the Principles . . . explaining why the first edition was going to be published, and I quote, 'Anonymously, as if it were by some goofy shaman wanna-be named Paj Nakasen.' "

Jak had never particularly believed in the Wager, keeping quiet mostly to avoid quarrels. Yet he felt a chill run up his spine. "So it was all—what did you find?"

"What I found basically is the 'Just Kidding' sign, stuck to the side of the box that your religion and philosophy, and mine, and almost everyone's, came in. It was a joke, Jak, a joke he had to hide because it was aimed at very politically powerful people. Writing anti-aristocratic satire isn't a healthy occupation now, and it really wasn't healthy then when there were still people around who were witnesses, or had known the witnesses, to the Age of the Dynasties. It was still common knowledge, then, and not a quaint old business, how the first generations of aristos had come up out of organized crime—pirates, druglords, gangsters, robbers, and thugs of all kinds.

"Well, Nakasen was a satirist. Or rather Bob Patterson was. That was what he preferred to be called, by the way, but I'm getting to that. Satirists make fun of things that other people go into rages and tears about.

"According to his letters to his friends, Nakasen's principles were—this is a quote—supposed to be the 'secret rules the upper class live by,' or 'a guide to helping the average person be as big an asshole as the average aristo.' He saw the way the aristos actually behaved, when you stripped away all the bowing and ceremonies that they insisted on, and being the funny heet he was, he couldn't help mocking it. He published it anonymously because he thought people would get the joke and the tyrants and monopolists might put a price on his head."

"So the Principles are actually—"

"About how to be a treacherous, murdering bastard and carve your way to the top over the bodies of your friends. Intended to make fun of that behavior. And if there's open access to the lifelog, people will be able to see Nakasen working on that, writing notes to people who we've recast, in history, as his bitterest enemies, and cackling with glee whenever he takes what he thinks is a really good shot. Then they'll get to see his dismay when the Principles become a self-help bestseller, and people start to talk about how behaving like this changes their lives.

"That's the saddest part, when you see the clown trapped in his own routine, trying to mitigate the damage and maybe use some of his influence for good, for the rest of his life. The Hive was a scheme to wipe out most aristocratic families, by forcing them to blend in.

"He wanted the Hive to be a republic because, and there's no getting around this, Paj Nakasen was a republican to the bottom of his heart. More so than our most radical republicans today. And it's clear that the people who got the joke, the ones who laughed along with him, were dear to his heart, and that Paj Nakasen was laughing, and not even up his sleeve, at every one of the Acolytes and Teachers and all those other people they taught us to admire in school.

"This is like an ancient Greek finding out that Socrates referred to Plato as 'that moron' ... or maybe a medieval Christian discovering a letter from Jesus that says, 'Dear Judas, It's so good to have a friend I can write to. Wait till I tell you the stupid thing that asshole Peter said today—'

"And I don't think that people nowadays are going to react one bit better than their ancestors would have. This is uproar and chaos, Jak, utter uproar and chaos, and when it gets out, the solar system will be looking at, oh, I don't know, a century of war and rebellion. That's why Hive Intel has to know about this."

Jak couldn't breathe; the huge python, cold as ice, was squeezing him too hard. He tried but could not budge his arms; he kicked frantically about, tangling his legs in the covers. His chest was agony where the freezing cold coils squeezed his upper arms down into his ribs, and his hands flapped uselessly, unable to touch any part of the snake. He could feel his ribs popping, and he knew that if he let himself exhale even a tiny bit, to ease the pain and pressure, that all would be toktru lost, for the snake—so cold that it burned him like a brush of liquid nitrogen—would bear down, driving the air from his lungs, so he kept his jaws clamped and endured the burning inside his chest as the air, now burning hot and devoid of oxygen, sought to force its way out of him.

His eyes adjusted and he could see that the snake itself was made of pale blue ice; he could see its spiky spine and tiny heart, watch as thoughts like little red and black worms crawled through its frigid brain. It turned and looked at him with the most beautiful blue eyes, like Martian twilight; Shyf's eyes . . . no, to Jak, those eyes were still Sesh's . . .

He wanted to scream, "What have you done with Sesh?" but Uncle Sib stood over the bed and shook his head. Jak's uncle was alive again, his sad expression distorting as if in a wavy mirror because a loop of the ice-python had flipped across Jak's eyes, the burned left side of his head bulging from steam and covered with crumbling black skin and hair.

Sib shook his head again. "Sometimes, pizo, you have to do what doesn't come natural, and sometimes you have to trust and let go. You want help, don't you?"

Jak tried to nod but the snake had wrapped his head down in more loops, leaving only his mouth and chin uncovered, feeling with its tail for an opening to get round his neck.

"I imagine you do. Well, you can't get any help from me."

Through the distorting clear coils, between the cage of the pale clear blue ribs and spine, Jak saw the blue eyes of the snake, with the fiery coal of the brain burning between them, closing in, and then felt its hard, smooth snout—taut elegant leather—bumping at his lips. He knew then that all the squeezing and choking was only to make him open his mouth; the ice-python intended to thrust down his throat and tear out and eat his heart.

"Sometimes," Sib said, casually, "you have to be willing to face the worst, head straight for the fear, go toward the pain, lean into the blade. Are all these metaphors making sense, pizo? Think about how you slip out of a hammerlock, masen? How do you do it? What are you most afraid to do right now?"

Open my mouth, Jak thought. *Dujuv is in the next room on one side of me, and Pikia is on the other side, and if I screamed for help . . . would the snake eat my heart before they got to me? Would they hear? I get one scream.*

He looked into the ice-python's Shyf-blue eyes, and nearly relaxed and let it come in for his heart; but somehow behind them he could see Sib, distantly, making frantic, confusing gestures, trying to tell him not to do one thing and to do another.

Well, might as well go out trying.

He shouted *"Help!"* as his chest collapsed, then felt icy leather on his tongue and throat as the big iron-hard head hammered a passage through his lungs.

"Jak?"

The lights came on and Jak was rolling over to his side and vomiting, a single hard surge that seemed to empty his belly completely through his mouth, spattering across the floor. He spat frantically to clear the taste and avoid aspirating it, and then sucked in a huge, lung-filling gasp of cold pure air.

"Weehu, old tove, did you need us here to do that on?" Dujuv's voice was shocking in its gentleness; Jak looked up to see his friend had jumped back two meters, to the other side of the room, to get out of the way of the spew, and on the way had simply grabbed Pikia over his shoulder, like a sack of potatoes, and taken her with him. He set her down gently, apparently unaware that she was in jammies and bunny slippers.

The world swam into focus and the last traces of sleep fled from Jak's exhausted brain. No snake. No Sib. Another nightmare. Jak climbed out of bed, watching where he put his feet, and spoke to his purse. "Uh, can you get some cleanup in here—"

"It's already on its way," the purse said. "I heard that sound and thought you would need it." There was a thundering sound of water in the bathroom. "I'm also drawing you a tub. And mixing you up a nice warm mouthwash, and I'll have something soothing brought in for your tummy." Jak massaged the reward spot firmly, making sure he got several loud cheebles.

"Well," Pikia said, "you still seem to be alive, despite those noises you were making. I was worried. Try not to have more than ten of these a night, masen?"

"Toktru," Jak said.

"Anyway, you've got Dujuv for company, and I'd just as soon not get home and tell Great-great-grandpa Reeb that I spent any time visiting with you in the bathtub, toktru. So I'm going back to bed, if I can find clean floor to get there on, and I'll leave you boys to bond with each other."

"I'm glad you came to see if I was all right," Jak said. "Thank you, Pikia."

"Any time, pizo," she said, all her attention on stepping only on dry spots on her way back to her door.

Dujuv stood by calmly as Jak stripped into the clothes freshener. "Need someone to talk to, or need to be alone?"

"Need to talk to someone, toktru. Even by the standards of nightmares, that was a bad one. Thanks for coming and waking me up."

"Just returning the favor. You screamed like something was eating your heart."

"Almost." Jak gargled and spat. He slipped into the warm water; a faint hum and whoosh told him his bathwater was being continuously scrubbed, and from out in the rest of his suite he could hear the cleaning robots getting to work.

Jak sat up, wiping the streaming water from his face, and shook his head to get it to stop dripping from his hair. The warm clean bath felt wonderful; a moment later his stomach-settler arrived, and with it a pile of sandwiches for Dujuv, who ate, for once, as if distracted, and without the full attention he usually gave to it. After he had finished the first sandwich, he asked, "So, was it about Shyf? Or about your uncle?"

"Both. And maybe about needing to reach out to my toves more. I'm glad you came to me."

"Weehu, you needed the help." Dujuv dug into the next sandwich, masticating it to pulp in a few mighty chomps and swallowing it in one gulp. "They told you this was going to hurt, tove. And hurt a lot."

"Toktru." Jak sighed. "Every time I succeed, I feel better; every time I slide back . . . well, I succeed more than I slide back."

Dujuv made a strange face around the sandwich he was in process of gobbling; he swallowed hard and took a big swig of tomato juice. "Have you thought about what we discussed a couple of days ago, Jak?"

He shrugged. "I don't know about you, but I trust King Dexorth. He and his counselors are going to do the right thing, I think. Maybe not what the scholars and teachers back on the Hive would want, but definitely the right thing."

"I hope you're right." The panth sat on the edge of Jak's bathroom sink with easy grace. "Never thought I'd see a problem I couldn't solve with food. Just shows you that the world is more complicated than we know." He took a sip of his juice. "I wish that lifelog had been destroyed before I found out what was in it. Because now I can't *not* know what's in there, and every time I think about that, the whole universe falls away from me."

Jak nodded. "I can tell you feel that way."

"And I can tell you don't. And I have to admit, old pizo, that puzzles me more than anything else. Don't you get it? It's not a guide to human beings living their lives, it's Nakasen's *satire*. He was *joking*. And the joke turns out to be that he's telling everyone how to behave like an aristo, what an aristo believes and does, *because he thinks it's despicable*. Worse than that. *Silly.* Jak, if this gets loose in the human noosphere . . . think about it. It could trigger enough war and revolution to match any of the big convulsions before. As bad as the Age of Dynasties. As bad as the Great Upheaval. Maybe as bad, in proportion of the population and in the amount of violence and change, as the Red Millennium itself."

Jak nodded. "So there's going to be plenty of trouble. Toktru. I get that. Didn't we always expect that there would be a lot of trouble? Wasn't that why we wanted the jobs we got? Uproar for the human race is adventure for us, old tove."

"But at what cost?"

"I don't think they'll charge us anything. Very likely they'll pay us."

"Jak . . ." Dujuv sighed. "I wish you'd burst out laughing right now and tell me you're playing dumb. It's weird. You've traveled as much as I have, but you've never been anywhere."

"What's that supposed to mean?"

"Jak, suppose human civil war breaks out. What's that going to mean on Mercury, which is a prime piece of strategic real estate, occupied by hardworking—god, nobody works harder than they do—people who are used to getting no reward at all, when all of a sudden everyone is trying to grab their world from each other? When ten different armies land there and start to fight and six different spatials try to blockade it and a whole planet that has to import food has all its space cargo facilities bombed out?

"Or what's it going to mean to the merchant crewies? Nakasen's hairy bag, old tove, with all that sail spread, you can see a sunclipper with binoculars from five AUs away, and their habitats are just thin-walled cans. And everyone will be trying to shut off trade with everyone else, and if there's general war and civil war and revolution besides, no one is going to be respecting all the old conventions about letting neutral shipping alone. All our old trusted pizos on the *Spirit of Singing Port* might as well be glued to the center of a bull's-eye the size of Jupiter.

"Or think about the Harmless Zone. Think of every castle and palace and every delicate little opera house and every beautiful museum and statue . . . think of all those people just living and making life good where they are . . . and have you noticed that it's a perfect place to turn into one big industrial park? Vast resources, great transport, educated population—it was an industrial belt once, and that's what it will be again, because some damned fool is going to take the chance to take a shot at starting the Third Empire, and the Hive and the Jovian League will both be down on that—and at each other's throats besides—

"Or think about the Aerie—two billion people living fifteen centimeters from vacuum—or remember Africa, on Earth, how beautiful it is? Right in the middle of it is the capital of Uranium, and most of the continent belongs to the duchy, and when big trouble starts, everyone will be gunning for that. At the bottom of the deepest gravity well that human beings live in. There'll be a second and a third and a two hundredth Bombardment, and then what happens to the grasslands and the wild horses and the elephants and all?

"Don't you see how much we're about to lose? And that our whole bet—the whole Wager itself—is toktru *lost?* Ninety-five percent or so of humanity *took* the Wager, and it turns out, no, we were all wrong, it's not the way to live, it's not the likely pathway to a decent world, it's a bitter joke! We don't even have a decent religion or philosophy to get the human race through the nightmare that's coming!"

Dujuv had been leaning forward, fingers locked together, speaking very fast but not raising his voice at all, as if whispering the most dreadful secret of all time to Jak. Now he stopped as if switched off.

The warm water and the relief of no longer being in the nightmare had relaxed Jak; he had sat and listened without reacting much, his soft comfortable muscles allowing his mind to just relax and accept his old tove's words. Jak breathed deeply, three times, tongue resting lightly against the roof of his mouth, gently opening and filling his sinuses, the way Sib had taught him to do when you were trying to perceive something difficult and unclear; he let the relaxation wash over him and the knowledge of the situation come in after it.

"Dujuv, maybe I'm toktru misreading you, and maybe this is completely wrong, but I have a feeling. I think there's some weird way that you're *glad* all that is coming, and you're *glad* that the Principles turned out to be what they are, and you're trying to talk yourself out of feeling that way, trying to make it feel like you don't want all that upheaval, when I think another part of you really just can't wait. And maybe you should tell me about that part before I try to say what I think about what you just said. Because I don't think I should answer only half of what a toktru tove has to say, and especially not the half that he maybe doesn't believe himself, or maybe he just won't say what he really feels about it, or something."

Dujuv heaved a sigh and buried his face in his hands. "Nakasen, Jak, I thought I had a better act going than that. Was it that easy to see through it? This feels like a case of Principle 29: 'If your friends see through your act, expect the blow from your enemies at any moment.'"

"The only thing I'm seeing, old tove, is that you're not telling me everything you're thinking, and you've just made a long speech to avoid saying whatever it is that you toktru want to say." Jak fiddled with the reheater, adjusting it slightly upward, and lay back to enjoy the warmth flowing in; he slowed his breathing and heart rate, the better to accept whatever Dujuv might be about to say.

The warm brown of Dujuv's bare head glinted in the soft indirect lights of the bathing room, but his face remained hidden in his hands for so long that Jak began to wonder if his oldest, most toktru of toves would ever speak. When he did, it was almost a whisper. "Yes, Jak, I think I *am* glad.

I've seen people dying young of *radzundslag,* on Mercury, and I've seen the hopeless expressions on the faces of the children born into peonage. I've seen proud crewies with generations of deep-space experience converted to virtual slaves on their own ships by one minor accident or one clever trick of an insurance company. I've seen some of the best artistic, musical, and literary talents in the solar system wasted—and I mean *wasted*—in the Harmless Zone, re-creating things that were old a thousand years ago, encouraged to dither and fiddle themselves away to nothing. I've seen that evil princess hold my best tove in thrall and torture him half out of his mind, and you and I both remember some of the things she was doing among her own people, and that still makes me sick. And I've seen my own nation help her do it.

"And the whole time, I thought *I* was insane, Jak. Because we judge right and wrong by the Wager and you know, there's not a word in the Wager against slavery or tyranny or war. There's not a thing in the Wager to say that children should be loved and cherished, or should grow up to be free and strong and unafraid. Oh, the Wager sometimes urges us to be kind, because it's an effective way to manipulate others, or brave, because it's an effective way to get what you want—but, Jak, that's all. I thought I was the only person who felt that way.

"And now, of all things, I find out Nakasen did. I find out he was making fun of the cruel petty tyrants of his day, writing out the guide to how they acted. And for the first time in my life, I really, truly, deeply wish I could have known Paj Nakasen, and served at his side."

"But I would have thought—"

"I want to make a new Wager. I want to bet that Nakasen

was right—that *Bob Patterson* was right—about us. Nobody writes satire for people who can't get the joke. You don't mock people for what they can't help. But you do for what they can. And he believed that people could do better than following all those blind stupid pig aristos on through the centuries, losing the best parts of ourselves so that the aristos can be . . . amused." He stared down at the floor for a long time, thinking of something or other. When he looked up at Jak, his voice was as neutral as a machine's. "I bet you can't dak what I'm feeling."

"Humanity tried democracy for a long time, Duj. Some places are still trying it. It spoiled and ruined most of the good things about life."

"Did it really? Or is that what they want us to believe?"

"Oh, come on, Duj, you're much too smart a heet to fall for conspiracy theories. Athens, where five percent of the people could vote, produced the Parthenon; they gave a lot of people the vote and they went down the tubes. The great cathedrals were built by kings and popes. The Taj Mahal was built by a monarch on a whim. Medieval America conquered a continent and gave us atomic bombs and reached the moon, then they freed the slaves and let women vote, and in no time at all they lost all their ambition and relied on the U.N. to protect them and got squished like bugs between the armies in the Quebec-Jamaica War. Now these are just facts, facts anyone knows from school. Oh, sure, a republic can work as long as not too many people have the vote—"

"Jak, what I'm asking you is . . . how did those get to be the facts? Who *wants* us to believe all that?"

"Facts are not true because people want us to believe them, they're true because they're true! Every democracy ends in ruin because there are so many worthless people and they vote themselves and their relatives into power and destroy all the beauty and glory—"

Dujuv stood up. "I'm glad you're feeling better, pizo. Keep up the deconditioning. I know it's tough but I think it's a good thing for you to be free of her. And if I hear you scream, I promise, solemn as a Rubahy, I'll run in to help. But right now we shouldn't talk more; we're both getting angry, and I want to stay toves." Dujuv grinned, so suddenly that it seemed as if a different man had been substituted for him at that instant, and added, "But you know, given that the solar system is producing twenty times the whole wealth of Charlemagne for every single human being—and yet we have hunger and people dying young—and this has been the way for five hundred years at least, I can't help pointing out that maybe it would be more glorious to feed and house and take care of everyone decently, than it is to hold a really fine parade or have a really great-looking ruler. Just can't help thinking that."

Jak shrugged. "I'd like to stay toves, too. But I can't help it either; I think if you did that, you'd have a race of slugs with no ambition."

"Do you have no ambition?"

Jak snorted. "Come on. You know me."

"And have you ever been hungry and not had access to food?"

Dujuv turned and left before Jak could answer. Jak lay awake the rest of the night, growing more and more angry that he couldn't think of the simple, obvious reply that Dujuv's cheap shot had demanded.

The next day, when Jak saw Doctor Falimoraza, he finally mustered the courage to ask why so little of his deconditioning time seemed to be spent on the deconditioning itself.

The doctor nodded a couple of times, leapt up onto a counter, and perched comfortably. "Well, what we do here in the treatment of anything is begin from the assumption that Paxhaven is a healing place. Things that come here get better—minds, bodies, friendships, marriages, even whole societies if enough of their members visit. So mostly we give you the good experiences you can have at Paxhaven, and encourage you to let Paxhaven work on you. For example, the conditioning itself is a trivial problem. The serious problem is that your personality has grown, more and more, to be the personality of a person who wants to be conditioned. So we need to get you past that. Healthy people, of course, don't want to be conditioned . . . it closes off too many other possibilities in their lives."

"I wish it didn't feel so much like love."

"It *is* love, Jak. Here's a saying of Paj Nakasen that you won't find in the Principles—'Love manifests the good the way the face manifests the person.' As we build up the good inside you, you'll find you can love in better ways, and conditioned love won't attract you much."

That evening, as Jak was drifting off to sleep, his door dilated suddenly. He sat up in bed and rolled toward fighting position, get time, get space, get room enough to work and see what's going on—Dujuv and Pikia were both out for the night, Shadow was in the other wing, no help close by—

A familiar voice said, "Calm love. Hard." The door contracted behind Shyf; the lights came up. "I have been overridden," Jak's purse said, its voice tinny and twisted by the difficulty of getting even that much of a message out.

Jak stared at the Crown Princess of Greenworld as a very

small mongoose might stare at a very big cobra; wanting the fight but hating the odds. He was aroused, but not uncontrollably; her giving the "Calm love" command had soothed him but not dangerously so. He could not quite trust himself to do the right thing if he moved.

Shyf took off her long nightgown in one smooth movement. She stretched out on the bed and said, "Hard, hard, hard, that's good, now, *hard rage.*"

It took less than a minute and Jak felt sick afterward. He was crawling toward the bathroom when behind him, as she was putting her gown back on, Shyf said, "Calm love. Calm love. You're sleepy, you're sleepy, you're sleepy—" and the world slowed down and became fuzzy and soft-edged, a warm friendly place, and he just needed to rest on the floor here—

His purse howled an alarm and then was choked back. The door dilated. Bex Riveroma walked in. Jak rolled as hard as he could, but he seemed to be at the bottom of a well filled with molasses, and Riveroma seemed to flash from point to point like a flea with hyperdrive. He bounded over Jak, landed behind him, hammerlocked him, and clapped a stunner onto Jak's forehead. The last thing Jak heard was Shyf saying, "Remember you promised not to hurt him," and Riveroma saying, " 'Unnecessarily,' Your Utmost Grace, you always forget, 'unnecessarily.' "

CHAPTER 14

All Right, What's the Plan?

When Jak awoke, the most astonishing thing was that he awoke. He knew plenty of good reasons Riveroma would have had to just kill him. But here he was, in his bed, flat on his back, with Gweshira bending over him and saying, "He's waking up—"

"Good," Shyf said. She leaned into Jak's field of view as well. "Takes a little while for the stunner to wear off," she said. "You won't be able to talk for another minute or so."

After a long time, Jak was able to form the words "What's happening?" so that they could be understood. It was the most obvious possible thing, but then the situation seemed to call for obviousness.

"Well," Gweshira said, "it so happened that there was some old Greenworld business that Sib had been involved in, and that Her Utmost Grace and I were taking advantage of the chance to talk it over. And the subject of you came up. And I happened to have a visit with Bex Riveroma later that day, for quite different reasons—a little conversation about relations between Circle Four and Triangle One, actually, perhaps leading up to an armistice, because our two zybots have been feuding rather a long time with no gain to either. And between all the conversations, we realized that it was high time to just get rid of that sliver, which has been forever making a mess of your life, old pizo. It was Bex Riveroma's chance to destroy it and to know it really was destroyed; your chance to have it removed with friends watching; my chance to put that whole intrigue to bed for Circle Four."

"And I had some personal reasons as well," Shyf said.

"We didn't think Hive Intel would approve if we asked you in the presence of your purse. And it was better for you to be given no choice—that way you can't be blamed. Anyway, except for a few millimeters of fresh scar, your liver is now just like anyone else's, and you probably won't ever need to see Bex Riveroma again."

"But what about Riveroma getting away, free as a bird, with all those crimes?"

"Oh, he always *was* going to get away. That was never the question. He was a pro—he'd probably never have been arrested, or not prosecuted, or not convicted, or he'd have escaped—one way or another. And he knew that, about the five crimes whose files we had loaded into the sliver. We, and he, knew that all of it was things that no government anywhere would ever actually touch. Every one of them was crawling with nascent disasters for any polity stupid enough to prosecute Bex. And unless Clarbo Waynong becomes supreme dictator, there will never be a government that dumb.

"That was always the whole point, Jak. He had kidnapped Princess Shyf on behalf of the Duke of Uranium. That was a pretty normal crime, as crimes between aristos go. Not a big deal. We needed to make Bex want to release her more than he wanted to keep her. So we needed some leverage, some threat that would make him change his mind, especially if he forced us to carry out our threat. That was all there ever was to it.

"So we made the sliver and stuck it in you and threatened him, but what we were threatening him with were things that would inconvenience him, make him do some running and hiding, force him to change some identities and abandon some schemes. The idea was that we'd threaten to put a kink in his hose for a couple of decades, that was all. It was never about killing him or locking him up, and still less about bringing him to justice (as if that idea meant anything!)."

"But he's ruined people's lives and messed up all of history—"

"We all have, silly boy. It's what we do. Now, I'm going to get out of here because you and Shyf have things to talk about." She got up and left. Shyf waited a moment. She drew a breath and gently ran a hand over Jak's face. "No doubt your purse is recording this and relaying it back to Doctor Mejitarian at Hive Intel."

Jak sat straight up struck as if by a kick to his solar plexus.

"Of course I *know*, silly," Shyf said. "I discuss it now and then with some of the Hive Intel psych people, keeping the right balance, making sure you don't become either too independent or too dependent, things like that, masen? Think about it. That big monkey Dujuv that you're so fond of was panth-bonded to Myx, and I also had Dujuv conditioned to me, and after just a few weeks of deconditioning, he's been completely free of his bonding to either of us. And he's a *panth*. The genies have programmed twenty generations of that bloodline to imprint and bond deeply, he's naturally the most loyal lover and friend you could have, the singing-on essence of the tove for life, and yet deconditioning worked on him in less than three months. You're an unmodified native-stock human, you get sessions a couple of times a week and at-home treatment too, and it *still* hasn't worked on you?"

"But I get deconditioned all the time! After every message from you! Plus I see Doctor Mejitarian twice a week and he puts me under and—"

"Jak, how do you know that what's being done is *decon*ditioning? Conditioning wears off naturally. I have to rework all the Royal Palace Guards all the time. Conditioning wouldn't last anything like as long as it has lasted in you, all by itself. And the messages I've been sending you haven't been the reason. It's nearly impossible to condition someone—at least someone who doesn't want to be conditioned—at a distance, and non-interactively. At least some big part of Doctor Mejitarian's 'deconditioning' has been 'reconditioning.' You didn't realize? Too bad. Of course it was all at my request, as you might guess. Greenworld and the Hive are old allies, masen?"

Jak gaped at her, as shivering-cold as if a bucket of ice water had been dumped over him. Shyf was certainly a skilled enough liar, but it was undismissably likely that at least some of what she was saying was true. "But why would they—"

"Oh, Mejitarian can explain all that much better than I can. And Dean Caccitepe better still." She dismissed the entire issue with a captivating little wave of her perfect, elegant fingers.

"Why are you telling me all this?"

"Because I don't want you conditioned to me anymore, Jak. I had to use the conditioning, one more time, to get that sliver out of you, but these nice people at Paxhaven have been working with you on deconditioning, and with me on—well, never mind, that's complicated. Anyway, I prefer you free to conditioned. So I am returning the toy Hive Intel gave me, and I'm maybe telling him I'd rather he didn't let Hive Intel play so rough with him anymore.

"It's obvious, Jak, that all men are *not* created equal. Not even close. But a few men are crated eagles. And I'm the one that crated you, and your crate-er has just decided to endow you with your unalienable rights. Sorry to give you your freedom in a series of bad puns, but that's the way it goes, sometimes, important gifts show up wrapped in old newspapers, masen? Send me a message or something sometime, if you like, but I'd rather hear about you in the headlines and the gossip channels. Go fly. Make me proud." She got up, bent to kiss him, her mouth already opening . . . then stopped herself. She asked him, "May I shake your hand?"

"Sure," Jak said, holding his hand up as if he were a dog presenting a paw on command.

"I don't know, strictly, what I'm doing this time, Jak. Maybe I'm giving you the freedom because I want you to have it. Don't think this means I became your friend. It only means . . . you're free."

She let go of his hand and left.

After a while, Jak walked out into the warm sunlight of the polar night, through the quiet dark alleys, hearing and seeing nothing, until at last he found a narrow stretch of sand, a dune that had blown into a crevice, where he could stretch out on his back and sleep in the sun.

Borcles woke him with a touch on his shoulder. "And a pleasant morning to you," Borcles said. "You're absolutely right, this is a lovely place to sleep, and it's a fabulous change of venue for practice today. Let's start on the te-waza, shall we?"

"So that's the issue; now that we know what's in that lifelog, do we turn it loose in the solar system? (In many places it won't be believed anyway . . .)" King Dexorth said.

"I don't think it matters if it all comes crashing down, as long as what grows to replace it is founded on truth," Dujuv said.

"But what if the Galactic Court issues an Extermination Order while we're having a solar-system-wide religious war?" Myxenna demanded. "And a lot of people are going to suffer in the upheavals. It's not such a bad world, even if it's founded on delusions—"

The argument went on for hours; the longer it went, the less Jak felt that he had a side.

After the meeting, Jak returned to his room to find Myxenna already in there, sitting on his bed. "I really don't know why I have a lock," he said.

"I was going to ask you the same thing. Your purse badly needs an upgrade; its security is about shot." She yawned and stretched. "So, you're rid of the Princess. She released you and the deconditioning seems to have worked. You'll have troublesome feelings now and then, but that will fade, and one day you'll be completely free of her. Even now, she doesn't really exert more than a mild influence on your decisions. I am authorized to ask you if you feel better."

" 'I am authorized . . . ' Are we still friends, Myx? Or do you just represent Hive Intel?"

"Depends on what moment you ask me, old pizo, but if it's up to me, we're always friends, solid pizos, toktru toves."

"But you also are a rising star in Hive Intel. Whereas, at the moment, I'm a resource of dubious value," Jak said. "And I speck that has something to do with your being here."

"That's right," she said. "There's a very simple plan that can completely redeem the mission for you. You'll get the lifelog for the Hive, and you'll get the credit to Clarbo Waynong, and you'll get a regular posting with Hive Intel. Or, of course, you can wander off in anger and self-pity just because the world isn't what you want it to be. Your choice."

"What if I decide I just want to walk away from everything? Take a regular civilian agency posting, maybe even see if PASC will take me back as a low-ranker?"

"You'd be the assistant administrator at some mine in the asteroids, you know."

"I could do that job."

"You could." She said it flatly, obviously agreeing that it was possible. "Shyf just turned you free because she thought you were too much of a hero, a do-er, an achiever, to be her slave. I always thought you were *the* friend of mine who was going places. And your Uncle Sib—well, that isn't really fair to mention him, at a time like this, masen? But you're right. I know you could put your head down, suck up the boredom, and do that." She looked at him. "I just don't think you will."

With a sinking feeling, Jak said, "All right, what's the plan?"

It occurred to Jak that this was his third attempt at stealing the Nakasen lifelog, and the first for which he had any faith in the planning. Myxenna had procured a Harris Fastbox recording block of a matching age and general description. She had penetrated Dujuv's and Xlini's purses to obtain passwords. The plan was simply that she would let Jak into the archive, he would switch the empty recording block for the Nakasen lifelog, and he would deliver it to Clarbo Waynong, who would immediately be picked up by a Hive submersible shuttle, which would then jump up to orbit with him, thus taking the Nakasen lifelog into Hive Intel's possession. Jak knew that though there were undoubtedly many partial copies, the full and authenticated copy was irreplaceable to begin with (since only the block itself could vouch for the recording within Nakasen's lifetime, as opposed to its being a clever forgery) and furthermore, since most lifelogs contained literally decades of vid footage, it was unlikely that it had all been copied even yet. Even if it had, without the physical block to authenticate, Hive Intel would always be in a position to disinform against anything unacceptable that came out of the Nakasen lifelog, making sure that respectable people thought it was a forgery.

Jak was wearing a gi, cloak, and high-tops to be less conspicuous, all black to blend in better. The side door of the archive opened to his purse's command just as it was supposed to. He walked through the silent shelves of books, papers, and recordings, following a tiny infrared sprite in his goggles.

The high security archive room opened easily, and Jak stepped inside. The little vault, just big enough for the lifelog, also popped open at his purse's command. He pulled out the lifelog and put in the fake; closed it back up; and retraced his steps, locking doors behind him. In three minutes he had the thing.

Waynong was waiting right where he was supposed to be. Myx had made it clear that Jak was to wait until Waynong was actually on the submersible before taking his eyes off the young patrician and the lifelog. So they stood there in the dark, on the narrow pier, waiting.

"I don't exactly know how to thank you," Waynong said, after a while.

"For what?"

"For being so good at your job. For letting me see how much I'm not good at it. For being polite to me when you had every reason not to be. King Dexorth was right, you know. There's a lot for me to learn. And I've been resisting it most of my life. You helped me to see that it really did make a difference what I learned, and how I did things. I'll probably never be very smart, nor even very well informed, but thanks to you, and Dujuv, and to King Dexorth, and Paxhaven generally, I don't think of knowledge or learning as some kind of nasty conspiracy intended to keep me from my rightful place. I might not even think I have a rightful place anymore. Not, at least, till I know a few things."

The smooth black water in front of them stirred. A dark smooth surface rose, and water ran off it. A hatch opened, forming a darker circle within the dark ovoid of the exposed submersible shuttle. Waynong and Jak clasped forearms, and then Waynong, carefully clutching the precious object to his chest, stepped down into the waiting craft. It closed up and was gone.

As Jak walked back through the narrow alleys, he thought about how little excitement there had been on that mission—tension, yes, but excitement, almost none—a textbook demonstration about how things got into textbooks—

Distant thunder—the submersible would have waited to break surface till it was over the horizon, and now it was rising from the Phobos-lit sea, ascending in a stream of water and flame.

Hisses and whooshes all around Jak; fifty big mounted lasers and dozens of fast missiles let go. Turrets all over this side of the atoll erupted simultaneously.

Thundercracks as the air rushed into the vacuums the lasers had cleared.

A searchlight pinned Jak. A calm voice told him to put his hands up.

Even through the glare of the Paxhavian police lights, Jak still saw the bright white burning cloud that plunged from high in the sky, over the horizon, and down into the pitiless ocean. They had shot down the spacecraft carrying Clarbo Waynong and the lifelog, and from a crash like that there could be no survivors.

"Jinnaka, hand over the lifelog," a hooded and masked man said, approaching him. "And then you can guide us to whoever that shuttle dropped off."

"The shuttle made a pickup, not a dropoff," Jak said, standing there with his head still ringing from all the artillery fire, and dazed by the sudden change of fortune. "The lifelog was on it."

For many hours afterward, he was hustled from room to room, and people shouted at him. He kept repeating what he knew, and finally they stopped asking.

Another part of the mission was utterly routine and conventional; once it didn't matter; all captured agents were released and exchanged. Paxhaven released Jak direct from prison to Dujuv's custody, in the dusty little Harmless Zone town of Blue Cyan Yellow Amber, whose major industry seemed to be being diplomatically neutral. Pikia was with

Dujuv when he came to pick Jak up; she hugged Jak, but Dujuv did not even shake his hand. "I am instructed to tell you that you should get your messages at once, in secure mode," Dujuv said, handing Jak his purse and goggles.

He put on his goggles and plugged them into his purse. There was one message from Myxenna; nothing more than the sentence "Sorry, Jak, they didn't tell me everything."

There was also a message from Caccitepe. The man was an ange, and that breed's long nose and long limbs always reminded Jak of some bird about to swoop down—some bird whose dietary habits were generally nasty, fixated on Jak. The message reminded Jak of nothing so much as Principle 203: "Nothing is so galling as praise from an enemy."

Caccitepe smiled constantly as he delivered the message. "You may not realize this, but you have had considerable success. Listen closely as this is a self-wiping message and it will play only once. Our possession of the lifelog would have been highly desirable, of course, but the destruction of physical authentication for whatever material anyone may have copied is more than adequate to our purposes. Thanks to you, and some censorship and some disinformation campaigns, the Wager will be secure. In the matter of the loss of Clarbo Waynong: Mister Waynong's performance on your joint mission had already caused us to reconsider the wisdom of helping him to high office; we had begun to think that a man of his competence could help no one, no matter how much he had been helped. He is no longer a possible future prime minister. This can only be seen as positive, whatever the personal cost to Mister Waynong may have been. And his heroic death on a vital secret mission will enhance the prestige of the Waynong family, with whom we retain close ties, and so the loss to the Hive, the Waynongs, or to Hive Intel must be reckoned slight indeed.

"So, in short, the Wager is secure, and the political future of Hive Intel is secure, and those were our purposes. If we did not achieve them in exactly the way intended, we still achieved them."

When Jak put his goggles away, and turned to Dujuv, his old tove said, "This waiting room is secure. Jak, I'm going to tell you a few things, and then leave. You can certainly get on the launch back up to Deimos without my help. First of all, I'm going to resign from the Roving Consuls and start a career in professional slamball, a little late but still I should do all right. The reason for doing that is partly that I still would like to play slamball for a few years, but also that I'm going to use it as a springboard for running for office. On the Socialist ticket. I intend to beat every damn patrician whose family has been running the Hive for the last five hundred years, and beat him or her so badly that he takes the long dive into the black hole. Remember how we use to tease Myx about how soon she'd be running for prime minister? She'll have to run against me. And I'll be running as the incumbent. And I'll kick her overheated ass.

"And I'm hoping I won't see you again. Because I don't think the way you always wang your toves harder than your enemies is deliberate, Jak. I don't think the way you use and hurt everyone who cares about you is on purpose, but it always seems to happen anyway, masen? It's bad luck to stand near you.

"Just the same, if you send me a message, I'll answer— probably—masen?" Dujuv said. The door constricted before Jak could even squeak out a good-bye through his suddenly

too-tight throat. He lurched to his feet, too late, and saw
Dujuv's hovercar already pulling away. Very tentatively,
Pikia put her hand under his arm; he rested his other hand on
hers, and after a moment, he began to cry.

CHAPTER 15

Find Your Path

Jak wasn't sure why Pikia had followed him back to his apartment, but she was company, and friendly company, and he was grateful to have her there. His bags had been sent on from the warshuttle and were sitting in his front entryway when they airswam in; Jak ordered coffee in bulbs and a box of mixed rolls vacced over from the Sweet and Flaky, and while they waited, he unpacked, just tossing clean and dirty clothing alike into the freshener's slot. The vac door in the kitchen chimed; he opened it to find two big coffee bulbs and a box of his favorite rolls with "Nice to have you back—Avor" scribbled on the lid. *At least I'm appreciated by someone,* he thought.

"So what are you planning on doing next?" Pikia asked, digging into an immense creamhorn.

Jak sipped the coffee and thought how much he wished he could say there would be a couple of months of pure bureaucratic boredom. Perhaps there would, but he was no longer willing to bet on it. "I don't have much control of my life, you know. So I guess I don't really need to do much planning. Later on, I might try to persuade Dujuv to sit down with me and talk it all over—but I doubt that he will, and chances are that neither of us will have the time, and, oh, well. I wish he saw things differently but toktru he's just responding to the way he really sees them. In his place I'm not sure I'd see it any other way, either. When I plot myself in his orbit, I come out the same place he does, masen?

"So . . . I've lost a tove." Jak tossed the last of his laundry into the freshener. He hung up his empty bags and gave his toiletry bag to the butron to be unpacked in the bathroom. "Well, that's all the unpacking. Home again."

Pikia watched him from the wall perch she had grabbed; the creamhorn had vanished and she was now making a similar assault on a prune danish. She looked as if she really wanted to say something, and watched Jak as if looking for an opening, but she didn't speak. Finally, after a few more bites had erased the danish, and a big squeeze of coffee had washed it down, she seemed to shrug at the obviousness of her own comment, but she said, "Well, maybe you'll think of some way to patch things up with Dujuv before you go."

"I don't think there will ever be time enough for that in all the world, Pikia. If it were just one thing I had done, something very out of character or something, and there were some reason for Dujuv to think that it wasn't ever going to happen again, I think he might manage to forgive me. But not the way things have gone."

"This is crazy." She had a strangely angry expression.

Jak looked at that for a long breath; Pikia's face was set as if for a fight, and her eyes were focused far away, as if she were lost somewhere inside her own skull, her jaw muscles tensing and flexing to the rhythm of whatever argument was raging there.

Jak could not even see, at all, what any of it even had to do with her. "This is really bothering you."

"Yes, it is." She didn't look away, exactly, but her eyes met his, and then returned to that faraway imaginary place.

"I . . . Jak, out of all the smart ambitious young people I have ever seen pass through Deimos, you're the one who has toktru come the closest to making any sense to me. I always knew what you were trying to do and why. And you were completely devoted to Dujuv. No question. No reservations about it. You just were. So for him to reject you because of a few things you *had* to do . . . well, it scares me. Toktru it scares me. Because I don't want to lose the few toves I've got to some weird set of rules and judgments that don't make any sense: I mean . . . I guess I mean that I think you and I are sort of two of a kind, Jak, maybe that's what I found out on this adventure with you. I want to be like you, if you can forgive my saying it. I think maybe in a way I already am. And I understand that we are friends, even though we might sometimes have to do some bad things to each other. So I can imagine what it must feel like to lose your toktru tove that way."

He dakked her singing-on, and he didn't feel like politely pretending he didn't. "You're right. People are weird."

Pikia smiled at him, looked down, and said, in a complete non sequitur, "So, are we going to stay in touch?"

"Is one of us going somewhere?"

"Both. Hive Intel won't leave you here long. And I'm going to the PSA. I talked with Great-great-grandpa Reeb and he said that to *not* be admitted into the PSA now, I'd have to be convicted of excessive cruelty while killing my pimp. The weird thing is that even though he now knows you were always working for Hive Intel, Great-great-grandpa Reeb really does like you, Jak, and he's very proud of both of us." She stepped closer to him, and not looking at him at all, said, "And I'm proud of you too, if that matters."

Smiling in what he hoped was a brotherly kind of way, he

caught Pikia's hands in his own (it kept her from closing into a hug). "Well, you know that it matters. You're a tove, Pikia. You and I are going to stay toktru toves forever. And in touch with each other. I would miss you if we didn't."

When she hugged him she held him close, but she didn't press against him. "Dujuv's a real gweetz," she whispered.

Something forced Jak to admit, "Uh, I think actually he just wants friends who are as good a friend as he's a friend, if you see what I mean, and I'm afraid Duj is a pretty good judge of character."

She held him closer. "Jak, you *are* a toktru tove. The *best*. You just aren't the kind that Dujuv is. But"—she pulled away, still holding him by the arms, but looking at his face seriously, as if trying to confirm that he heard and believed—"you're the kind of tove that I want and that I need to have. Someone who is going places, and won't be happy unless he goes places, and wants *me* to go places."

"Well," Jak said, "as far as I know, tomorrow, I'm going to the office, and so are you. After that, who knows? But I'm glad we got to know each other."

"Me too." She let go of his arms as if she had only just realized she was holding them. "Hey, want to do something stupid and dull like catch a viv together?"

"Oh, sure. Anything without sex or Mreek Sinda."

"Then I guess the new 'Sex with Mreek' series would be out . . ."

It was a feeble joke, but he laughed anyway. They ended up just hanging around in one of those endless conversations that is really about nothing except the friendship itself—no matter what the subject may appear to be—and it was late before she left and he got to bed. His last thought before falling asleep was that he used to have conversations like that with Duj, often, and that he couldn't remember when they had stopped.

Next day, at work, just as he had made his last pointless note on the last bit of uselessly referred trivia, his purse announced, "Message from King Dexorth Verklar of Pax-haven, marked highly confidential and personal."

"All right, 'prepare to receive eyes-only message.' "

The door locked, the windows opaqued, and in a moment the screen flickered to life on the back wall. King Dexorth gazed out at Jak calmly; behind him, the Korolev lagoon rippled with the big slow waves of low gravity, as the long slow twilight of Mars crept across the sky.

"Dear Jak," he said, "I have been thinking about recent events here. I have some thoughts I should like to share with you.

"Let us start with that so-slippery issue, the truth. It is unlikely that the truth is the best thing for anyone to believe, but it is surprisingly easy to agree upon for most cases, and its secondary effects are more predictable. It is therefore very valuable and like any valuable intangible, it should be given away freely.

"So my decision is that the truth will be given away, freely and soon. Make your plans accordingly."

"Pause!" Jak barked at his purse.

"Got it. Back up two seconds and wait?" the blue fingerless glove asked.

"Please." Jak sat back and stared into space. Perhaps the King just meant that they would release their partial copies—

It was as if Sib sat at his shoulder, laughing and saying, *"Old pizo, think of the oldest trick in the book. It's the one they did. Tricks get to be old because they work. So you were escaping with the fake . . ."*

Uncle Sib's presence felt so real at that moment that Jak nearly turned and spoke aloud, but he checked himself; in a universe with an almost infinite supply of listening devices, you *"never say an unnecessary bit of the truth out loud,"* Sib's voice seemed to remind him, as it had so often as he was growing up.

I miss you, you horrible pushy rude pigheaded old gwont, Jak thought.

Yeah, well, so what's the answer?

They left a fake in the vault, Jak thought. *And I swapped them a fake for a fake. Clarbo was blown to bits trying to steal it for Hive Intelligence, and to restore his own mess of a résumé. Nakasen's hairy bag, what an absolute waste of effort by everyone.*

At least the King had had the decency not to look smug.

And his meaning was utterly clear: Paxhaven would release the lifelog and let whatever happened happen. "Unpause."

The King's face appeared on the wall again. "—and soon. Make your plans accordingly.

"Now, some people will be very upset by the truth that is about to come into the world. Large numbers of people will begin to run in circles and scream and cause trouble.

"It may seem irresponsible of us to unleash this thing, but when a mighty tower is built upon a narrow foundation in soft ground, and story after story and annex after annex are added at the upper levels year by year, it is inevitable that the djeste will fall. It is only a question of when. The longer it stands before it falls, the more will fall, from a greater height. It's not whether there will be a smash, but how big a smash there will be. The later, the bigger, you see. So we choose sooner rather than later.

"You can therefore expect that forces will be put in motion which will change the world around all of us, drastically. For Paxhaven—well fortified, safe, and thoroughly dakking who we are—this will be no very great change. But you, Jak Jinnaka—new, raw, open to the world, not yet wise, and unknown most especially to yourself—will be slung, hurled, and yanked every which way, like a single electron in a solar storm, your path always determined by forces vastly greater than yourself, and yet incalculable to anyone.

"There is nothing any of us here can do for you," Dexorth said, his eerily calm eyes never wavering from the camera, "nor would any of us care to, if we could. But a medieval American poet said that 'Home is where, when you have to go there, they have to take you in.' Strictly speaking, we will never have to take you in. But still we'd appreciate it if you think of us when you have to go somewhere. Meanwhile, find your path, Jak."

The message stopped and the room lights came back up to full. "Know where you are, Your Perception," Jak Jinnaka said to the sudden chill of the now-so-blank wall in front of him. He swallowed hard as he thought of how alone he now truly was.

He was just reluctantly opening the large file of nonurgent approvals—things where his judgment was not really needed but his handprint was legally required—when his purse said, "An urgent message, eyes only, has just arrived."

"Well," Jak said, " 'prepare to receive eyes-only message,' again. Screen it as soon as you're ready."

The crossed magnifying glass and dagger insignia of Hive Intel appeared on the screen, then the long vulturish face of Caccitepe. "Hive Intelligence hereby invokes its rights under Code Article 83, to cross-list or transfer such personnel from either Hive agencies or from other Forces, as Hive Intelligence may require. That's the officialese, Jak.

"Informally: I'm sending you on a mission for which you are well suited. It does not require more than what we covered in Advanced Intelligence Operations, at the PSA, and I know you did quite well in that class. You were, in fact, one of my star students.

"Your mission is this: you will be infiltrating a sunclipper crew, specifically the crew of *Umbriel's Glory,* which as you know is making a flyby very shortly at Deimos. We have created an identity for you in the UAS as a Crewman-Second, and made you look like exactly the fellow they have been trying to hire.

"Report to Hive Intel Deimos Office, two hours from now, for an orientation session, identity chip for your new identity, quick body makeover, pack of clothing, cache of concealed weapons, and of course a new purse in your new identity. All of these will be waiting for you."

Jak had taken a few chances, in his teens and early twenties, to accumulate union points to join the UAS, because it had been more interesting than traveling as a passenger; he only hoped that his skills weren't too far below those of a real Crewman-Second.

"*Umbriel's Glory* is upbound to Triton. We know from some of your previous reports that you are acquainted with the Canaan legend. *Umbriel's Glory*'s crew, both officers and regular crewies, is thoroughly penetrated by the Canaan cult. Also they are carrying contraband to the Tritonian underground, and there has been Tritonian penetration of the crew. We have been trying to prove a connection between the Tritonian government in exile and the Canaanist faction in the Council of Captains for decades; we are sure that crewie society is not maintaining the strict neutrality it claims, and we can make excellent use of any clear evidence of this. Your job, then, Jak, is to get that evidence. It need not be anything that would stand up in a court and I need hardly mention that there are no restrictions on how you get that evidence.

"Do be careful. *Umbriel's Glory* is Jovian League registry and therefore you are committing espionage, which is a capital offense.

"You need not revisit your apartment as our crews will store everything there; you may not take along any mementos or keepsakes. They will all be waiting for you, along with your purse, when you return to the Hive after this mission. Your two hours are intended to give you time to message friends and relatives so that they won't come looking for you, thereby possibly accidentally compromising security, in the next few months. Tell them enough to keep them quiet, but for your own safety we advise you to be vague in your good-byes.

"You could, of course, avoid this mission by resigning, and hope that PASC is not going to fire you, and will find some suitably punitive backwater for you. But you will instead do no such thing. This is exactly what you have been wanting—a deep-cover mission in which you can use your crewie skills. So I know you will take the job.

"Therefore, in advance: thank you for your cooperation. Good luck."

The message clicked off. It was immediately followed by three lower-priority nonconfidential messages, in which Jak successively authorized his own transfer (he had no choice anyway), signed up for the considerably better benefits package available to him in his new position, and authorized Hive Intelligence to grab everything out of his apartment and move it to the Hive for storage. (He was very glad he'd never gotten the kitten he had been wanting.)

He looked at the clock. One hour and fifty minutes to go. He set up his purse for messaging, faced the camera, checked his hair and made sure nothing was between his teeth, and spoke. The first one he recorded was:

"Dujuv, old tove, I hope you are not so angry that you're going to wipe this message without reading it. I've received new orders. I will have to be out of touch for a long while. I am going to hang on to my hope of someday renewing our friendship, and therefore, as soon as I am able, I will be back in touch. That will not be until I am done with this present mission which is going to take months or years and about which I can say no more than that. I am sorry for any pain I have ever caused you. I know that there has been plenty. I don't deserve your forgiveness but I would love to have it. Take all care of yourself, succeed at whatever your heart most wishes to achieve, and as they say in Paxhaven, 'Find your path,' old tove."

His next message was shorter and more formal:

"My oath-friend Shadow on the Frost, our paths diverge for the moment. Take care of Dujuv; he will need your protection. I have not forgotten my oath-friend and could not in any case. You *will* hear from me again. It will be a long time. It is an honor to have my name mentioned with yours. Be strong and well and don't lose that sense of humor."

His last message was shorter still.

"Myx, that was slick. Hive Intel assassinated a potential disaster of a future politician and established a basis for claiming that anything coming out of the Nakasen lifelog is a forgery, and if anything had gone wrong, it would have been me holding the bag. Was that Caccitepe's trick, or are you just his best pupil?" He thought of a dozen crude remarks he could make, swallowed them with difficulty, and clicked off.

He had an hour and forty minutes left.

He could drift around saying good-bye to his staff and to various Deimons he knew slightly, but he could see little reason for that; he had always preferred to come and go like a cat, saving the big productions for the hellos and simply vanishing for the good-byes. What to do with all this time?

He told his purse to unlock the door, and airswam out by Pikia's desk, where she was plowing along, obviously desperately trying to stay awake, through a collection of business even more routine than what Jak had just dismissed.

"Your boss has gone mad," Jak said, cheerfully, "and has decided that for today only, you are getting a long break, and you are having coffee with him, to discuss a variety of things around the office. This actually has to do with yet another chance to distinguish yourself. Unless you'd prefer to keep filling out forms."

"I was wondering how you could claim to have gone mad till that last sentence," she said, grinning. She pushed a button to complete an approval, told her purse to shut down her desk screen, and bounced out of her chair.

It was an odd time on the shift, so it was no trouble to find a café that had no one else in it, where no one knew either of them. They chose a centrifuged booth for greater privacy. Jak bought coffee and rolls and briefed her quickly. "You may have trouble staying awake, but your résumé is about to be spectacular," he said. "You're a line officer. The only one. You're going to be in command of the civilian side of Deimos. Of course, good as it all looks on your résumé, you have to do well at it for it to really count. But your great-great-grandfather gives very wise advice, there's a good chance that not much will come up, and the staff know much more than they admit to. If you really get into trouble and you've been nice to them, they might pull out some of that knowledge to save you. And if you succeed—I think you will—it won't hurt to enter the PSA with a reputation already walking in ahead of you—especially a good reputation. I could tell you a few things about going in with the other kind of reputation."

Her eyes twinkled. "Bet you could."

Jak smiled. "Well, once upon a time, Dujuv Gonzawara thought it might be fun to climb a light shaft—"

It wasn't necessarily the greatest story, but she laughed at it, so he counted it a victory. Then he heard a couple of accounts of how her feelings were terribly confused because . . . well, she just had so many of them . . . and was reminded of why he was glad not to be seventeen anymore. And the time crept on, and finally he said, "Well, I'll have to go. I'm sorry that I can't tell you anything other than sudden transfer, I'm going out on *Umbriel's Glory*, and I can't be in touch for a long time. Don't come to see me off. There are security considerations and besides I don't know which ferry I'll be on, masen?"

"Toktru. Find your path."

"Know where you are." He got up, and they shook hands.

It was only about ten minutes' airswim to the Hive Intelligence office. Machines swore him in and did the medical examination; more machines walked him through the briefing in the unreal world of viv, so that in three hours he experienced three weeks of briefings. While he was "under" for the briefings, yet more machines worked on altering his body, changing his skin color to two shades darker, a sort of rich chocolate; reshaping his face for higher, sharper cheek- bones, fuller lips, and a softer chin; erasing the tanpatterning he'd been wearing and putting in something more old- fashioned and bland, to fit in better with the more conserva- tive crewie society. When he staggered off the treatment table, he knew a great deal more about a very wide variety of subjects than he ever had before, and his skin and what was immediately under it had been stretched, pulled, abraded, poisoned, and depoisoned. He wasn't sure whether his brain or his body hurt more. He was now Pari Patzeron, a crewie, his second class badge still shiny and new and marginally qualified for, with a brief record of violent crime calculated to be unalarming (to any ship's security officer) but interesting (to anyone looking to recruit rebels).

After the surgery and the pumped learning, they left him twenty minutes to unpack Pari Patzeron's bags and repack them, becoming familiar with what was in them, and form- ing another impression of his persona.

The time came. He was supposed to make it to the ferry in the last few minutes, so that there would be as little time as possible to mess up his cover, since there was always the risk, even with all the modifications, that someone might recognize him.

So since he had to start late, he had to airswim through the corridors quickly and with many push-offs. When he hurried through the departure area, his new appearance fooled Pikia, who was waiting near the departure gate de- spite what she had said. He swam right by her, per orders, glad that she had been there and sorry that she would think she had missed him.

He had just time to strap into the ferry before it began to move up the track onto the loop, for launch to *Umbriel's Glory*. Through his viewport, he could see the great sails of the sunclipper, much farther away than Mars, enclosing a greater volume than that whole planet with a mass less than that of Deimos, a thin tissue over a vast nothingness.

Jak had not known that he would have a new face, name, and mission this morning. Now he did. Perhaps life would get busy, and he might remember his old life only rarely.

He was looking forward to that.

With a slight tug, the ferry whipped around onto the superconducting loop, Mars whirled by the viewport in a blur of red, blue, green, and white, the sun's reflection flashed in the great sails ahead, and they were hurtling around the loop to launch. Jak settled into a mental review of the Disciplines, blanking his mind, getting ready for a nap. As Uncle Sib always said, you never know what's coming next.

ACKNOWLEDGMENTS

I need to acknowledge an error; many thanks to the about thirty people (so far) who have noted to me that the home-world of the Rubahy cannot possibly have been orbiting Alpha Draconis, since in these books there is no faster-than-light travel (or at least humans and Rubahy don't have it), and Alpha Draconis is about three hundred light-years away, much too far. Special congratulations to the person who didn't want to be named who realized that, long ago when I was planning this series, I must have misread the Greek letter sigma as an alpha; in fact, the Rubahy are from Sigma Draconis, a mere 18.5 light-years away. I promise, young lady, that I shall get new glasses and stop having that third beer at breakfast. When you get to college, don't forget to correct your instructors at every opportunity; they'll appreciate it at least as much as I do.

Meanwhile, for the rest of you, be sure to buy the previous two books in the series, *The Duke of Uranium* and *A Princess of the Aerie,* so that you can pencil in the necessary correction. The Rubahy are from *Sigma* Draconis. Really.

As usual, I'd like to thank the people who made a tough job easier: William Barton, from whom I borrowed the term "the Red Millennium" for the 1450–2450 era; for the aftermath of a very different Red Millennium, you ought to read his excellent *Dark Sky Legion,* and while you're at it, everything the man's ever written.

Dr. Stephen Gillett, whose book *Worldbuilding* is the definitive treatise on the subject; technical errors in this book are almost certain to be caused by my misunderstanding Steve, and whatever is accurate here, chances are his hand is in it.

Betsy Mitchell, for her guidance in the creation of this series, and her early perception of, and insistence on, good qualities in the idea that I didn't see myself.

Jes Tate, my research assistant, for her usual amazingly efficient and thorough research (the most amazing thing of all is that it's so usual). You can have your old job back anytime, kid.

Jaime Levine, my editor, for being always there and always incredibly patient, and for asking the sort of questions that cause me to whack my forehead.

Devi Pillai, her assistant, for constant help with all sorts of annoying matters.

Nancy Wiesenfeld, the copyeditor, for cleaning up after me.

Ashley and Carolyn Grayson, my agents, for endless encouragement and for standing in my doorway as wolf-deflectors while I finished the book.

ABOUT THE AUTHOR

John Barnes lives in downtown Denver and writes full-time. At various times he has worked full-time as a gardener, systems analyst, statistician, theatrical lighting designer, and college professor. More than fifty entries by John Barnes appear in the fourth edition of the Oxford Encyclopedia of Theatre and Performance. His most recent books include *The Sky So Big and Black, The Merchants of Souls, The Return* (with Buzz Aldrin), *Candle, The Duke of Uranium,* and *A Princess of the Aerie.*

VISIT WARNER ASPECT ON-LINE!

THE WARNER ASPECT HOMEPAGE
You'll find us at: www.twbookmark.com then by clicking on Science Fiction and Fantasy.

NEW AND UPCOMING TITLES
Each month we feature our new titles and reader favorites.

AUTHOR INFO
Author bios, bibliographies and links to personal Web sites.

CONTESTS AND OTHER FUN STUFF
Advance galley giveaways, autographed copies, and more.

THE ASPECT BUZZ
What's new, hot and upcoming from Warner Aspect: awards news, bestsellers, movie tie-in information . . .